Sexual Exploits of a Nympho II

By

 W9-BFK-258

Richard Jeanty

RJ Publications, LLC

Newark, New Jersey

RJ Publications
rjeantay@yahoo.com
www.rjpublications.com
Copyright © 2007 by Richard Jeanty
All Rights Reserved
ISBN 0-9769277-7-2
978-0976927778

Printed in Canada

October 2007

1 2 3 4 5 6 7 8 9 10

Acknowledgement

I would like to thank all the usual suspects who have supported me throughout my writing career and other endeavors. You know who you are.

To my baby girl, Rishanna, it's been a joy watching you grow up. I love you Thanks for coming into my life. My family will always be first.

To Stacey Murphy, thanks for your understanding, love and support. My heart is always with you.

A big shout out go out to my nephews and nieces as well as my brothers and sisters.

A big "thanks" goes out to my dad for continuing to be my biggest fan. Special thanks go out to all the book clubs and readers who continue to inspire me to get better with each book. I would like to give a big shout- out to the street vendors and booksellers around the country and all over the world for keeping the world in tune with Black literature. Thanks to all the book retailers and distributors who make it possible for our books to reach the people.

A special shout out go to all the New York book vendors and entrepreneurs.

I would also like to thank my new editor, T. McDaniel for coming through for me at the last minute. I think we're going to work out.

Last but not least, I would like to thank my fellow writers for keeping their stories close to home.

Introduction

Since I've overcome the discomfort associated with the whole exploration of this sensitive subject known as "sex" from the last publication of the first part of this book, I hope that by now my critics and fans alike should also have a better understanding regarding my approach in this matter.

While many of us would like to dismiss sex as being one of the most important aspects of a relationship or marriage, time and time again we have heard the same complaints from men and women about their lack of satisfaction in the bedroom by their mate. However, the problem is deeper than it appears. Some people can never be satisfied, but they're not honest enough with themselves to admit it. It's not even a gender thing. Men and women risk losing their great relationships everyday to sneak a peek on the other side of the fence. Usually it's just curiosity, but most of the time it turns to devastation.

We live in a society where men are not as forgiving as women when it comes to infidelity. Perhaps the reason could be that there are far more suitable women available to men than there are suitable men available to women. Whatever the reason may be, one thing is for certain, men's egos are easily bruised. It's interesting how so many relationships are based on more important issues than sex, but somehow many of them end up destroyed because of sex. It only takes a few minutes for a great relationship to be destroyed because of lust.

There are different types of lust, but most of the time it is accompanied by sex. A woman might lust over a man who's in a powerful position because her man may not be maximizing his potential. The lust that she has may not necessarily have anything to do with sex, but if she decides she wants to pursue that lust, it will most likely end up in sex, whether or not she intended it to. Sex is the natural way for many people to bond and the minute there's no more conversation left, someone has to have sex. While many women can be very discreet about their sexual encounters, it continues to be an uphill battle for men. It's not that the men don't care about their partners, but their egos usually outdo their sense of secrecy.

Men don't always lust because of sex either. Some men lust after women that are in powerful positions as well, but most often they lust after women that are domesticated because they want to be taken care of. Whatever they feel is lacking in their relationship, they tend to lust after. Sometimes there might not be anything lacking at all, but a figment of their imagination can lead them to believe that they will find something better somewhere else, until they get there.

Lust is usually a search for bonding that we go through, but it can also destroy the relationship that we worked so hard to establish with our partners. Once we realize that we have to start controlling our lusting appetite for our created illusions, maybe then, we'll start to have better relationships and long lasting marriages. I'm no expert in this field at all; I just wanted to share my opinion.

A Note to My Readers

First of all, I would like to take this opportunity to thank all of you for your continued support. For without you, I would never be able to call myself a writer.

I would also like to inform you that I'm trying my hardest to bring you the best stories that I can possibly write. While some readers may enjoy reading the struggles of certain characters through many different episodes of my stories, I try to bring something different to my stories every time, even if it's a sequel. To be frank, I get bored with writing about the same thing all the time, and that is why I have never written the same story twice. For me, the joy of writing is to bring a new dimension to an old story every time I write. If I can't continue to do that, then I'll know it's my time to bow out from this profession and put my pen down.

As in life, I enjoy watching my characters grow. I try to take away the monotony and the predictability because life is not predictable. Those people who live a predictable life have no idea what predictable means. Tomorrow is not promised, so no one can predict anything. Monotony, I can understand, but I'll never get predictable. People with sense don't struggle with the same issues forever; they deal with them, and then move on to the next.

I hope to continue to quench your thirst and fulfill your fantasy as a reader. By all means, if I ever fail you, feel free to let me know about it. I can only grow as a writer with constructive criticism. I'm not looking for malicious rants about what I lack as a writer in anyway, but I will consider positive feedback so that I can become one of the best writers in the world so you can enjoy my work.

I've heard comments from people about me being all over the place as a writer with my writing. Well, that's exactly what I intended to do when I set out to be a writer. I want people to understand that I am versatile as a human being and it's just the same in my writing. I enjoy writing about different things and subjects because it keeps me motivated. I'm not asking everyone to keep an open mind if that's not their character, but I would like them to understand that I don't want to reach out to a limited audience. The world is vast and I think we should venture only to the parts of the world that are interesting to us. Fortunately for me, I seem to be interested in all of it. I feel it's a good thing, since there's so much to write about.

With that said, I would like to once again thank you. And please, always look for the unpredictable in my work and let your voice be heard. If sex is not your interest, you can always pick up *Neglected Souls, The Most Dangerous Gang in America: The NYPD* or some of the other books that I've written. I answer my emails as often as possible. Please reach out to me at rjeantay@yahoo.com to let me know how you feel about any of my books. Now, it's on to the next book.

Enjoy!!!

CHAPTER 1

Never Satisfied

Sweat was pouring down my body as I banged Tina every way possible around the bedroom. It started from the time I entered the house through the kitchen door from the garage entrance. She was standing there in a red teddy wearing my favorite high heel pumps and ready to work on me. "I couldn't wait for you to get home, baby," she whispered in my ear, while licking her way around my ear lobes. I was tired, but I couldn't resist her sexy body. I pulled her close for a long, passionate kiss. As our tongues tied, I could feel my dick rising to its peak almost as quick as a tornado traveling through the Midwest. Tina had been a good girl for the better part of the last twelve months of our relationship. However, she was easily agitated when I turned her down for sex. She would entice me by pulling out a ten-inch vibrator she kept in the top drawer of the nightstand on her side of the bed, but I didn't always succumb to her alluring ways.

I was starting to feel like sex with Tina was becoming a duty. She was horny 24/7 everyday of the week, and my dick hurt sometimes from banging her for hours. I'm sure my semen reserve was dried up because Tina and I had so much sex. Anyway, I didn't even have time to choose whether or not I wanted an early evening treat when I got home from work. I shouldn't fully blame Tina either because my dick got hard ninety-nine percent of the time when I saw her naked body.

As the passion from our kiss rose, Tina glided her way down to my crotch and pulled out old faithful Da'ron. It was Tina's idea to give my dick that nickname, and she chose the alter ego I created and named my dick after it. Old faithful Da'ron was standing hard and ready for action. After a little massage at the hands of Tina, my dick was looking for her wet spot to release the pressure from a long day's work. And Tina always made it available. Without saying much to me, she unfastened my belt and unbuttoned my trousers. I found myself standing in the kitchen with my pants down to my ankles, receiving the blowjob of my life.

My relationship with Tina had flourished for almost six months without a hitch. She continued to see her therapist for an additional three months until they agreed it was okay for her to cease her sessions. Tina's sexual appetite never slowed down, though. There were times when I came home from work feeling tired and completely exhausted, but Tina would hear none of it. She wanted to be satisfied. She felt it was my job as her boyfriend to keep her sexually fulfilled, all the time. Most of the time, I gave in at the touch of her sensual hands on my dick. Tina is a very attractive woman, so no straight man in his right mind should be able to turn down such a sexy, gorgeous woman for sex, right? We'll get to that. She was everything that I wanted physically, intellectually and emotionally in a woman. I was proud of the fact that she was able to overcome her sexual addiction. Not wanting to be the reason that Tina would revert to her old ways, I tried my best to satisfy her sexual needs every time she wanted me to.

Still in my mid-twenties, I walked around with a hard dick most of the time, anyway. The sight of Tina's silky, smooth skin, her curvaceous body and her perky breasts send blood rushing down my crotch even when I'm tired. This woman was my aphrodisiac. I enjoyed the soothing touch of her soft hands caressing my chest. And she knew how to get me in the mood. It wasn't unusual for me to arrive at my apartment to find Tina wearing a negligee and a warm water filled tub waiting in my bathroom so she could bathe me, or we could take a bath together. Oh yeah, my dick couldn't stay soft in those situations. And when I tried to act like I was too tired to make love to her, she easily convinced me that I really wasn't by taking all of my twelve inches inside her mouth at a whim. The warmth of her mouth always had my dick extended to its full length whether I wanted it to or not.

It was not like sex was the only recreational thing we did all the time, but Tina had it on our schedule most of the time. We were like any other normal couple, except for the fact that Tina's sexual appetite was bigger than most people's. As she nibbled around the tip of my dick, I felt like I had just drunk an energy drink in one gulp. She stared up at me while my dick was in her mouth and I stood there enjoying every minute of it. Tina made sucking a dick so sexy. I felt like she was an adult film star making my every dream a reality. My shoes disappeared in no time so I could ease my legs out of my trousers in order for Tina to continue with her rhythm. She made me feel like my dick was the most precious thing to her. I kept flexing and she kept running her hands over my six-pack as she continued to slob on my knob making me feel weak at the knees.

I couldn't stand it any longer. Her breasts were calling my name and I was salivating like a baby. I pulled her up towards me and lifted her off the ground and placed her on the kitchen counter. I took her knockers in my mouth and I could see the instant gratifying sensation in her eyes. She moaned softly and I sucked harder and longer. The more I sucked, the hotter she became. She started holding on to my head as I maximized the sensation to her nipples. I licked my way down to her navel. Her belly button tasted sweet and I licked around it leisurely until I was ready to go down to her pussy for the main course. Tina spread her legs on the counter like a gymnast doing a full split and her pinkness kept calling my name. I licked her clit slowly while stroking her hair with my hand. She had especially let her pubic hair grow for me. Her pussy had been bald for so long, I wanted it to have a different look even if it was just for a few days.

Tina's hair was soft and curly and somehow it added to the intensity of my desire to eat and please her. I licked her clit like it was my favorite *Now and Later* candy. I wanted to eat her now and fuck her later.   Completely energetically refueled by the aroma of her pussy, I stuck my tongue inside her as she held on to the back of my bald head. Her legs shook uncontrollably as I hardened my tongue and extended it all the way down near her sugar walls, motioning back and forth and in and out of her. "Eat that pussy, daddy. You're so good at eating pussy. Eat me. Oh, God! Don't stop. I love you, Darren," she screamed at the top of her lungs. Tina knew she had me whenever she whispered those little three words to me. While my tongue was in her pussy, I pulled back the skin covering her clit and started rubbing it with my finger creating a harmony with my tongue and fingers all over her pussy. As her legs tightened around my neck, I knew that ecstasy was near. I increased the intensity of my tongue and slowed down the movement of my fingers to allow Tina to maximize her orgasm. As predicted, a few minutes later I heard, "I'm cumming. Oh, God! Yes! I fucking love you. Oh, shit! Damn!" She continued to shake uncontrollably for five minutes like it was an aftershock from a recent earthquake. I knew she was satisfied because she smiled at me from ear to ear and threw her arms around me for an embrace.

CHAPTER 2

Supply and Demand

Over time, I became very familiar with Tina's body. I didn't have to work too hard to make her reach an orgasm, but often times she wanted to reach multiple orgasms as much as she could. I wanted to please her as much as I could, but there was a big problem. I didn't have the supply for Tina's sexual demands. Due to the nature of my job, my time was starting to be limited with Tina. I worked long hours from December to April. As an accountant, I had no choice but to work overtime. My company was flying me all over the country to do audits for most of the major companies on their client roster, and I received a very handsome salary. My career was very important to me and I never wanted to jeopardize my chances for upward mobility within this white dominated field that I am a part of.

Morning, noon and night was a little too much for me. Like I said, it was fun to fuck Tina two to four times a day when we were younger and before I had a career, but now it was interfering with my life. I was starting to second-guess her sex therapist who felt that Tina had made great strides. I didn't think that her sexual appetite lessened in any way. She spent most of her time at my place, so it was normal for us to wake up together every morning to get ready for work. However, Tina had a bad morning habit. She wanted to get a nut every morning before she left the house, not to mention that she also had to have one before she went to bed at night as well. Her sex habit was starting to get in the way of my work, because I started showing up late at work and even missed my flight a couple of times when she enticed me for a quickie or two.

Most people probably believe that a man would welcome the endless supply of pussy from a sexy woman, right? But that was not the case for me. Just imagine if you had to wake up everyday and had to eat your favorite food twice and sometimes three times a day. After a while, it wouldn't be your favorite food anymore and it would surely become less tasteful. Well, that's what was starting to happen between Tina and me. Sex wasn't special to me anymore. It became a chore; a chore I despised at best. When Tina and I first got back together, I wanted to keep her happy at all cost; even if I had to compromise my own happiness. The fear of Tina stepping out on me again was always lurking around in my head, so I agreed to her oversexed ways. I never thought anybody's life could revolve around sex so much until Tina and I started spending a lot of time together.

I didn't want to add to my stress, so I tried as much as I could to avoid thinking about what she could've done with other men when she was in college. Sometimes I felt like Tina was probably the campus hoe at her school. *With a sexual appetite like hers, one single man would not be able to fulfill her desires*, I thought. She had to have been sleeping with a bunch of men, but it was a new beginning for us and I tried not to think too much about it. And she hadn't even begun to see a sex therapist in college. Damn! I loved her. At that point, I was really hoping that love would conquer all. Despite her addiction, I could only see a long life happily ever after with Tina.

According to the therapist, Tina had a high sex drive and it was normal. I'll be damned if fucking three times a day is called normal. And I knew she was using those toys that she kept in the top drawer of her nightstand whenever she went home. She always made sure we had sex first before she went home to her house. I wanted to tell Tina that I needed a break from sex, but I had no idea how to approach her with it without offending her. I started giving her the cold shoulder or I would try to bust a nut as quickly as I could when we were having sex so she could get the hint; but that didn't work because Tina just wanted a dick inside of her at all cost and it didn't matter how long it was for.

Since I saw no way out of the situation, I started using my job as an excuse to abstain from sex with Tina. Honestly, my body needed a break, and I needed to focus on my career a little more; not to mention that I wanted to study for the upcoming CPA exam. I felt a little drained emotionally because I was becoming a Tina pleaser while I wasn't pleased with myself. I was about to cut off Tina's dick supply and disregard her demands all together.

CHAPTER 3

What Do I Do?

I started noticing a change in Darren that I hadn't seen before. In the past, he was always willing to satisfy my sexual needs whenever I needed him to, but lately he's been short-changing me. I still looked at him with lust in my eyes and he still got my juices flowing. I didn't want to assume he was cheating on me because he hadn't been giving it to me the way he used to, but I was watching him. Usually, I would spend three nights at Darren's house every week and he would spend at least two nights at mine, meaning we would see each other five times a week. He changed that drastically. I've only been getting one or two nights week from him and I was starting to feel neglected. It was unlike Darren to not fuck me at least ten times a week, especially since I had been going to the gym to keep my body nice and tight for him.

Every time I looked at Darren, something came over me. I couldn't quite explain the feeling that I had; all I knew was that I got extremely wet and I wanted to feel him inside of me. Darren walked around with that swagger that made me want him all the time. The way he looked in his suits, his walk, his sexy lips, his tight, sexy body and that butt. That man made me melt and I knew that I loved him with every ounce of red blood in my heart.

I really didn't know how to approach Darren about his lack of attention towards me. I didn't want him to think that I was needy and certainly didn't want him to believe that I was still a nympho. So what was a sister to do? While Darren

14

immersed himself in his work, I decided to keep myself entertained with my toy collection. By then I had bought every sex toy imaginable that was available on the market, and had one to fulfill whatever need I had. I always felt that Darren and I were the best of friends, but for some reason I couldn't talk to him about the things that bothered me the most in our relationship. How could I call him my best friend and lover and I couldn't really talk to him without feeling bad about it? It was more like a tormenting feeling because I knew what I wanted to say to him, but I was afraid of ruining his image of me. I worked hard with my therapist and made enough strides for her to suggest that we terminate our sessions, but I was still yearning for dick, his dick.

I fantasized all day everyday about Darren. My panties were wet on a daily basis while I was at work. Once I was sitting at my desk and my dirty mind started to wander off in a dreamy state. I saw Darren walking towards me wearing a hard, yellow hat, a flannel shirt, construction boots and carrying a lunchbox. As he made his way towards the door into my office, I let loose a couple of buttons on my blouse to expose enough cleavage to pique his interest. Immediately as he saw me, he developed a bulge in his tight jeans and I could see all the twelve inches he carried. I spread my legs across the table and started playing with myself. First, it was my clit. I started rubbing it slowly with my middle finger while Darren stood in my office watching and rubbing his dick through his jeans. Instead of joining me, he decided to take off his shirt to expose his muscular chest, teasing me even more.

While my eyes were fixated upon him, I pulled my breasts out of my bra and started licking my own nipples. I was getting hot and I really wanted him to put out my fire, but he didn't want to. Instead, he commanded me to pull off my top so he could get a full view of my breasts. His commanding tone was sexy and I obliged. I took both of my nipples in my

15

mouth licking them like a porn star who was faking it for the camera, but my feelings were real. I was lusting for him. He then ordered me to pull my underwear to the side so he could see my bush, and I did. I had shaved my pussy in a heart shape especially for Darren. He loved playing with my curly hair. He started licking his lips when I exposed my pussy to him. To entice him even more, I inserted my middle finger into my pussy. Out of the blue, Darren pulled his dick out of his pants and started playing with himself. I tried to make my way towards him to put it in my mouth, but he backed away. He ordered me back to my desk with my legs spread wide open. Darren was only interested in watching me masturbate.

Masturbation had become an art to me and I didn't mind indulging every now and then. With my pussy running wild like a river, I inserted my index and middle fingers while I used my thumb on my clit for maximum satisfaction. I was using one hand on my pussy while the other caressed my breasts. Within minutes I could hear a loud groan coming from Darren as he increased the speed of his hand strokes around his dick. I knew he was about to cum and I wanted to join him. I could hear him say, "Rub that clit, baby. Rub it!" as he exploded all over the floor in my office and my own nut wasn't too far behind. While trying to capture the vision of a good nut exiting Darren's body, I exploded in spurts, busting multiple nuts without ever putting my hands on Darren's body.

I've always had a mind of my own when it came to sex, but I especially had fun when I thought about Darren. I also fantasized about other men as well, but they were mostly out of reach and I could only create images of them based on the characters they played on the big screen. Yes, they were mostly actors and Denzel was always my favorite. I busted so many nuts because of that man. Thank heaven for Denzel Washington.

Lately, I had been feeling like Darren and I were at an impasse. There were things that I wanted him to know about me that I was afraid might turn him off. He had no idea that I masturbated two to three times a day. I wasn't even honest with my therapist because I really felt that I could control my sexual appetite on my own. I led her to believe that she was doing a great job and like any doctor with an inflated ego, she bought into my lies and cut our sessions short and completely off eventually. I can't say that I wanted to be cured of my sexual addiction because I enjoyed the fantastic feeling of a good nut too much. Yes, I had realized that I had been preoccupied with my own feelings of self-gratification more than anything, but what was wrong with that? I wasn't hurting anybody. I especially didn't want to hurt Darren.

The looks that I used to get from Darren when he laid eyes on me were slowly fading away and soon I knew they would disappear altogether. How does someone approach a situation where preconceived notions are already formed? I knew that Darren felt that I was a freak when my skeletons were exposed in the news, and I had been lying to him the last few months, acting like I was no longer a nymphomaniac. That was only making things worst. I thought I could be a functional nympho, but it was proving to be harder by the day. I craved a dick inside of me everyday and I didn't know if anything could psychologically be done to help me with that. I'd hoped that I didn't have to put up with my rejected advances towards Darren for too long. It was embarrassing to be turned down for sex as a woman.

CHAPTER 4

I Really Love Her

Even though I wanted to sexually shun Tina for a while, I started to feel bad about it. The enthusiasm she demonstrated at the sight of me was enough to make me want to satisfy her every need. This woman anticipated my presence like I was the president of the United States. The flashing smile, the excitement, the joy she exhibited around me forced me to give into her wants and needs. I started to allow her to manipulate me. I felt manipulated because I wanted to please her, but her character could've been true the whole time. I didn't want to be a sucker for love, but Tina had me hooked. The love I felt for Tina was definitely everlasting. The more I wanted to find reasons to stay away from her, the more reasons I found to love her. Since I didn't have a child, I had no idea what unconditional love was, but my love for Tina came pretty close to it. How many guys would take back a woman who had been with so many men knowingly? Yes, I had a hunch that she had slept with more men than I could count on my hands and toes together. That part of her life didn't matter much to me because I had done my own dirt back in college.

I remember when Tina came up to see me one weekend and I kept her in my room the whole time because I didn't want her to run into the other four women that I was boning on campus. I think she was smart enough to know that I was a pipe fitter back in college. That weekend I ended up having sex with Tina at least ninety percent of the time. She arrived on campus late that Friday evening and we drove straight to

18

my dorm. There were a few parties going on, but I didn't want to bring Tina anywhere near one. I was able to take her mind off partying by pinning her up against the wall in my room the minute after we entered.

Tina's baggage was on the floor along with her coat, pants and blouse within seconds. She leaned her back against the cold plastered wall as I voraciously shoved my tongue in her mouth for a wet kiss. We tugged on each other's tongue for a while until my hand found the clasp on her bra and I started to make my way south down to her breasts. I took them in my mouth while I palmed Tina's ass like a soft volleyball. She held on to my neck for security as I unleashed the power of my tongue all over her breasts and navel. As she started to moan, I kneeled down between her legs and gently pulled aside her underwear so I could commence eating her while she was still standing against the wall. Her body started to shiver, not from the cool temperature in the room, but from the sensation of my tongue on her clit. "I miss you, Darren," she whispered. While briefly coming up for air, I whispered back, "I miss you, too. I miss this pussy." "It's yours whenever you want it," she said. Tina knew exactly what to say to stroke my ego. I knew that pussy was somebody else's when she was back on her campus, but I accepted her statement. I continued downward towards Tina's knees and down to her ankle, licking every inch of her body.

Honestly, I really missed my baby and I wanted to make love to her like it was our first time all over again. True, I had pussy on campus, but none of it was like Tina's. Making love to Tina took me to another place. As I made my way back up towards Tina's luscious lips, she started moving down towards my dick. Without saying anything, she took my twelve inches in her mouth, and I was trying to hold on to the wall for balance. She sucked me like I needed it. I felt like I had been in solitary confinement for months and she was my tension reliever. I watched Tina take a good nine inches of me down her throat, and the amazement of it all almost caused me to bust a premature nut, but I pulled back. I wanted to enjoy the royal treatment she was laying on me. I started grabbing her hair and I felt as sexy as a man could feel while Tina sucked my dick to perfection.

While contouring her hands around my ass as she sucked me, I whispered, "You do that shit so well, baby. I love it." I knew Tina's mouth was hurting from sucking me for so long, so I pulled her up to me and lifted her left leg up and placed it on my arm for comfort while I penetrated her with her underwear pulled to the side. Something about Tina in her sexy matching underwear and bra fueled me. As I stroked her with her back leaning against the wall, the passion between us rose when she took my tongue in her mouth. Our bodies were moving uniformly. Tina held onto me for comfort and balance while I held on to her legs and ass for pleasure. Her moans intensified as my strokes became harder and stronger. I could feel her cumming when I started winding my hips faster, and she made it known by screaming, "Right there, baby. You got it! I'm cumming. Oh God, I'm cumming, baby." I increased my movements to share the moment with my baby. With a few more harder strokes, I reached a level of ecstasy with Tina that I had been missing since I last saw her.

Thinking back to moments like those, I knew that Tina was always the woman for me and I loved her more than anything. No other woman could ever replace her in my life and I wanted her to become my wife one day. As prissy as some people thought Tina was, she was also very domesticated and clean. I enjoyed the fact that she couldn't stand clutter and filth. She kept her house clean and when she came to my house, it wasn't unusual for her to tidy up the place when I neglected it. She didn't do much cooking, but she was good at it and everything else around the house. I didn't have to ask her to help me with my laundry and if my shirt and pants needed ironing, she wasn't shy about putting a nice crease on my pants and ironing my shirt to give me that neat look that I enjoyed sporting so much.

There were many things that I loved about Tina, but a few of them needed to be highlighted. I enjoyed the fact that Tina wasn't caught up in the excessively materialistic world that most of the women I met were driven by. She didn't make a big deal of things that didn't matter to her life and I enjoyed that. The latest Prada bag wasn't a priority and Gucci and Louis Vuitton weren't always in her vocabulary, even though she could afford them. Most people would find it unbelievable that Tina came from an affluent family with great wealth. She had priorities and that's hard to find in a woman these days. Perhaps it was the way her family came up from the gutter to their fortunate status in life.

CHAPTER 5

I Love Him to Death

Analyzing my relationship with Darren now, I understand that I love him. He knew how to make me feel special. It was the little things about Darren that impressed me and made me love him so. There was one time when he asked me for my class schedule and he called this florist and had a bouquet of flowers delivered to my Psych 101 class in the right building and room for no reason at all. He sent me flowers because he missed me and wanted me to know that I was in his heart. All the women in the class were jealous that day because Darren made me feel so special. Even my professor was a little flattered by his gesture. That was only part of the stunts that he has pulled to make me fall so deeply in love with him. I knew they weren't really stunts because Darren did what came naturally from his heart and he was a man of action most of the time.

I remember how he surprised me one day back when I was in college. I had no idea that he had driven six hours from Syracuse to come to Mount Holyoke to see me until he popped up in my room with a couple of helium balloons with the words "Missing You" inscribed on them. Luckily, I had no male visitor that day and it was a pleasant surprise because I spent the whole weekend in my room with Darren doing what we did best. As a college student, I found his gesture romantic and deserving of the best blowjob that I had to give. I pulled him towards me for a long hug and somehow I managed to get his belt unbuckled; before he knew it, his pants were down by his knees and I was on my knees with his twelve inches wrapped in my hands.

Darren stood in the middle of my room and enjoyed the acrobatic movement of my tongue around his penis like it was a balance-beam and my performance was perfect, leading to the right landing. I maneuvered my tongue around his nuts, taking them in my mouth like I hadn't tasted them in months. I savored the sweaty taste of Darren's nuts in my mouth until he couldn't stand it anymore. He pulled me up for a kiss after pulling off his shirt to expose his ripped bare chest. I started suckling on his nipple while stroking his dick with my right hand. I wanted him inside me. I could feel the veins popping on his dick and I knew he wanted me just as much as I wanted him. While I continued to kiss Darren's chest, he extended his hand around my back and started caressing it. His touch was soothing and welcoming. There was something about the way Darren handled me that was different than all the other men that I was sleeping with. He stood out above everybody else.

Just when I was ready to shove his dick inside of me to fulfill my desires, Darren picked me up and placed me on top of my desk. He kneeled in front of me and proceeded to eat my pussy until my whole body started trembling from a tremendous orgasm. I held on to him for comfort as I exploded in his mouth. Darren was never a selfish lover. He always tried to make sure I got my nut off before penetrating me. It didn't always work because I was not always so patient, and that day I didn't want to wait a minute longer. I leaned back on my desk with my legs wide open as I welcomed Darren's penetration with a big grin. I had been missing the thrust of his dick inside of me. The motion of his body towards me alone almost caused me to climax before his penetration even began. He slowly eased his way inside me giving me about an inch and a half at a time. His dick felt so sweet as he unloaded the rhythmic movement of his waist on me. He extended his right hand for me to hold as he slowly stroked and caressed my breasts with his free hand.

23

With each thrust of his dick, I was getting closer to a climactic state.

Darren knew exactly when I was cumming because of my body language and the aggression in my pelvic movement, so he pulled back a little to allow me to enjoy his love-jones. He pulled his dick out and started brushing it against my clit, causing me to collapse still under the pressure of a suppressed orgasm. If I came like a man, my cum would have sprayed the entire room. That was the extent of my orgasm. Then, he reinserted his dick in me for a more direct affect. I could feel his thrust against my g-spot and I knew that I was about to cum at any minute and he knew it, too. Darren soon got in the perfect position and I could feel another orgasm coming again. He grabbed my ass as he stroked me to yet another orgasm while he enjoyed one of his own. Afterwards, we hugged and kissed each other on my bed for a good half hour, catching up on what had been happening in our lives up to that point; then it was time for another round.

Darren was thoughtful and kind in many other ways as well. Little walks in the park with me were frequent and it gave us the opportunity to talk and also have more sex, sometimes. I had talked about wanting to go to Vegas because I had never been, and one day I opened my glove compartment and found a pair of tickets to Vegas for two for a weekend getaway. I had no idea he had snuck the tickets in there and he knew that I kept a stick of lipstick there that I used everyday. There was really no reason for me not to be in love with Darren. I won't even mention the fact that he had forgiven me after all that bullshit that I went through. Darren is a real man and I will love him forever.

CHAPTER 6

Now That Love Is Established, What Are We Gonna Do With It?

Okay, Tina and I have admitted our love for each other and we knew that nobody could tear us apart, but it seemed like we were tearing ourselves apart. My long days at work continued, and my lack of interest in sex was that of an impotent man who had completely given up on pussy all together sometimes; and Tina was getting tired of it. There was definitely a lot of spontaneity when we did have sex, but the obligating feeling that I had to please Tina all the time started to take over and I was disgusted with myself. It was time to request another break from our relationship. I knew the risk that I was taking when I decided to ask Tina for a break because of the amount of stress I was under at work. I really didn't want her to feel neglected, but I was drained.

It was a regular Friday evening and I had just gotten home from Houston, Texas. I had spent most of the week in Houston doing audits for this retail company whose home office was based there. I called Tina on her cellphone to ask her out for dinner. I could hear the excitement in her voice because she missed me and probably thought we were gonna be having sex all night that evening after dinner. I did plan on sleeping with her, but not before I told her that I needed a break from our relationship for a little while, anyway. Tax season at my job was hectic and I couldn't focus with Tina on my mind all the time. We made arrangements for eight o'clock that evening and I told her that I would pick her up. I wanted to go to this little cozy Thai restaurant in Brooklyn on Seventh Avenue called Rice Kitchen. We had been there before, but it had been a while.

When I showed up at Tina's place, she greeted me at the door wearing a sexy little brown dress with a cashmere sweater, her long coat and purse in hand ready to go. Tina was very stylish and I could've sworn I felt a boner coming on at the sight of her. I didn't want to smear her lipstick, so only a kiss on the cheek and a nice hug was appropriate. She also smelled like she had walked out of the Garden of Eden. Her light scented Chanel No 5 perfume ran up my nostrils and straight down to my dick and I couldn't help the elevated reaction in my pants. *Maybe it wasn't Tina who was a nympho all the time*, I thought. I was starting to feel this sexual high around her and I almost walked back into the house for a quickie before we headed to the restaurant. I realized that would defeat the whole purpose of me telling her that I needed a break. Tina was not naïve at all about my reaction to her. After getting in the car, she saw the noticeable bulge in my pants and she asked if I wanted to detour back inside the house for a quick round and I vehemently said "no."

She thought she could trap me for a quickie with her fine ass and I was tempted, I thought to myself. On our way to the restaurant, Tina kept flirting with me. She rested her hand on my crotch while whispering, "I want you to fuck the hell out of me tonight, baby. I missed you so much. I want to feel you inside of me. It's been five days since I had my fix and I can't wait anymore." Her plan was obvious and my dick acted like it was my primary brain because it kept rising and rising like Tina was hypnotizing it. I was being thrown off course and I needed to refocus. Initially, I had invited Tina out to eat because I wanted to talk to her about taking a break from our relationship, but I was no fool to think that she would want to fuck me after telling her that I wanted to take a break from her. And there was no way I was gonna go

26

home with a hard dick and blue balls. So over dinner, I opted for light conversations about our time away from each other and everything else in between. I decided that I was gonna wait until after I got some from Tina before I brought up the subject of a break to her. I was lusting for Tina, and I needed one for the road.

Through dinner, she kept flirting with me. The way she flirtatiously licked the spoon after every bite got my blood boiling. Tina also had this look in her eyes that I was all too familiar with. It was that "I'm gonna eat you whole tonight" look. I couldn't pass that up. A few minutes later her foot was in my crotch and she was massaging my rising passion. Suddenly I wanted to hurry up and finish my dinner. That was another problem that I had with Tina, she turned me on so much that I couldn't help wanting her. I felt like I was under her spell whenever I was around her. I wanted to take back control of myself, not just because of my ego, but also to find out if my relationship with Tina was purely physical. Yes, I know I said that I love her and everything, but that love has never been tested since Tina and I got back together. I wanted to feel the experience of missing Tina the person, not Tina the sex symbol. However, it would be the wrong time when I opened my big mouth to tell Tina about my plans. That night, she got me in the mood for some hot sex and there was no turning back.

CHAPTER 7

Dessert

Darren looked so good in his black trousers and striped, button-down, gray shirt. I could see his outfit under his long, wool trench coat. He had exquisite taste in fashion and I have never been disappointed by one of his outfits yet. Darren was the type of man that made me want to get naughty all the time. His closely shaved bald head and clean-shaven face made me want to pour some ice cream on him and just lick him down. How dare he go to Houston for five days and came back without giving me a quickie before we went to the restaurant. And he had the nerve to show up at my door looking and smelling all good. I knew just what to do while we were in the restaurant to get him back home in a hurry. I know he knew what I wanted to do when I saw that bulge in his pants after we got in the car. He wanted me just as much as I wanted him, but it was all about maintaining control for him. I knew that Darren was weak around me because no matter how tired he told me he was, I was always able to get at least a quickie out of him. That night, my plan was to tear his ass up to pieces for making me wait so long to get my fix.

Dinner couldn't be quick enough. When we got to Darren's house, I dropped my coat right at his front door and walked straight to his bedroom and with each step I took, a piece of clothing came off. By the time I made it to his room, I was in my high heels, bra and panties. It was his job to take off the rest. I took my commanding pose by the foot of the bed, with one leg leaning up on the bed exposing my pussy and the other on the floor for balance. It was that "come eat my pussy" power pose. He was right behind me half naked as well and ready to please her majesty. I grabbed the canopy post on the bed while Darren kneeled down to eat me. Nothing was said between us. Darren and I had developed this different type of language with our bodies that signified everything that we wanted from each other whenever we were getting ready to fuck. I was in no mood to make love that night, I wanted to be fucked.

As he passionately took his tongue to my clit, forcefully pulling back the skin and taking my clit in his mouth, his hands hovered over my ass for shelter. He squeezed and massaged my ass with his hands while his tongue did the tango with my clit. My pussy was hot and I wanted to take control. "Stick your finger in my pussy," I ordered. The position I was in couldn't be satisfied with just one finger, I needed a couple and Darren knew exactly what to do. With two of his fingers inside my pussy and my clit fully erect in his mouth, Darren created an orgasmic rhythm. In and out with the fingers and up and down with the tongue on my clit, and the only destination I saw was climactic heaven. He had never finger fucked me like this before. I could feel the thrust of his fingers deep inside my pussy and he was hitting all the right spots. I started winding and grinding on it while I hung onto the bedpost. Then he eased up on the fingers and took my pussy lips in his mouth and started sucking on them like chewable vitamins. I could feel a nut coming on strong and Darren knew it, too. He took the tip of his index finger to my clit and stuck his tongue inside of me while I exploded on his face. I really needed that nut.

It was business as usual with him. I took his dick in my mouth until he was ready to serve me on a platter. He bent me over the base of the bed and he penetrated me from the back just the way he liked it. The light smacks on my ass began and Darren started stroking me to submission. His

29

long strokes came from the base of his knees and I braced myself each time. "Fuck me!" I screamed. "You missed Da'ron, huh?" he asked. "Yes baby!" "Well, this is the last time you're gonna have him for a while," he said. Did I hear this motherfucker right? Did he say something about me not having this dick for a while? Everything just slowed down for me at that moment. "What did you say?" I asked. "I want us to take a little break from each other after tonight," he said, while he gave me his best strokes. I knew this motherfucker didn't think that he was about to bust a nut on me while telling me he wanted a break from me. I pulled my ass away from him and turned around to face him. "Why did you move away?" he asked. "I think we need to talk and we can't talk and fuck at the same time," I told him.

Here I was thinking that I was about to have my favorite dessert after dinner, but Darren had to fuck it up. "Is there something that you want to tell me, Darren?" I asked with an attitude. "Calm down, I don't want you to be upset over this. It's just that I feel that I need a break from our relationship because I have a lot of stress from work," he said. "Oh, I see. So this was one last hurrah before you hit the road, huh?" I said with sarcasm in my voice. "What are you talking about? Ain't nobody hitting the road. I just want to focus on my job for a little while. You know I also have to start studying for my CPA exam, which is coming up very soon. I just don't think that I can keep up with the demands from you, my job and the CPA exam all at the same time," he answered. "So how long do you want to propose this break and what are the bylaws? I want you to tell me everything you want because you have a funny way of interpreting things," I told him. "Why it gotta be all like that? I'm just saying that you demand a lot of attention and I don't want you to feel neglected by me, so I want us to chill out for a little while," he said.

Darren thought he was smooth. He was trying to leave one foot in while he goes off and deals with whatever he wanted to deal with. "Okay, if we're taking a break, that means I'm free to do whatever I want," I said to him. "What do you mean by whatever you want?" he asked. "I know I did not just speak French and you understand well what I just said. In a nutshell, I won't be sitting around the house waiting for you to come see me when you're ready. I'm gonna go out and have a good time," I warned him. "What do you mean by having a good time?" he asked. "You know what having a good time means, Darren. Don't play dumb. You know that I love sex and I need to be sexually happy all the time." I wanted to put him on guard. "Oh! So you wanna go fuck every Tom, Dick and Harry like you did before!" he tried to insult me. "I'm not gonna stand here and argue with you. Please take me home. It was your decision to take a break and you think you can also dictate what I do with my life? Think again, buddy!" I yelled angrily, as I started putting on my clothes.

CHAPTER 8

Where Do We Go From Here?

As Darren drove me home, it was total silence in the car. Maybe I overreacted to his suggestion, but I didn't want Darren controlling me or my life. He wanted to have his cake and eat it too. Darren knew that I loved sex and if he wasn't going to supply me, I was gonna get it from somebody else. I didn't want to be with every Tom, Dick and Harry like he assumed, but I wanted my sexual desires fulfilled. See, I'm not like most people who equate sex to love. My love for Darren had nothing to do with my personal satisfaction. Yes, I love him dearly, but I wanted him to fulfill my needs as well. I wasn't going to deprive myself enjoyment just because I love Darren. I didn't feel like I was being unfair. All I wanted from him was to keep me happy and satisfied. It wasn't even like he thought. I know that he thought that we were having sex everyday, but the reality of it was that Darren and I had sex about three times a week. When we did have sex, it was more than once in one day, but the total number of days never exceeded four days out of the week. He was traveling like crazy, how the hell were we having sex everyday? There are always two sides to a story and I'm sure his side will always be different from mine.

I was pissed at him for even thinking that he needed a break from me. I didn't see him enough as it was. I could see that he was pissed with me as well because Darren gets very quiet when he's angry. He didn't as much as cough in the car. He kept his eyes straight on the road and didn't even bother to read my body language or the expression on my face. Since he and I got back together, I didn't even go out or talk on the phone with any of my friends. I wanted to give him the respect I thought he deserved. Now that he was taking a break from my life, what was I going to do with myself? Even when Darren went away on his business trips, I didn't go anywhere because I was too busy missing him or thinking about him. I always anticipated his return and that was enough for me.

I felt that Darren was being selfish and it was time that I became a little selfish myself. I always felt like I was walking a fine line with him because of my past, but I couldn't go on living in fear of Darren leaving me. He'd never thrown my past in my face before, and out of respect for him, I played my role perfectly as a girlfriend. He crossed the line that night.

When we finally made it back to my house, he just dropped me off without saying a word. *How could he be so cold?* I thought. I didn't even get one last good nut out of the deal. He could've waited until after he fucked me well to say something and perhaps I wouldn't have reacted in haste because my mood would've probably been mellowed after a couple nuts, but he had to blab his mouth in the middle of everything. Why do men always ruin shit at the wrong time? If Darren wanted a break, a break he was gonna get and maybe even a permanent one at that.

I hadn't yearned for the touch of another man since Darren came back into my life, but now I was starting to think about other men again. For almost a year and a half it was just Darren and me. Neither of us had friends, so we hung out with each other most of the time. When my little case came to light, very few people wanted to be my friend. We were in our own little world and I was happy with that. I thought that's what he wanted. I didn't even have a girlfriend that I could hang with if I wanted to go out, and my brother, Will,

33

who was my ace, was busy playing football for the Atlanta Falcons in the middle of November. It was the worst time for Darren and me to break up because winter was fast approaching and I needed someone to keep me warm at night.

If Darren thought he was gonna have total access to my pussy while we were "on break," he thought wrong. Anyway, as far I was concerned, our break-up was permanent after he dropped me home without saying anything to me. No back door will be left open for easy access to my pussy. I wished that he would make up his mind soon about what he wanted to do because there were plenty of men in New York City who wanted to get my attention.

CHAPTER 9

I Should've Known Better

I never anticipated a complete break-up with Tina. As much as I wanted to believe that she was going to understand my position, I also knew that Tina would've reacted the way she did. She was a control freak who wanted to be in control all the time. Sometimes there was no "give and take" with her and I tended to overlook that most of the time. She was my love and nobody's perfect. I couldn't believe she sat in the car without saying anything to me. I figured the long ride back to her house would've given her enough time to think about the situation and reconsider what I was asking of her, but she didn't. If she didn't want to speak, I wasn't going to speak to her either.

I dropped her off thinking that our relationship was over. Put a fork in it, it's done! I wasn't going to call her anymore and I didn't care whether or not she called me. However, there remained the problem that I had no friends and Tina was not just my lover, she was also my best and only friend. Yes, I thought about burying myself in my work, but how long was that going to work? I had a boring job where I crunched numbers all day. I was elated everyday when my workday ended, so I couldn't see me burying myself in my work. Tina was my habit and I wish it was a habit that I could control. But I was willing to test my limits without her in my life for a while. Given the way we left each other, I didn't feel any guilt about my newfound freedom either.

In the past when I went away for my job, I didn't hang out much after work. I would go straight to my hotel room after leaving a job until the next day when I had to wake up and go back to work again. It was inevitable that I ran into a lot of fine sisters in my line of work. Most of these sisters, half the time, were complaining about the lack of college educated, sophisticated, and all around intelligent good black men. I heard it a lot from them and they were disappointed by me most of the time, because I wore my relationship on my sleeves. I was never shy about telling other women about my relationship with Tina. *This time around, I'd be the prize that all these women were looking for*, I thought. I was educated, handsome, well versed and most of all, funny. Oh yeah, I got jokes. I've always known the way to a woman's heart was through laughter. When I met Tina, I didn't have to dig too deep into my bag of tricks, because it was empty then. I hadn't fully developed as a man and I was still trying to learn the game, much less play it. It was my turn to become a player and I wanted to be at the top of my game like Michael Jordan. An overall number one draft pick. *Ladies, here I come*, I thought.

CHAPTER 10

My Brother and Me

My brother's agent was able to negotiate a new contract with the Atlanta Falcons after he became a free agent from the Miami Dolphins. His stock had also gone up tremendously as he worked tirelessly to improve his game on the field. He sold his home in Florida and settled in a mansion in ATL that was left empty most of the time. Times like these, I needed to be next to my brother. I needed to talk to my brother.

I picked up the phone and dialed his number. "Hey, Will, what's going on?" I said through the phone, after he picked up on the second ring. "Who this?" he asked, like he had no home training. "It's your sister, fool. I'm calling to see how everything is going with you." "Hey, T, what's up? I thought you were this girl that I've been avoiding. You wanna talk about a stalker...and I only hit it once," he said. "Well, stop hitting 'em just to be hitting 'em," I shouted at him. "Anyway, I was calling because I know you have a by-week this week and I wanted to come down to Atlanta," I told him. "You know my door is always open to you. I have to practice three times this week, but after that, I'm all yours," he said. "Cool! I'm gonna go make my reservation for Wednesday and I will call you with the details." After Will and I hung up the phone, I immediately got online to make reservations to Atlanta. I was able to book a six o'clock flight leaving the upcoming Wednesday and returning on Sunday. I couldn't wait to see my brother.

Will and I didn't see much of each other during the football season because of his busy and demanding schedule. I missed my brother and wanted to be in his presence even for just a couple days. Will was becoming a notable player in the NFL and had wowed the critics who had underestimated him when he was drafted in college. His great work ethic, which he inherited from my dad, kept him focused and determined. He was always a leader, but not the most athletic. But over time, he developed skills that made up for his lack of athleticism. As a linebacker, Will knew that his career-span in the NFL at best was about twelve years and he needed to make sure he maximized his earning potential while he was still in his prime. At first, he relinquished the idea of relocating to Atlanta because he had become accustomed to his life in Florida and had developed friendships with a couple of Dolphins' players. However, the Dolphins' management wanted to pay him less than he was worth so they could sign this sensational running back. Will wasn't having it!

As spectators, most people just enjoy watching the game and most of them don't understand the physical demand associated with the sport. Quite often it is publicized when players are bickering about their contract, because the media and sometimes the public feel that they should be grateful for earning a seven-figure salary. But no one ever sees the preparation and dedication behind becoming a great player in any sport. Most of the time, the players are only seen on game day when they're in college and only if they attend a marquee school. Often times, the public also wants to determine how high paid players should comport themselves, not knowing that some of these players come from disadvantaged backgrounds and newfound wealth and fame can sometimes lead their lives in the worse possible direction. Fortunately for Will, he had a grounded family that was there for him from the time he was born to the time he signed his first contract with the NFL. Not all his friends or colleagues fared so well.

Atlanta, known as "Chocolate City," had my parents fearing the worst when Will decided to sign with the Falcons. With the tag "Chocolate City," it also became known as the city with the highest number of reported AIDS and HIV cases as well, according to the Center for Disease Control. Traveling to many cities and running into groupies on a weekly basis was one thing, but to actually have some of the most gorgeous, intelligent, independent as well as the most trifling and gold-digging women living just a fifteen-minute drive away from Will, was something that concerned my parents. Not to say that Will couldn't meet a productive woman in Atlanta who had it going on, but he had a habit of going after the easy ones who saw green first. Even though Will was a grown ass man, my parents were still very involved in his life. The female flesh is the strongest weakness known to mankind, and my dad had known about Will's weakness for the female flesh since he caught him masturbating in the bathroom as a teenager; so that put him on alert. He wanted to make sure that Will didn't fall victim to some scandal that could ruin his career and reputation. It was bad enough that their normal, average citizen of a daughter brought shame to their doorstep, but Will was in the spotlight and that would be national attention. So they decided to take a proactive step in order to help keep Will out of trouble. Honestly, my parents weren't trying to control Will's life; they just wanted to be involved in some of his decisions. They called him often and talked to him as much as they could.

Both Will and I went through sex therapy for our sexual addictions, but I personally learned during therapy it was more about self-control than anything. I honestly don't believe that a therapist can help deter a pattern of behavior. Any pattern of behavior that needs to be curbed, most of the time has to be curbed because it is a destructive pattern. And it's only when we start to take a look within that we can discover a clear path to recovery. Yes, therapy helped me a little, but it was ultimately up to me to change my behavior patterns and I was glad I did it. Say what you will about me, I still love sex and perhaps I'm still a nymphomaniac in some ways, but I was not fucking as many men as I used to fuck. I was not interested in fucking a bunch of men just for curiosity sake anymore. This time I did it for the love of the dick. Puuuhlize!! I know people didn't think that by sitting on some chick's couch three times a week it was gonna take away my appetite for the dick. Most women are too afraid to admit that they don't have the willpower to live without dick, but I'm not one of them. I never was and never will be. I have the willpower to control my behavior, but I'd be lying if I said that I could do without dicks. There's a bunch of women out there sticking dildos inside their pussies and vibrators all over the clit to get the satisfaction of a good dick. Shit! Even I do it sometimes, but it's no replacement for a real dick. You can't hug a fucking vibrator. A vibrator ain't gonna lick my nipples or caress my body. I need a man with a hard dick to give me the full Monty. I got lost in translation for a minute. I just got so excited talking about dicks.

Anyway, the only thing I could hope was that Will had used the same willpower he used on the football field to help deviate from his sexual addiction. I love my brother so much. The only thing I ever wanted for him was to be a respectable and successful person in whatever he was doing. We had strong-willed parents and I hoped that he inherited the traits more than I did.

My highly anticipated trip to Atlanta kept my mind off Darren, for the most part. Of course, there were times when I wanted to pick up the phone to call him because I missed him, but I was too pissed to do it. I kept myself busy by reading a few good books. I checked out *Me and Mrs. Jones* by K.M. Thompson and I was enthralled from beginning to end with the story. Then I picked up W.S. Burkett's debut novel, *Chasin' Satisfaction* to pass the time, but what I found was entertainment beyond belief. Sometimes I wonder how these writers come up with such fascinating stories. It must be a gift.

Wednesday couldn't come any sooner. I was bored out of my mind and didn't know what to do. I was in a funk and didn't really feel like doing anything in New York. I simply went to work and came home. That monotony was starting to get to me. I needed something different, something new and exciting.

Finally Wednesday had arrived. After sitting in the terminal at LaGuardia Airport for close to two hours, the agent's voice could be heard over the intercom announcing that they would start boarding for the flight to Atlanta in five minutes. It couldn't be any more perfect. I had just finished reading an article in the *New York Times* about another rapper getting shot over some ridiculous beef that was brewed over territory. It was time to get my ass on that plane to get some much needed sleep before we landed in Atlanta. Since I booked a business flight, I was one of the first few people to board my Air Tran flight to Atlanta. If I could find a bargain, I would take it and that's how my black ass ended up on a two-hour delayed flight on Air Tran. It really didn't make any difference because all the other airlines' flights were delayed as well, but Air Tran is notoriously known for this crap, especially their evening flights.

I flopped myself onto the leather chair and within minutes, I started dozing off. There was some guy in a gray business suit sitting next to me who attempted to strike a conversation with me, but I was too tired to carry on any conversation. Besides, the foul odor coming from his breath would've knocked my ass right out, anyway. I turned my face towards

41

the window to avoid his breath as sleep took me away. I was sleeping like a baby, and the next thing I heard was the flight attendant announcing that we had landed in Atlanta. I normally couldn't sleep through a flight, but I was happy that I did because my body needed some rest. I grabbed my carry-on luggage from the overhead compartment and stood in the aisle for another fifteen minutes before they finally opened the door to the gate. I can never understand why people can't keep their asses in their seats after a plane has reached the gate. It ain't like anybody's going anywhere until the gate is open anyway, but everybody wants to get up, including me. I had to fight for my position before I ended up being the last one to deplane.

I was happy to finally walk off that plane and on to my destination. I called Will back at LaGuardia to inform him of my delayed flight. He promised that he would pick me up at the new announced arrival time. I took that underground train to baggage claim and as I made my way up the escalator I could see Will's big ass standing behind the line waiting to welcome his little sister to Atlanta. It seemed like he had gotten as big as a horse since I last saw him. As I made my way towards him, I knew he was about to pick me up to give me one of those signature bear hugs that he always gave me whenever time had passed since we have seen each other. I was so happy to see him, I didn't mind. Will picked me up like I was his favorite piece of fried chicken and the boy had my feet dangling in the air while he held me up for close to thirty seconds. I held on to him tightly for safety as well as comfort.

There were flashing lights from people taking pictures of us because Will was apparently a big celebrity in Georgia. He was an easily recognizable guy because of his size and stature. After gently placing me back on the ground, he took my luggage and carried it out to his truck that was parked in the parking lot. Will must've thought he was a real G because he was blasting Jay Z's "Can I Get a What What" like he owned the world. We peeled out of the parking lot after paying the attendant and off to Alpharetta we went. Will lived in a posh neighborhood with high-end homes. Every house on that street would have probably cost at least ten million dollars in New York City. In Atlanta, people get a lot more house for their money. I was shocked when we pulled up to Will's mansion and he told me that he only paid seven hundred and fifty thousand dollars for it. The house was beautiful. It was four-sided brick sitting on three-quarters of an acre with five bedrooms, four and a half baths, a family room, living room, dining room, recreational room, a spa, swimming pool and a freaking steam room. The bedrooms were carpeted with Berber carpet and the main areas of the house were outfitted in the best cedar hardwood that money can buy. I was almost out of breath after touring his house.

I was really proud of him because the place was nicely decorated and cleaned spotless. He didn't live like a messy bachelor. He knew better because my parents didn't raise us that way. After Will and I got through talking, I could hear through his voice that he felt lonely in Atlanta. Even with all his admiring fans, he felt alone. He wanted to meet that special someone that he could settle down with, but most of the women he met saw him as a meal ticket; something that Will has always been able to recognize since he was in college, but he didn't mind it then. However, Will was changing. He was becoming a man.

I spent my first night in Atlanta sitting on the couch in my brother's family room kicking it with him like we did when we were kids. He had matured a lot and had also taken the right steps to change his life for the better. Will's biggest worry was always the fear of disappointing my parents. He was definitely not a disappointment, and my parents were very proud of him. From the look of things, my brother didn't have to worry about that. His house was in order, and there weren't too many women calling him. Other than his loneliness, he seemed at peace with himself.

Staying away from clubs and wild parties was very important to my brother. He witnessed the destructive behavior of some of his teammates and saw how their fortunes turned to misfortunes and he didn't want that. I worried that he was becoming a homebody, though. "Will, it seems like you haven't been getting any lately. What happened to all the girls that used to call you all the time?" I asked. "I left all that back in Miami and I'm turning a new leaf. Don't sleep on me; I also got a couple of booty calls that I have total access to any time I want. I just don't give them access to me," he told me conceitedly. "Call it my booty stash," he joked. "So you've become Mr. Moderation," I joked back. "Life is about growth and I'm at a point in my life where I'm growing and growing and growing...." he said laughingly.

We stayed up to watch Jay Leno and conversed a little more about his new situation in Atlanta. He really liked his new team and the prospect of going all the way to the Super Bowl. He had one of the best quarterbacks in the NFL in Michael Vick to lead the team, and felt it was a matter of time before they'd be crowned champions. Will was a confident guy with a keen eye for reality. Realistically, he didn't stand a chance of going past the first round into the playoffs when he was in Miami. Miami's focus was to build while Will was looking to get a ring at the time. Every great competitive athlete wants to ultimately walk away from the game with a championship.

Will was very honest about his life and he didn't feel ashamed to tell me that one of the women he was sleeping with enjoyed splurging with his money. "Her body's tight and the sex is crazy," he told me, trying to justify her taking advantage of him. As kind hearted as he wanted to be, I was

about to put a stop to it before I left. This girl in particular
named Marla was especially fond of my brother because of
his wealth. When he started telling me about her shopping
sprees and how she always wanted to go the Phipps Plaza to
shop at exclusive boutiques whenever they were together, I
was angry. "How can you allow someone to take advantage
of you like that?" I asked. "It's nothing but money and I have
enough of it. It's not like I would ever marry the girl," he
cautioned. "Well, you might as well go out and find you a
prostitute because it would be a lot cheaper. She sounds like
a high class prostitute to me," I said to him with concern in
my tone. I continued, "I bet she only gave you ass after
spending a couple thousand bucks on her, huh?"   "Not all
the time, but we do have the best sex after shopping," he said
smiling. "You got yourself a hoe. Mommy and daddy would
be disappointed to know that you're down here sleeping with
hoes," I said to him, while shaking my head. "You're not
gonna tell 'em anything, are you?" he asked. "All you gotta
do is get rid of her and I won't have to say a thing. Look,
Will, you're an intelligent, handsome, charismatic and very
successful man; you can have almost any woman you want.
Why would you settle for someone who's using you?" I said
passionately to him. "T, it's not like I purposely look for
these women. It's just that they're more accessible to me and
I can control our interaction as long as I spend a little money
on them. I don't have time to go out there and mingle and get
to know people. I spend most of my time training and the
rest is spent on the football field. And the fact that you don't
have one fine girlfriend that I can kick it to doesn't help me
out either," he said to me, smiling. "Don't worry, your
sister's gonna hook you up with the perfect girl. But first,
we're gonna have to get rid of your chickenheads," I said
mischievously.

I wasn't about to let this little hoochie take my brother for a
ride. I didn't mind my brother spending money on a woman
that was down for him, but from what he told me about

Marla, he was nothing but a trick to her. He told me she didn't even come by to see him when he had the flu, but she was right there when he recovered and was able to drive to the mall. I realized when it comes to ass, some men are just plain dumb and my brother was no different. Well, that was about to change.

CHAPTER 11

Cleaning Out Will's Closet

It just so happened that there was going to be a celebrity fundraiser taking place that Will was invited to the upcoming Saturday, and Marla knew this and she wanted to go, badly. She wanted to be seen on the arm of the celebrity guest. She was calling Will every half hour on the phone asking him when he was gonna take her shopping for a new dress for the event. I overheard their conversation and I knew instantly that I had to step in before this woman walked over my brother any longer. "I just got you four dresses last weekend that cost me almost ten thousand dollars. Why don't you wear one of them?" he said to her. She must've told him that she gave away a couple of the dresses after she realized she didn't like them, because I could hear him tear into her. "You did what? How you gonna give away some shit that I just bought you? I don't care that you gave it to your sister, I bought that dress for you," he said. It sounded to me like that trick was using Will to buy shit for her family as well. She probably returned the dress and kept the money. The conversation went on and I didn't know what she must've said to him, but his whole demeanor changed and he suddenly agreed to take her shopping for a new dress. "You know I like that thing you do with your tongue. You better make this up to me, good. I want the ass tonight, too. That asshole is so tight girl you got me going crazy," I overheard him on the phone. This dumb ass negro was being played because of some anal sex. *Got damn! Men just go crazy for anything that is out of the ordinary*, I thought to myself.

Before my brother got off the phone, I could hear him making plans to take Marla shopping on Friday afternoon, the day before the event. Now I had to conjure up a plan to get his ass away from her for good. Women like that give a lot good sisters a bad name, because all they care about is the depth of a man's pocket. I checked out this website called *"Whatshappeningatlanta.com"* to find out what was going on in the city on a Thursday evening. Level 3 was the happening spot and scores of women showed up to find their Prince Charming every week. I also heard that Justin's restaurant was a good place to go for drinks and dinner during the early evening hours. So I decided to make plans to go have dinner at Justin's with my brother and then take him to Level 3 for a night of fun. Honestly, I was hoping he would find a professional woman with more to offer and way freakier than Marla without all the gold digging characteristics.

Thursday couldn't come soon enough. My brother and I got decked out in our best gear. Since it was very chilly out, I decided to wear my brown leather pants, a dark cream-colored suede shirt and my suede boots. My hair was done to perfection and I made sure Will looked as good as a Big and Tall model from a high-end boutique; all three hundred pound of him. Will wore a button–down, white, designer shirt with gray pants and a black, striped suit jacket to accentuate his pants, black shoes and belt. He smelled good courtesy of Armani Code. I sprayed a little of Burberry's latest perfume around my neck and wrists. We smelled and looked good and I planned on making sure that my brother had a good time. I had to get his mind off that gold digging trick.

We arrived at Justin's around eight o'clock in the evening and the joint was packed with people. There were a few celebrities maxing out their celebrity status with the hangers-on clinging to them like leeches. And there were other successful brothers making it known to the world that they had made it by boasting about their houses and cars and the multi-million dollar deals that they've brokered. I felt like I was eavesdropping on everyone's conversation. Of course, there were also the fakers. The women who sounded too independent and lonely and the braggarts who could only wish that they possessed all the shit they were talking about so loudly in the restaurant. Some of them talked so loud, it seemed as if they were just short of using a bullhorn. I even heard one of them pronounce Versace as "Verse Ace." My brother and I were rolling when we heard that one. All that bullshit to impress someone, only for the truth to come out later, that's too much work. After waiting at the bar for close to thirty minutes, the maitre d finally offered us a table by the window facing Peachtree Street.

As my brother and I made our way to the table, this wonderful gorgeous man caught my eyes. He was tall, clean-shaven and medium complexion; not too light and not too dark. He looked like a young O.J. Simpson, very handsome. I couldn't help smiling back when he flashed his pearly whites my way. I also enjoyed his confidence. Despite the overbearing size of my brother, he wasn't afraid to flirt with me. He had no idea if my brother was my man, but he was bold enough to think that it was worth a try to get at me. He sat at the bar on a stool and was being admired by a few ladies, but his focus was on me. A few of the groupies at the restaurant recognized my brother, but they were too scared to approach him while he was with me. The gorgeous man wouldn't let up, so finally I extended my index finger and commandeered him my way. He walked up to the table without fear and with the balls of Godzilla. "I noticed that you've been staring at me all night," I said to him, after he reached my table. "I think you meant to say that we've been staring at each other all night," he answered, as my brother rolled his eyes. "Let me introduce you to my brother, Will," I said, to ease any apprehension he might've had. I introduced

49

them and they exchanged their manly daps. "Are you here alone or waiting on someone?" I questioned. Will was scoping out the place while I was talking to my new friend. "No, I'm here alone, but I would love to join you and your brother for dinner," he chimed in. "That would be great except that I want to spend some time with my brother and I don't want anyone to feel left out or neglected," I said to him. "Well, how about I invite this fine, young lady over there who's been drooling over your brother from the time he walked in?" he said in a deep sexy voice. I could tell that my brother had never seen a man that smooth before and I had to kick him under the table before he got ignorant in front of the man. He kept rolling his eyes as if to suggest that my new friend was laying it on to thick. It seemed all natural to me.

Will was not like me, he didn't pay attention to his surroundings as much as I did and I knew exactly who Mr. Gorgeous was talking about because I could hear her say, "Tall, dark, handsome and taken," when Will and I walked in. Her comment was about Will. Mr. Gorgeous had no problem walking over to the lady to invite her to join us for dinner. Besides, he offered to treat everybody, and Will wanted to make him regret ever offering to pay because the boy could eat. "I never got your name. Why don't we go around the table and introduce ourselves by name?" I suggested. We were sitting at a table for four even though it was supposed to be just Will and me, initially. So it was no inconvenience when Terrence, as he revealed his name to us, and Cassandra joined us. We told our waiter that it was going to be four instead of two people for dinner.

While waiting for our first order of drinks, Terrence, Cassandra and I were doing most of the talking. Will was a little more laid back. I was starting to think that he didn't find Cassandra attractive. She was more attractive than any woman that I had ever seen him with and I was wondering when he was going to start wheeling her in. Cassandra worked as a corporate attorney for a well-known firm in Atlanta, she had no children, no husband. She was a perfect size six for her 5 feet, 9-inch-frame. She was brown-skinned with light brown hair and light brown eyes that I envied. The woman was perfect in every way physically. I became even more envious of her when she smiled. Her teeth were straight and white, and she told us she never wore braces. She was also well-spoken and well mannered. *Now, that's some good genes there*, I thought to myself. Mr. Terrence wasn't too bad himself. He was an attorney turned sports agent with his own firm. He had a few reputable low profile clients. I figured he was one of those six-figure-earning brothers from his attire, confidence and swagger. However, some of those qualities were secondary to me. I was more curious about his bedroom skills. He was charming, intelligent and smooth at only thirty-two years old. I started to question the fact that he was even available, but I stopped myself short because everyone at the table was a great catch, including myself.

CHAPTER 12

Go! Go! Go Darren Go! Go!

Since I no longer had Tina to worry about, it was time for me to start enjoying my freedom. Maybe I only believed that I loved Tina because I was around her so much, I started to question. I needed to explore my options and see what was out there. While I was on a business trip to Atlanta, I met this beautiful flight attendant named Tamika who wanted more than my attention. I usually didn't fly to a new location in the middle of the week, but this was an audit that needed to be done and I had to fly out that Wednesday evening. It was a delayed flight and while I waited in the waiting area for my Delta flight, Tamika walked past me and smiled. This was not the usual smile that I encountered from women in the past. It was the "You better holler at me or else" smile. She had the most beautiful, whitest teeth and she forced a big Kool-Aid smile out of me. The form fitting uniform she was wearing on her 5 feet, 6-inch-frame and what seemed to be a perfect size six had me thinking about the kind of overtime I would love to put in on her. As she walked by me strutting her stuff with her baggage in tow, she reminded me of the sixties when being beautiful was a prerequisite to becoming a flight attendant. She was confident and sexy.

I really didn't know what I wanted to say to her, but I knew that I had better say something. She went to the desk to talk to another agent who was on the intercom keeping the passengers updated on the delayed flights. After talking to the agent for a few minutes, she decided to leave her baggage behind the counter and headed towards me. She came and sat down right next to me. This woman looked so good I even forgot how good I looked that day. She made me look ugly. "You look good in your suit," she said to me. I was caught off-guard because no one had ever said that to me out of the blue before. "You look good in yours, too," I responded, but she wasn't wearing a suit. "I mean, you look good in your uniform," I corrected myself. "What's your name?" she asked. "My name is Darren. What yours?" "I'm Tamika, but Tammy for short. So, Darren, where are you on your way to?" "I'm going to Atlanta to do an audit for this company," I answered. "Are you an accountant?" she asked. "Yes, I am." We continued to make small talk and found out that Tammy was a recent graduate of Spellman College. She'd just completed a bachelor's degree in business administration and she wanted to take a year off to travel before pursuing an MBA. She took a job with Delta so she could see the world.

For the next hour while I waited for my flight, Tammy told me about the perks of being a flight attendant. On her days off, she could go anywhere in the world that Delta flew to for free. She worked four days a week and had three days off. I also found out she was working my flight to Atlanta and I was happy. She was definitely the kind of woman I wanted to get to know better. She was going to be in Atlanta for a couple of days and we made plans to go out to dinner. Tammy was the finest sister that I had ever laid eyes on. Light skinned, with jet black hair, dark eyes, a beautiful smile, legs to kill for and a body that I couldn't wait to see naked and caress, she was heavenly. I knew that my trip to Atlanta was going to be the best ever.

CHAPTER 13

Let the Good Times Roll

After a great dinner and conversation over drinks with Terrence and Cassandra, my brother was able to loosen up to draw enough interest from Cassandra. I was afraid that she was going to think that he was one of those dumb jocks who could not put together a sentence without adding "you know what I'm saying" at the end. He surprised her with his articulation and intellect, and she loved every minute of it. Both Terrence and Cassandra agreed to come to the nightclub with us. I didn't know what my brother was thinking about, but my intention was to get me some from Terrence before I left Atlanta. That man looked delicious and I wanted to take a bite. If my brother wasn't with me, I probably would skip the club all together and go straight home with Terrence. He had my juices flowing like a faucet and my panties could hardly withstand the wetness. It was one of those thrill moments because I had been out of the loop for so long.

When we made it to the club, VIP was automatic as the big bouncer escorted my brother and his guests to the front of the line, and a generous tip was snuck into his hand on the low. The bouncer also appeared to be familiar with Terrence as well as they both acknowledged each other with a sly grin. It wasn't my business to try to read anything more into it. Maybe Terrence was a frequent visitor at the club, who knows and who cares? We went upstairs to the VIP room where we enjoyed each other's company away from the huge crowd. Whenever I wanted to get a little freaky with

Terrence, I took him downstairs to the main dance floor. That man was packing, too. I could feel the thickness of his dick against my backside when they started playing this old style southern music. The freak in him came out and I was enjoying it. I sized him up to be about ten to ten and a half inches in length and just the right amount of thickness to satisfy me. That man was desirable and I wanted him to take every inch of me. After exhausting ourselves on the dance floor for about forty-five minutes nonstop, we decided to go back to the VIP room to check up on my brother and Cassandra. I really wanted to stay downstairs with Terrence the whole night, but I wanted to make sure that Will and Cassandra were getting along.

I came back upstairs and found my brother and Cassandra engaged in an intimate conversation. They were whispering in each other's ears and we didn't want to break his flow. We decided to go back downstairs unnoticed by them. We found a comfortable little corner and that's when Terrence decided to plant a big wet one on me. His lips were soft and tasty and I welcomed his tongue inside my mouth as I tastefully relished his kiss. Our tongues intertwined a few times more before we decided to hit the dance floor again. After the kiss, Terrence felt a lot more comfortable dancing with me and I with him. He turned his back to me so I could freak him, and my hands found their way across his muscular chest. It was a good thing that he left his blazer in the VIP room because it was getting a little too hot for us on the dance floor. We saw the looks of envy from some of the single women dancing with corny, awful looking men, and also saw the player haters with their cornrows so tight that they could've burst a blood vessel from hating. Terrence and I were having fun and enjoying each other; we paid no attention to the jealous ones.

I'm sure Terrence knew that he could've had me that night if my brother didn't come along. In a way, I was hoping that

55

my brother would leave with Cassandra so I could go home with Terrence. However, I knew it was a long shot because Cassandra, by my assessment, was not the "hit it on the first night" type of woman. She looked like the type who wanted to be courted right, before she put out. Honestly, I didn't think there was anything wrong with that. I also didn't see anything wrong with two people clicking, and if they both wanted to fuck each other's brains out on the first night, why not? I left those societal standards alone a long time ago, but I knew out of respect for my brother I had to wait another day to get a taste of that juicy Kielbasa Terrence was packing.

The foreplay on the dance floor was marvelous and Terrence left me wanting more. The man moved his hips like a true African prince and I couldn't wait for him to get between my thighs. If his moves on the dance floor were any indication of his skills in the bedroom, I knew I was going to be satisfied. The throbbing between my legs was calling out to his dick and I just wished that I wasn't with my brother.

CHAPTER 14

Let the Fun Begin

After hooking up with Tammy the next day on Thursday for dinner at the Cheesecake Factory, she insisted on treating me dancing at a local nightclub. I've never been the nightclub type, but I wanted to spend as much time with her as I could, so I agreed to go. She informed me that her cousin worked as a manager at the club and that we would be in the VIP room most of the night, away from the crowd. I didn't have to be at my appointment until ten o'clock the next morning, so I told her we could party until about 2:00 a.m. because I needed at least six hours of sleep. I took into consideration the fact that I might get some ass from her after the club. Tammy was looking so good I would've functioned on two hours of sleep, if I had to. This woman was wearing one of my favorite spaghetti strap dresses that flowed around her curvaceous body. I could tell she was wearing a thong and no bra because her breasts were perfect and a perky C cup. Since Tammy drove, I had no idea where we were headed. After a short ten-minute drive from the restaurant, she pulled up in front of this club on Peachtree Street. The line was long, but the bouncer at the door recognized Tammy right away. She handed her keys to the valet and the path was clear for us to go straight to the VIP room.

Tammy later told me that she decided to live in Atlanta after graduating from Spellman after her cousin convinced her that Atlanta was a better place for black folks than her native city of Boston. He had moved down years prior and was doing pretty well financially. After being in the VIP room for a few minutes, as Tammy and I conversed, her cousin came up to give her a huge longing hug. I didn't have to ask who he was because that kind of hug only came from family. Any regular man would have tried to cop a feel of her beautiful, shapely ass while hugging her. "This is my cousin, Mario," she introduced. "What's up, man? I'm Darren," I said in my deep baritone. Mario was obviously busy and couldn't sit around much for small talk, so he told Tammy that they would catch up later. I later found out that Tammy and Mario were first cousins. His mother and her father were brothers and sisters. They even looked a little bit alike.

As I was sitting on the couch trying to whisper sweet nothings in Tammy's ear, I swore I saw someone who looked like Will, Tina's brother, talking to a woman. I didn't pay it any mind even though I knew that he was traded to the Atlanta Falcons. It would be a great coincidence to run into him. I continued on with Tammy trying to lay my best game on her. I wasn't ready for a relationship of any kind, but I was definitely ready for some ass. Tammy was working my loins and I could see myself working that ass all night long. In any case, she also appeared to be a great catch if I happened to fall in love with her, but that was the furthest thing from my mind at the time. And just because she was packaged right, it didn't mean she was gonna be right for me. I never considered myself to be much of a dancer, but it didn't matter to Tammy because she wanted to dance with me.

I was a little eager to get my arms wrapped around Tammy's fine body. She was great on the eyes and as we made our way down to the main dance floor, a lot of guys were extending their hands out to her for a dance like I didn't exist. I was right behind her and talking over her shoulders to make my presence felt, but these fools in Atlanta were completely disrespectful. One of them almost tried to grab her ass until he looked up and saw this killer look on my face; then he wanna talk about "my bad." I'm not one to fight over a woman, but I wouldn't allow a woman that I'm with to be disrespected by some chump who can't keep his hands to himself.

"Baby, when you're grinding, I get so excited...." were the lyrics blasting from the speakers from this group called Next. It was just the right song because my plan was to dance real close with Tammy. I'm not one of those MC Hammer guys who feel the need to get buck wild and sweaty on the dance floor to draw attention to myself. Tammy pulled me close to her and my hands found the back of her waist and that was going to be my post all night. I didn't know what kind of perfume she was wearing, but she smelled very sweet and I didn't want to let her go.

CHAPTER 15

No Parking On the Dance Floor

Terrence was wearing my ass out on the dance floor as he held on to my waist to do his magic. I could feel his throbbing dick rubbing against my pussy as his pelvic movement to the smooth rhythm of the group Next, got me wet and excited. I was feeling his whole body and I wanted to become one with him. I moved in for a kiss with a lot of tongue because I was really feeling this man. He didn't disappoint. His smooth tongue met mine and we locked lips for a good forty-five seconds while dancing slowly to the music. I wanted to feel Terrence's hands wrapped around my body, so I turned around to give him my backside. I could tell that he found my butt irresistible and I wanted him to get a feel, and that's when I noticed him staring dead at me. "What the fuck is he doing here?" I said to myself. "And who's this pretty chick he's dancing with?" I could see the disappointment in Darren's face as he locked eyes on Terrence and I. He must've seen me tonguing Terrence down like he was my man and that pissed him off.

I wondered if I should've gone over to him to say something, but I didn't. As far as I was concerned, he and I were broken up and I could do whatever the hell I wanted. Suddenly, Terrence wasn't so fine anymore. I was now thinking about Darren and that trick had her hands all over my man. Terrence could sense something was wrong because I just stopped moving and was just standing there while he grinded on me. His dick was hard as steel and my pussy became dry as a desert because I was pissed at Darren.

60

Darren suddenly shifted his position and had his back to me while the girl faced me as he worked his wonders on her. She looked almost innocent, like she just got out of college or something. I was a little intimidated by her looks. Blemish free skin, nice height, beautiful body and envious hair, this chick was hot. She had her arms over Darren's shoulder as he glided his hands down to her ass to infuriate me even more. Darren was looking great that night in his black pants, and fitted black shirt showing off his ripped body. As he started to pour it on the girl, she started flirting with him by turning around so he could get a better view of her ass. I knew right then that this chick wanted to fuck Darren. A woman just knows these things. My woman's intuition about other women had never been wrong in the past. I wanted to convince myself that Darren wouldn't sleep with her, but she was gorgeous and I didn't think he would be able to resist.

I didn't want to just stand there and let Darren think that I was still head over hills for him. I decided to make my own move as he made his. I pulled Terrence towards me in a tight embrace to show Darren that I wasn't going to let him ruin my night. Whether or not Terrence knew I was using him to make Darren jealous was not my problem. I turned him around with his back to me so Darren could see his pretty face, and I started feeling his body up and down hinting to Darren that I may let Terrence fuck me that night. Terrence was a great participant as he displayed his sexiest moves on the floor, making me feel like I was the only woman in the world that mattered to him at that moment. I turned around to feel his Bobby Brown copycat pelvic movements up against my ass. He was humping and grinding as he grabbed my waist while I felt the rhythm of his vibes through my soul. I could feel moisture reappearing between my legs. I grabbed his ass to infuriate Darren. Terrence was unknowingly being used and abused on the dance floor, and he enjoyed every minute of it.

After working up a good sweat, it was time to walk away and let Darren be with his little girl. I was devastated to see him so wrapped up in a new girl so quickly. I hadn't thought about him since he dropped me off at my house without saying a word to me, but now I was bothered by his presence. Terrence could sense that my mood had changed, but like most men, as long as he got what he wanted, he didn't care about my feelings. Terrence was not selfish or anything, but he didn't even ask why my mood changed all of a sudden because I allowed him to have his way with me on the dance floor. By then, I was thinking about two things: I could fuck Terrence to piss Darren off or I could go home and sob because I saw Darren with another woman. The idea of pissing him off was easier to swallow.

Terrence and I went back upstairs to see if Will and Cassandra were ready to leave. I didn't want to be in the club anymore. I wanted so badly to go home with Terrence to fuck the hell out of him, but respect for my brother kept me from doing it. He and Cassandra must've had a great time because she decided she wanted to come by the house with him for a nightcap. There I was, thinking about showing respect to this fool and he was about to bring some chick home while I slept alone in my bed. I invited Terrence over after making sure it was all right with Will. I didn't want to cock block, but I could tell that whatever my brother had planned for Cassandra was not going to happen. He may have been thinking with his dick, but she was definitely thinking with her head.

I knew the four of us would end up either playing cards or having great conversation all night. First, I wanted to make sure that Darren saw me leaving the club with Terrence. I wanted to piss him off. I purposely walked by him holding hands with Terrence as we exited the club. I could tell that he was fuming, but Darren wasn't the type of guy to cause a scene, and I was confident of that. Walking out with

Terrence empowered me and hinted to Darren that I was moving on, even though I knew that I wasn't.

CHAPTER 16

Two Can Play That Game

I couldn't believe Tina was playing me like that. It hadn't even been that long since we broke up and she was down in Atlanta with some new dude. That pretty boy had nothing on me, that fucking Bobby Brown wannabe. Busting moves so old that Bobby Brown has made it his prerogative not use those moves anymore, anywhere. That dude needed to step up his game if he wanted to keep up with me. It was okay if Tina wanted to be scandalous. I could be just as scandalous. Not only that, she walked right by me with dude in tow. And as horny as she always is, I knew she was gonna give him some. I played it cool, though. I just needed to make sure that Tammy and I were on the same page. The only way to get even was to make sure I got some ass of my own. I know that shit sounded vindictive and Tammy was about to become a piece to my chess game, but hey, I didn't really give a damn at that point.

Tammy seemed nice enough and deserved to be treated like a lady, but that frame of mind left me when Tina walked out the door with that fool. Everything was going great between us, and Tammy was starting to loosen up after a couple of drinks. They started playing some of that "shake that ass" style of music and Tammy acted like she was a native Georgian, a Georgia Peach of some sort, as she threw her ass all up on me. The serpent in my pants was about to meet the rainbow. She turned around and had her ass bumping against my dick like she was a stripper trying to get more tips. Suddenly, the conservative personality vanished. Tammy had been living in Atlanta a little too long because her southern moves started the blood flow in my pants. Her slow grind against my crotch had my dick extended to its full twelve-inch length and Tammy wanted to feel it as she continued to back me up against the wall.

After feeling my dick against her ass for a good fifteen minutes, working me like she wanted me to bust a nut on the dance floor, she turned to face me and pulled in close so she could rub her crotch against mine as we danced. It was worst than a sexual simulation act by the worst R&B act that I had ever witnessed on stage. K-Ci & JoJo were tame compared to what we were doing. I looked around and saw a bunch of other women busting far worse moves on the dance floor. It was like a competition of women trying to outdo each other while the men enjoyed the whole thing. Shit, I was worried that her cousin might have me thrown out the club for trying to fuck her on the dance floor. Whether it was just a dance, Tammy didn't have to say much for me to know that I was gonna tap that ass that night. It was time for me to leave the club and go do what I had to do.

"Can we go finish this at the hotel?" I whispered in her ear. She smiled and said, "What took you so long?" My instinct was correct. Tammy and I drove down to the Windham Hotel so quickly I didn't even get a chance to check out the scenery because my hands were all over her in the car. I wasn't shy about touching her because she had made her position very clear at the club. There was a strong physical attraction between us and I enjoyed the fact that all her attention was focused on me. I wish I could've said the same about her because I was distracted by Tina. Well, she was about to have all my attention and all the jealous rage I was holding in me for Tina.

Tammy's skin was soft, and as my fingers made their way down to her crotch, I found out that she was a little hairy,

65

which turned me on even more. I started massaging her thighs in the car and all she kept saying was, "You're gonna make me crash. I see that you're a bad boy." I think Tammy was fascinated by my physique. She was probably hoping and praying that I would be able to deliver in the bedroom. We finally made it to the hotel and I hurriedly handed the keys to her car to the valet after she parked the car. I didn't care that my dick was trying to bust out of my pants while some of the people standing around were frowning in shock. They shouldn't have been up so damn late, anyway. The elevator seemed like it took forever to get to the fifteenth floor. My tongue was in her mouth caressing hers as the automated voice in the elevator blared through the speaker, "Fifteenth floor." We got off the elevator and walked down the hallway while my hand palmed her ass.

Tammy surprised me by dropping her dress to the floor in the hallway while I was trying to slide the card into the slot on the door to get it open. My eyes were lost on her breasts and I started losing concentration. I had the wrong side of the card up. "Hurry up, papi," she said, while trying her best to sound Puerto Rican. Her body was to die for and I got the door open just in time. Tammy's naked body had my head spinning. She walked through the door and I followed after her while picking up her dress from the floor and brought it to my nose to inhale her sexy scent. The room was dark as all the lights were off, but I couldn't fuck this woman in the dark. I wanted to see her beautiful body; no I needed to see her beautiful body while I brought pleasure to her body and soul as well as mine.

We didn't even make it to the bed as we stopped short against the wall for a long sensual kiss. My hands were all over her body like a little boy overly anxious to open his gifts on Christmas Eve. But this gift was open and it was mine for the taking. As Tammy stood by the door near the bathroom, she could see her reflection in the mirror located

66

on the closet door. I slid my way down to her breasts as I took each one of them in my mouth, alternating every thirty seconds or so. Her nipples were hard and tasty and I applied just enough suction to get her pussy moist. Tammy was moaning loudly and it brought out a more fierce determination to please her. As my hands glided across her body down to her navel, I kissed her softly and slowly. She looked so sexy in her high heels against the wall; I didn't want to have a premature situation, so I slowed down. Tammy grabbed my head after I finally made my way down to her pussy, tasting first her elongated pussy lips, drenched in her flowing juices.

She must've felt some kind of sensation as I slowly licked and slightly sucked on her pussy lips because she held on tighter to my head like she was bracing for a major storm. That storm soon came and hit her right on the clit. I softly brushed my tongue against her clit and Tammy started shaking. I could tell that she liked it slow, so I slowed the motion of my tongue so she could experience my cunnilingus technique, the way she imagined she would when we were at the club. Sensing that the soothing touch of my tongue against her clit was making her lose control, I retreated so I could allow her time to breathe. "Don't stop. Why are you pulling back? I was almost there," she said. "I know, but we have all night and I want to enjoy you," I told her. "What about work in the morning?" she asked. "Let me worry about that," I answered.

I grabbed a towel out of the bathroom and took Tammy to the loveseat at the other end of the room. She sat on the towel with her legs wide open while I ate her pussy the best way I knew how. With the simplest flick of my tongue against her clit and in and out of her pussy, she started moaning and screaming, "I'm cumming. Ooh, Darren, you're making me cum and it feels goooood!" It was just the reaction I was looking for. I hadn't yet taken off my clothes, and while Tammy was in a climactic trance, I decided to drop my pants to the floor and pulled my shirt off. She dove face first into my six-pack abs and almost caused damage to her face as my twelve-inch flagpole stood up waiting for some attention. It was one thing to feel my dick against her ass at the club, but when she saw my twelve inches, a look of shock overtook her face. She extended both hands and wrapped them around my dick as she tried to jerk me back and forth while I stood in front of her. The face to dick meeting was perfect as she sat on the couch. I tilted my head back and waited for her to take me in her mouth, but the jerking back and forth continued.

Suddenly, a blowjob was not part of the equation, but her hypocritical ass enjoyed every nut she busted while I ate her. She was holding on to my dick like it was a snake waiting to bite the hell out of her tongue if she took it in her mouth. I wanted to help ease the situation a bit, so I tried to appeal to her humorous side. "I feel so free with you. I'd do anything to please you. You shouldn't deprive yourself the pleasure and freedom of tasting a new kind of beef because this is our first time. Think of this as a taste test. If you don't like it, you don't have to eat it; I mean lick it. Girl, I ate your pussy like we've known each other since kindergarten," I jokingly said to her. She laughed after my comment and slowly eased her head forward and her tongue was wrapped around my dick like a comforter around a cold child in the dead of winter. The shit felt great! I knew that Tammy was worried about whether or not I would think she was easy for sucking my dick on the first night we went out, as do most women. But the vibe was perfect and everything felt so natural. I ate her pussy because I wanted to and I didn't care what she thought of me.

As Tammy continued to take a thousand licks up and down and around my dick, I felt she was a little hesitant. She didn't want to showcase her expertise for lack of a bad reputation of a dick sucking queen. That was because she never met Tina and I could care less about what other people think. I brought her to the couch to take her mind off the fact that she had a dick in her mouth. It was time for us to take the sixty-nine position so she wouldn't have much time to hesitate about what nature intended. As I stuck my tongue inside her pussy with her round booty all over my face, she reached for my dick and her talent started to shine through. My job was to make her feel good enough so she could relax and do the best that she could with the talent she had acquired from experience. I was no fool. I could tell that Tammy had sucked more dicks than she wanted me to believe, but I didn't care. I wanted to enjoy the moment with her. She started grinding on my face as my tongue took over her clit and I knew that she was about to cum. She sucked harder on my dick and was trying to make me cum along with her. I inserted my index finger in her pussy while my tongue continued to float up and down with ease against her clit. Moments later the uncontrollable shake started again and I knew that Tammy was about to reach an explosive orgasm. The warmth of her mouth around my dick took away my control and before I could warn her, I released a couple of warm teaspoons of high protein down her throat and she took it down like a champ. Pussy juice took over my face as well, as Tammy exploded in my mouth.

After the first round, I was ready for the main event. Tammy's body was looking as delicious as ever and I hungered for more. After a quick trip to the bathroom to get a wet rag to wipe Tammy's juices from my face, I went into my suitcase to wrap my hard dick in an extra large Magnum condom. Tammy was lying on the bed with her legs wide open waiting for me to penetrate her. I couldn't help giving her pussy a few licks before I slowly inserted my dick into her pleasure dome. After mounting her and a good nine inches inside of her, I proceeded to caress her breasts and kiss her while I winded and grinded her to ecstasy. "Your dick feels so good inside me. Ooh! Aah! Keep doing it, baby. Oh, yes! I'm loving this dick." Tammy was a talker and that fueled me with even more energy. I was trying to take it easy on her, then I heard, "Give me all of it, daddy. Fuck me with that big dick!" With those encouraging words, I started humping her with all my might. I could feel her walls on the tip of my dick and she continued to scream in pleasure. I slightly lifted one leg up and that's when I found it, her g-spot. "Oh, shit, you got my spot, baby," she warned. I stayed in position and continued to wind and grind to the best of my ability. Tammy was enjoying every minute of it. I could feel her slowing down to keep from climaxing, but I would have none of it. As she slowed down, I picked up speed and just like that, the convulsions started and her orgasmic face appeared. With eyes rolling to the back of her of head, Tammy held on to me tight. I kept on until every ounce of ecstasy was reached.

Tammy's ass was my destination that night. I wanted to fuck her doggy style and that's exactly how I wanted to bust my next nut. With her ass propped over a pillow, I slowly eased my dick inside her sugar walls and I started banging away softly. With every stroke, I slightly tapped her ass and Tammy was once again saying a lot of sweet nothing to me as she enjoyed my long strokes. I couldn't help pulling on her hair while I smacked her ass harder. She became the sexual beast that I always fantasized about. I started laying down the pipe like Tammy wanted me to tear her pussy to shreds. "Harder! Fuck me harder!" she continued to scream. All my twelve inches were inside of her and her freakiness was turning me on. Without a second thought, I inserted my index finger in her ass and Tammy went crazy. Her hip movements accelerated and she was starting to reach climax again, but I wanted to get mine, too. Now my thumb was in her ass after pulling out my index finger, and while caressing her ass and stroking her, I felt the eruption of my thick semen running through my body. I quickly pulled off the condom so I could jerk every ounce of semen all over her ass, but Tammy didn't want that. Instead, she reached for my dick and took it in her mouth while playing with her clit. Since Tammy reached hers first, it was only just that she made sure I got mine. She welcomed my warm semen down her throat. I could only stand back and watch her because I was one happy brother.

CHAPTER 17

Sexual Tension Reliever

Things were going exactly as I imagined when we got back to my brother's house. Cassandra was more interested in getting to know Will better on the couch in the living room than fucking him, while Terrence and I lounged in the family room. Terrence and I talked about our lives a little more and he started getting a little touchy feely on the couch, which I didn't mind. A little massage to my outer thighs and a kiss in between conversation was very welcoming. However, it was getting late and I knew that Terrence had to be in his office early the next day for a meeting with a new client who was seeking a trade from the Minnesota Vikings. It was hard to watch him leave without as much as satisfying my throbbing pussy that was screaming his name. His departure also prompted Will and Cassandra to take their conversation to the bedroom. Oh shit, I was pissed. This motherfucker was about to get his freak on and I allowed my dick supply to walk right out the door.

I couldn't wait to find out the details of Will and Cassandra's "nightcap." My original hunch was that she was not the type of woman who would give it up on the first night, but I could be wrong. Anyway, after getting pissed at Will for thinking that he was about to fuck the hell out of Cassandra, I went to the guest room and dialed Terrence's cell phone number. I knew he hadn't gotten home yet because it had only been a few minutes since he left. "Hello," he answered in a sexy baritone that moistened my panties. "It's nice to hear your voice so soon," he charismatically said to me. That man was smooth and I wanted to bust a nut that night before I went to bed. "You know I really wanted you tonight, but the situation with my brother is the only reason why you're driving home alone," I said to him. "I know. I wanted you too and hopefully I can have you sooner than later." There he went with that smooth shit again. "How about you have me now?" I said to him. "Are you asking me to come back because I can make a u-turn and be over there in less then ten minutes," he said calmly with a sexy "you know you want to fuck me" demeanor. "No, silly," I responded quickly and continued, "I want you to have me now, on the phone." "You want to have phone sex with me?" he asked hesitantly. "Do you have a problem with that?" I asked. "No, not at all, baby. I'm just pulling into my garage, just give me a minute to get comfortable and we can both do what was meant to be done in person together." He was still smooth.

I wanted to find out how freaky he could be and phone sex was just what the doctor ordered. If Terrence was freaky enough to make me cum through the phone, I knew it wouldn't be long before I started erasing Darren from my thoughts. I needed to be naughty after I saw him all over that woman at the club. There was a point at the club where I noticed his excitement for her because he couldn't contain his erection. For a man with a big dick, he sure as hell doesn't know how to keep it inconspicuous.

Terrence kept me on speaker while he got undressed, and never once did he lose his sexy edge. By then I had a couple of fingers in my pussy and was waiting for Terrence to talk me through my nut. Phone sex was something that Darren and I never got into, but I always wanted to see if a guy could make me cum over the phone. Just as I was playing with my pussy, Terrence's sexy voice reemerged through the phone. "What are you in the mood for tonight, baby?" he asked with ease, as the words rolled off his tongue and out of his mouth. "Ooh, I like that. A man who cares enough to ask a woman what she wants," I replied and continued, "I want you to make me cum like I've never cum on the telephone before." "That's gonna be a little hard to do since I'm not physically there with you, but I'll try my best to paint a mental picture of what I would've done to you if I were there. Is that ok?" he asked. The sound of his voice had me dripping wet and that was just the beginning. His voice was a cross between Barry White and the soothing baritone of Gerald Levert with the looks of Boris Kodjoe. My pussy was on fire just talking to the man. "Be easy with me because I'm a virgin at this," I said. "Don't worry baby, you're in good hands," he assured me.

He started, "Well, I want you to close your eyes and imagine our tongues intertwining in a long, sensual kiss. While I'm kissing you, my hands are also wandering your body... Your lips are so soft and they taste so sweet...I'm sucking on your bottom lip while you suck on my top lip. It's so sensual you start grabbing my ass and reaching for my crotch, but I stop you because I want it to be all about you...I'm taking the straps of your teddy off your shoulders because I want to kiss your neck and shoulders as I make my way down to your firm breasts. Your skin tastes like honey and I'm indulging." I briefly interrupted him to say, "Yes, baby." He continued, "Your breasts are now in my hands and my tongue is salivating over your nipples. I take the left nipple in my mouth and I'm wrapping my tongue gently around it and continue to suck on it. You can feel the sensation of my tongue surging through your body from the suction on your nipple. You ask me to suck harder and I oblige. I'm gently rubbing your right nipple with my hand while sucking on the left one. They're both very erect and I bring your large breasts together so I can have both nipples in my mouth. I alternate my suction between the two and your pussy's getting drenched because you want me to fuck you. You can feel the hardness of my dick against your thigh, but you don't want me to penetrate you just yet."

Before Terrence could get to his next move, I had already busted my first nut. The soothing sound of his voice had me under a temporary spell that kept my juices flowing. "You know I just came, baby," I whispered to him. "Good! I wanna make you cum again," he said. "Believe me, I would love to reach another orgasm right now, but I'm too tired and too drained to stay up. How about we continue this tomorrow evening in person?" I suggested to him. "Sure. I'm looking forward to it. Get your rest because you're gonna need it for tomorrow," he said playfully. "I hope you don't end up eating your words, because this sister has a lot of energy and a big appetite for good dick," I told him. "My supply never runs out, baby. I always make sure I meet the demands of every satisfied customer," he said. "Customer?" I questioned. "It's just a figure of speech. It's all in fun and games," he responded. "We'll see about that tomorrow. Goodnight," I warned him before I got off the phone.

I fell asleep within a few minutes after I got off the phone with Terrence. I woke up the next morning feeling refreshed and looking forward to seeing him again. The thought of Darren boning that woman had completely staggered off my mind. If Terrence's bedroom skills were anything close in person to what he was like on the phone the night before, I knew I was gonna be satisfied. After having great thoughts about a wonderful day ahead, I decided to make breakfast for my brother and his friend.

CHAPTER 18

Da Hook Up

Will and Cassandra woke up to the smell of crispy bacon, scrambled eggs and blueberry pancakes. I credit my brother for keeping his fridge and cabinet stocked with food during my stay with him. Will came downstairs with his breath smelling all funky and grabbed a piece of bacon from the serving tray. "You might wanna go rinse your mouth with Listerine before your company comes down here," I said to him. "What company?" he said. "Didn't Cassandra spend the night with you last night?" I asked with a nosey flair. "Yeah, but she had to get up very early at six to go home and get ready for court. She's due in court at 9:00 a.m.," he told me. I must've slept like a baby because I didn't hear when she left. "That must've been some kind of nut that I busted last night," I said to myself. "So did you hit it?" I asked. "T, you're starting to sound like a dude. How you gonna ask me if I hit?" he said. "Just like I said, did you hit it? It's either yes or no and don't lie on your dick because I'm your sister and you don't have to impress me like I'm one of your boys," I said to him. "See, that's what I like about you; you keep it real. I'm glad you're my sister, but for your information, I did not hit it nor did I try," he said. "You mean, she didn't let you hit it, or you saw no window of opportunity to hit it last night," I said to him. "Damn, T, why you gotta put me on blast? It ain't like I won't hit it. I'm just taking my time. She's special," he confirmed.

I had to give my brother the benefit of the doubt because Cassandra seemed special and I almost started to feel that she was a little out of Will's league. The sister was very well put together and I would welcome her as a sister-in-law. Will had gotten used to so many chickenheads, I was afraid he was going to blow it with Cassandra, but he held his own. "So you ended up holding her all night with a woody?" I said, teasing him. "For your information, I did not have a woody and I did not hold her because I slept on the pullout sofa in my room. I really respect her as a person and I didn't want to cross the line with her intentionally or unintentionally. Are you satisfied?" he said sarcastically. I wanted to tease him a little more. "You might want to go wash that funky breath before you get all funky with me. Oh shit, it's already too late 'cause your breath is humming." He ran upstairs to go wash his mouth before coming back down to eat breakfast with me.

I assumed that Cassandra would be eating breakfast with us, so I cooked enough for three people. It was a good thing that Cassandra wasn't there because Will almost ate my portion as well. That boy could eat! We hardly said anything to each other at the table as he buried his face in his plate to devour the food like a hungry lion. By the time he came up for air, his plate was empty and I still had two pieces of bacon left on my plate that he had his eyes on. "Sis, when'd you learn how to cook so good?" he commented. "You act like I spent no time in the kitchen with mom," I said to him. "I was always at practice, so I didn't know," he said. It was time to change the subject because I really liked Cassandra and I wanted my brother to drop the gold-digger as soon as he could. "When are you going to see Cassandra again?" I asked. "She works a lot, so I'm not sure. I told her if we don't make the playoffs that my season will end early and we can pick it up from there." That window of opportunity was very small and I needed to make sure that Will got to know Cassandra quick before Marla came by shaking her ass like a dangling carrot in front of him so he could chase it like a rabbit. "Why don't you invite her over for dinner tonight?

I'll cook for you. Just don't go bragging about your culinary skills like you cooked the food yourself," I warned him. "I don't want her to think that I'm sweatin' her," he said. "Women like Cassandra aren't small minded. They like men who show interest, know what they want and come after it. It's only the chickenheads with nothing to offer who feel that way about men. It's a self-esteem boost for the chickenheads when a man is a little persistent. I'm sure Cassandra would welcome your invitation," I advised. "Well, she said she'll call me around lunch time. I'll bring it up when she calls," he told me. "I bet you she'll accept your invitation. You have to stop messing with small minded women," I said to him.

While I was working hard to make sure that my brother didn't let a good catch slip away, I was also making my own plans to have Terrence serve me on a platter later that evening. I figured my brother would need his privacy and that would give me time to go see Terrence. Honestly, my female intuition told me that Cassandra was a good woman and she would be a great addition to Will's life.

As promised, Cassandra called Will while court was in recess around lunchtime. She rarely spent time in court because her job basically dealt with negotiations with other companies, but she was working a special case that required litigation in a courtroom. Will was pleasantly surprised when Cassandra accepted his invitation to dinner that evening. That meant that it was going to be one more day without Marla and Will might even ask Cassandra to go to the benefit dinner with him after spending time with her. She would be a better fit for the event, as Marla only cared about being seen in a new expensive dress. Will's plans were confirmed and I had to start cooking for his evening date.

Will, my big spending brother, thought it would cost at least a thousand dollars to cook him a complete meal, and he handed me a thousand dollars in cash to go grocery shopping. I was surprised and shocked at the same time. "Why would you think it costs that much money to prepare a meal for two? I asked him. "Marla always says the best meals are expensive and when she comes by to prepare dinner, she usually asks for about a thousand dollars. The food usually lasts me a couple of days. She's no great chef like mom, but she can throw down a little," he said. "Will, please stop acting like a fool. You know damn well that it does not cost a thousand dollars to prepare a meal even if it was by Wolfgang Puck himself. This woman has been taking you on a ride for too long." I continued, "I'm so pissed at you for acting so dumb and gullible around this girl because of pussy. You used to be a mack, what happened?" I said angrily. "T, I can't explain it. This girl came into my life and I became complacent because I was getting good sex and a good meal every now and then, so I didn't complain. However, I can see where you're coming from. I'm gonna be more careful from now on," he assured me.

"Just so we're clear on a few things, I want to know what you feel like eating tonight. I want to show you how much an extravagant meal will cost you, so that no one can ever think of you as a dumb jock throwing money around for no reason," I said to him. "Let's make a list of everything you want for tonight and you can be as extravagant as you want." I waited to hear his list. "T, I know you don't know how to cook everything I wanna eat tonight," he said sarcastically. "Try me," I answered. "Okay. I definitely want shrimp cocktail, lobster, and t-bone steaks with rice and vegetables. I also want chocolate éclair for dessert just like mom used to make for us," he told me. "Is that all?" I asked. "Yes. Oh, one more thing; I want a nice bottle of wine, too," he said. We got down and wrote a complete list of everything he wanted and the total cost was less than two hundred dollars. He was shocked. The most expensive item on the list was the bottle of wine, which cost about fifty bucks. When he asked for his change back, I told him I was gonna keep the rest of the money as a reminder of his stupidity. No wonder Marla was coming by once a week to cook for him. She had a part-time job earning full-time pay with extra benefits. I also found out that Marla claimed she was in college trying to earn a nursing degree at the University of Georgia. However, when I called the registrar's office, there was no one enrolled there under the name Marla Peoples. I couldn't wait to meet this woman.

I dragged Will to the grocery store with me so he could see for himself how much everything cost and that he didn't have to rely on a woman to feed him. I knew that my brother had enough money to bring a chef to his house to cook for him everyday, but I wanted him to be self-sufficient, just in case. Money comes and goes, but self-sufficiency lasts forever. It was great spending time with him because I discovered a lonely soul in my brother during my first couple of days there. The sexual romps with Marla only gratified a temporary void because after she left, he would feel lonely all over again. Marla only came around to fulfill her financial needs. My brother needed someone to be there for him and with him to make him feel whole. It's human nature for people to want companionship. My brother was ready to start a family. He wanted to have someone at home to help heal his wounds from the football field. Cassandra was going to be one lucky lady, I hoped.

While I had empathy for my brother, I couldn't keep my panties from getting drenched every time I thought about Terrence. I imagined that he was going to rock my world later that day. When I was in the kitchen cooking, I called Terrence to solidify our plans for the evening. We had plans to hook up at six o'clock just before Cassandra was scheduled to be at my brother's house. I wanted to be out and gone by the time she got there so she could feel comfortable alone with Will. I don't know where this saying came from, because pigs don't sweat, but "I was sweating like pig" in that kitchen. My brother wanted a three-course meal and I worked my ass off to cook it for him. By the time I was done, he had battered shrimp, shrimp cocktail, shrimp scampi, steamed lobster, a few t-bone steaks, steamed vegetables, white rice, buttered garlic sauce and chocolate éclair for dessert. I was happy to cook for him and I was excited about the prospect of a new relationship between him and Cassandra.

By the time I was done with everything, it was time for a long soothing bath before Terrence showed up. While I took a nice bath filled with bubbles, great thoughts of Terrence making me feel like a woman filled my head. My mind drifted for a few minutes and my Calgon bubble bath took me away to a place where I imagined Terrence walking through the bathroom door with his shirt off with a towel wrapped around his waist to join me in the jetted tub for two in the bathroom. I could see the bulge under the towel before he finally dropped it to the floor. There it was in front of me, finally; all ten and a half thick inches of him. I sat up to get a taste of the mighty beef standing before me, but he stopped me short to plant a wet kiss upon my lips. It started with a peck then a slight slip of the tongue. It was hard to let go, so we French kissed a little while longer as he bent down to caress my breasts with his hands. The water pressure in the jetted tub only added more complexities to my horniness. I wanted Terrence to hurry in and take me, but he was slow with his hands and even slower with his tongue. As his hands reached around my backside for a light soothing massage, his tongue had already reached my breasts. My nipples stood erect and waiting for mouth to nipple resuscitation. Terrence provided just enough life in them to increase the estrogen waiting to explode from my body.

The bathroom was quiet for a long while before my brother woke me out of my day dream to ask, "T, are you alright? You've been in there for a while now. You didn't pass out, did you?" I was nearing my nut and this fool messed up the whole thing. "I'm okay," I answered trembling at the afterthought of a well orchestrated orgasm. I promised myself I was going to wear Terrence's ass out. I couldn't wait for the clock to hit six on the dot. I had been in the water long enough and my skin was starting to get wrinkly. I needed to get out and get ready for my stud. I wanted to wear something that was going to be irresistible to him. I wanted him to lose control and I knew just the right outfit to do that. My dress had to be fitted, alluring and sexy.

Without looking too much like a hoochie to my brother, I wanted to be sexy and elegant leaving the house. I wore my black mini skirt with a black, buttoned-down shirt tied around my waist. I wore no stockings to show off my smooth legs, and if I as much as sneezed, that skirt was going to roll right up my ass exposing my bare pussy. There was no room for underwear in that skirt. I buttoned my shirt up while I was in the house with my brother, but my plan was to undo a couple of the buttons the minute I stepped out of the house to entice Terrence with my cleavage. I'd planned to wear the hell out of my breasts while they're still perky. Soon, children are gonna make them sag and I won't be able to show them off as much. I was getting as much wear out of them as I could. I was done getting dressed at exactly six on the dot, and Terrence was at the door ringing the doorbell as I stepped out of the room. He showed up right on time, and I was impressed with that. Promptness always impressed me.

I opened the door to find a handsome looking Terrence in a black suit and white striped shirt and smelling so good, like he had just walked out of the Giorgio Armani cologne factory. I wanted to lick his neck while I hugged him. "These are for you," he said, as he handed me a bouquet of a dozen roses. I pleasantly replied, "Thank you." "I have this great little restaurant that I want to take you to," he said. I was in no mood for food because I ate enough during the day while cooking for my brother. "How about I bring some of the food that I cooked today to your place, so we can a have a great night in," I suggested. His face lit up like I just offered him a million dollars. That man wanted me and all I wanted was for him to deliver and fuck me well. I went to the kitchen and packed some food in this fancy serving set that Marla probably forced my brother to buy. I took enough food for Terrence because I wanted to stay light and right for the evening.

My brother was in the shower when Terrence showed up, so I lucked out because he didn't get a chance to see my sluttish attempt at seducing Terrence with my outfit. My tities damn near fell out of my shirt, and my bra was so tight I felt like I was gasping for air. He was trying his best to be a gentleman when I opened the door, but keeping his eyes away from my breasts was even harder. "I'm leaving," I screamed to Will through the closed bathroom door. "Leave his number on the fridge in case I have to hunt him down for any reason," Will said playfully, but I knew he was serious and Terrence had better taken him seriously. My brother wanted to make sure that I was going to be okay. "I'll be home late, so don't wait up. I'm taking the spare keys with me," I continued to talk through the door. "Okay. Have a good time because I know I will tonight," he said clowning.

Before I walked out the door, I wrote down Terrence's phone number on the pad hanging on the fridge door in case of an emergency. I also wrote down Terrence's plate number. He was still standing in the foyer waiting for me. He couldn't see what I was doing in the kitchen. I looked over to his car to memorize his license plate number while I hugged him at the door. He may have smelled good, but I was not going to be that fool again, not after that episode with Vinny. I've had my guard up ever since.

CHAPTER 19

A Night of Passion

Terrence allowed me to walk in front of him so he could watch me strut my way to the car, and that I did. I felt like there was a runway in front of me as I sashayed my stuff in four-inch heels, mini skirt and legs Tina Turner wish she had, in front of Terrence. I felt good because after I reached the car and turned around, I noticed a big Kool-Aid smile flashing across Terrence's face as he leapt forward to hold the car door open for me. He took the scenic route to his place in Buckhead to show me all the luxury that Atlanta has to offer. We drove by the Governor's Mansion, the Lenox Mall, Phipps Plaza and the exclusive gated communities of Buckhead. Terrence wasn't doing too bad himself. We pulled up to his house in this gated subdivision with multi-million dollar homes. This brother was living it up. I never get too impressed with other people's material possessions because I grew up a spoiled brat who led a fortunate life, but Terrence's crib was like whoa! Even my brother's house didn't compare to his.

We pulled up to this four-sided brick home with a three-car garage and a circular driveway in the front. Terrence pressed the automatic garage door opener to reveal his black Range Rover and a red, hot convertible M class 645 BMW CSI. He parked the silver S550 Mercedes Benz in the unoccupied space. His lifestyle was grand and I started to wonder what kind of clients he was representing. We entered the house through the door in the garage that led straight to the kitchen, and what a kitchen it was. I placed the food on the counter top and stood around to just admire the whole kitchen. Italian marble tiles covered the floor, stainless steel appliances accented the oak wood cabinets that filled the walls, and an exquisite solid piece of marble sat atop the island in the middle of the kitchen. The stainless steel faucet and sink were breathtaking. I never aspired to be a housewife, but his kitchen made me feel like putting on an apron and start cooking.

Terrence either had great taste or enough money to hire an overpriced home decorator like Collin Cowie to decorate his house. The Italian furnishings were impeccable and the house was completely breathtaking. Each room had a different theme and each one was welcoming. For a relatively unknown agent, Terrence was living large. I had never heard of him before I met him. Even my brother didn't know anything about him, and my brother was an athlete. Terrence was showing off his house in a subtle way, but I didn't see anything wrong with a man who was proud of his accomplishments. I was even a little surprised that Terrence didn't have much more of a flair of arrogance. Given that most brothers in his situation are usually overly arrogant about such great accomplishments. He gave me a tour of the whole house and talked about how each piece of furniture was especially picked to his liking.

The high ceiling throughout the house made it look even bigger. A grand piano sat in the living room and I wondered if he even knew anything about music. I was in awe of everything that I saw. As we walked towards his office, framed, autographed pictures of him and many well-known athletes lined the walls of the hallway leading to his office. Terrence's office was grand. His office was laid out like he was the CEO of a Fortune 100 company. My panties started getting wet, and I started thinking about all the places that I wanted to be fucked that night. He had enough couches in the house for me to get fucked on fabrics from five different continents. The house was too grand for me to tour it all. I suggested we take a seat in the family room where the fifty-inch plasma television was located. Terrence made an even better suggestion by going downstairs to his custom movie theatre with enough seats for twenty people.

After taking off his jacket to make himself more comfortable, we headed downstairs to the custom designed home theatre. The latest clear version of *Daddy's Daycare* starring Eddie Murphy was what we ended up watching. I was a sucker for comedy and I still feel that Eddie Murphy is a comic genius. Since I had never been fucked in a movie theatre before, my mind was wandering all over the place. While I was sitting next to Terrence with his arm wrapped around my shoulders, I imagined him fucking me in the most awkward positions. We were about a half hour into the movie before he gave me a kiss. It was an attempt to make his presence felt and make me feel wanted. His kiss was my opportunity to basically have my way with him. I liked Eddie Murphy, but not that much.

Terrence intended to give me a light peck on the lip, but I clutched on to the back of his head and turned it into a spectacle of a kiss that led to my skirt rolling up above my thighs, and his fingers searching for my g-spot. One of my legs stretched across the arm of the chair that separated us while the other one lay dormant on the floor. Terrence's controlling voracity took over as I started breathing heavy, enjoying his fingers deep inside my pussy. He leaned over toward me with his tongue steady in my mouth while he figured out a comfortable position to have me. He finally pulled up the arm on the chair and we were now lying across the two chairs with Terrence on top of me, kissing me and finger fucking me to a drench. I leisurely unbuttoned his shirt so I could run my hands across his bare chest. As I caressed his back, Terrence was reaching for my breasts. Access was easy because he only needed to undo the top button before my tits spilled out of my bra. My erected nipples found their way in Terrence's mouth in no time and I had a stream running down my legs, I was so hot.

As my juices flowed downward, Terrence found a comfortable enough position where his tongue landed directly on my clit. He maneuvered his tongue like a kitten trying to clean herself. With each stroke of his tongue I was nearing ecstasy. With two of his fingers still inside my pussy, Terrence never came up for air as he licked my clit softly. The man knew what he was doing and I was enjoying every minute of it. Then finally, he used a technique that I couldn't even describe properly. While he held back the foreskin on my clit with his right thumb, he wiggled his fingers inside of me and his tongue on my clit simultaneously to force my juices to squirt out all over his face. I clamped Terrence's shoulders and screamed at the top of my lungs, "I'm cumming! Yes, I'm cumming! Oh, shit, I'm cumming!" I noticed a satisfied look on his face, and I knew then that he wasn't a selfish lover. The man was happy to see me cum.

After finally shaking out of my trance, I noticed Terrence sitting on the chair next to me watching me and smiling. But more importantly, I noticed his ten-inch dick standing straight up waiting for action. I leaned my body across the chair to lie down on my stomach and I slowly took the head of his dick in my mouth and circled my tongue around it. I licked it slow and all around, and Terrence just sat back enjoying the motion of my tongue around his dick. As I increased the pace of my oral tactics, he started stroking my hair with his hands confirming that I was doing a great job. Confident that my head game was up to par with his expectations, I started relaxing to enjoy the sweet taste of his dick in my mouth. His dick tasted so good and I wanted him to feel just as great as he made me feel. I took about a good seven inches of it in my mouth as he watched in amazement and hummed to himself. I started sucking harder and he

87

reacted more. The more I sucked the more reaction I got out of him. I tilted my head back and went for the gusto. I took all ten and a half inches of his dick in my mouth and played with the head of his dick with the back of my throat. Terrence couldn't control it anymore as he let out a loud roar, "I'm cumming!" I quickly pulled my head up to avoid swallowing him. I jerked the semen out of him as his body crumbled in the chair losing total control in my hands. He felt like a little baby going into a commotion as he lost himself in my mouth.

As good as the little episode inside Terrence's home theatre was, I wasn't satisfied enough to let him off the hook that easily. I always want to be fucked well before walking away from a great dick supply. We left the theatre and walked up to his monstrous sized bedroom. He had a bed that was so huge, Shaq, Tim Duncan and Yao Ming could all sleep on it together. He threw himself on the bed with his dick still standing straight up waiting for my tunnel of love to be wrapped around it. I had never been on a bed so huge, so I took the opportunity to roll around with Terrence as he lay on top of me with his dick inside of me after wrapping himself in a condom. It was rhythmic the way we rolled around on the bed without his dick slipping out of my pussy. The exhilaration from our tumbling sent a magnitude of energy through Terrence's body and before I knew with it, I was on my knees facing the glass mirror on his headboard while he pounded me from behind. I got off on watching the grimaces on his face as he tried to conquer my pussy. With each hard stroke he started asking me, "Are you gonna make this pussy mine?" I was thinking, *You keep fucking me like that, I might not have a choice.* Terrence's dick felt so good, I didn't want him to cum. I eased my ass away from him to help slow down his strokes so I could enjoy the cadence of his dick inside me.

He took notice of my direction and slowed down the pace so we could both enjoy the moment. I could see the joy on Terrence's face as he brought his hands to caress my ass while his dick continued to thrust my walls of pleasure to ecstasy. He pounded my pussy for about fifteen minutes without breaking his stride. I arched my ass up so he could get a better view of his penetration, and just like that, he picked up the pace another notch and I knew that he was going to have very little control over his dick. I adjusted my position so his dick would hit my g-spot just right so I could cum with him. As he held onto my ass and unloaded his exact strokes on me, I felt the uncontrollable urge to cum. I pushed my ass back against his crotch to take all of him inside me as I started to shake, making sure that every ounce of my orgasm was exasperated. Terence's freaky ass followed me into ecstasy seconds later as he tried to push his body into my ass while shaking violently. I enjoyed the fact that he lost control, which told me he was a little vulnerable.

Terrence and I went at it a couple more times before the night was over. And each time my orgasm would get stronger and more earth shaking. This was a man that knew what he was doing and I wanted to maximize those benefits like he was a premier health plan. By the time I decided to leave at three o'clock in the morning to go home, I was exhausted and my pussy couldn't take anymore. I was feeling happy inside as Terrence dropped me off at my brother's house and sealed the night with a passionate kiss. Hell, I could see myself having this man's children. His sexual techniques reminded of a particular guy that I used to fuck back in college who ended up moving to Maryland. Terrence made me feel like a college student all over again.

That night, I had no problem sleeping and apparently neither did my brother because I could hear him snoring all the way down the hall when I got home. I knew Cassandra didn't spend the night because her car was not in the driveway, but by the sound of his snores, I knew she gave it up. A man could only snore that loudly only after he got some good pussy and busted a couple of good nuts. I was happy too that they connected because it was time to kick Marla out of his life.

CHAPTER 20

Getting to Know Tammy

Tammy and I had great sex. Other than Tina, I had never met a woman who could satisfy me so well sexually. However, I wanted our relationship to be about more than sex. Tammy was undeniably gorgeous and I could tell that she had potential and was very smart, but I needed to get to know her. I have to admit that it was hard controlling my blood flow around Tammy. Her curvaceous body always got a rise out of me for no reason. I knew it was going to be a task getting to know her without trying to get in her pants every time I saw her. Tammy also didn't make it easy for me either. She was very straightforward and had no problem with her sexuality, whatsoever. It was normal for her to say things like, "You look delicious in your suit." Those words would travel straight down to my dick and I would have a problem hiding my twelve inches from her. She also knew that she turned me on in the worst way. Maybe we were going through the honeymoon period in our relationship, but I could tell that I was always going to be turned on by her. She didn't make sex a task as Tina was starting to do. It was spontaneous and natural.

I must've sexed Tammy a hundred times while I was in Atlanta. We spent most of our time indoors and most of it was naked. She also took interest in my work, as she was a business major back in school. Tammy was showing me the kind of attention that I never received from Tina and it was refreshing. She made me feel like a new man, and the fact that she lived in Atlanta gave me a chance to miss her. We talked on the phone often and I found out many of her likes and dislikes. Her conversations were always interesting and we often made fun of people who use made-up words like "conversate and tooken," and think that they are actual words. She and I were on the same page most of the time. Tammy was not the typical woman. She knew what she wanted to do with her life ever since she was a freshman in high school. She had everything mapped out and had a plan to execute everything accordingly.

We were having a great time. I even went back to Atlanta twice to visit her. We went to the Museum of Art, the King Center, Underground Atlanta and a few other visitors' hotspots. She was my tour guide and we had a ball, but more importantly the sex got even more intense and frequent when I saw her. My dick just would not go down every time I was in Tammy's presence. I remember one time while we were at a show at the Fox Theatre checking out Malik Yoba's play called "What's On the Hearts Of Men," I found my hands creeping up Tammy's skirt and before I knew it, I was on my knees in the aisle eating her out while the play went on. It was a good thing that we got VIP balcony seats where we were the only ones in that section. The thrill of someone peeping at us set off what was a tumultuous orgasm for Tammy while I displayed my tongue skills between her thighs during the show.

Malik was trying his best to hone his skills as a stage actor in his first play, but our attention was elsewhere. I can't even recall what the play was about. I recall slipping my tongue in Tammy's mouth for a nice, sweet, French kiss. "You're making me wet," she whispered, and that's all it took for my desire to please to accelerate. We tried our best not to be rude while the show was going on by minimizing the moaning and groaning. Tammy was breathing heavily as my tongue hit her favorite spot around the base of her neck. "Don't start nothing you can't finish," she quietly moaned. Not one to disappoint and leave a job undone, I placed my index finger over her mouth, signaling for her to be quiet as I ran my free hand up her thighs. I pulled her thong to the side with my index finger as my middle finger found solace in the warmth of her wet darkness. It was slippery and very wet. I brought the finger to my mouth to taste her juice. She tasted good. I wanted more. I knew penetration was out of the question, so I resigned with the fact that I could only eat her.

We continued to kiss while my fingers found their way back inside her pussy. It was magic the way I inserted two of my fingers upwards inside her pussy to find her g-spot. She was trying her best to keep it quiet and low-key, but it wasn't good enough. I had to place my hand over her mouth and apply a little bit of pressure to keep her from screaming in pleasure. I could feel her climactic convulsions as my fingers ever so gently touched her g-spot. She held on to the armchair for support. I was just in the beginning stages of the theatre experience with her. Without a moment's notice, the playbill found its way to the bottom of my knees to keep my pants from getting dirty. My head was arched back as I took in the pleasure of savoring Tammy's pinkness.

The tingling sensation of her juice on my tongue tasted like my favorite strawberry flavored Starburst fruit candy. Her pussy smelled fresh and clean and my tongue found her hole to be a soothing comfort. I hardened my tongue up and started stroking Tammy back and forth until she grasped the back of my head with her head tilted to the ceiling and eyeballs somewhere in the back of her head. She was humping my tongue like a hard dick. No, she was fucking my tongue hard and I allowed her to enjoy every minute of it. Each time I came up for air, I replaced my tongue with a finger or two to keep the flow going. Her thighs were gyrating against the seat and Tammy loved the voyeuristic risk we were taking. I wanted to make sure that she got her best orgasm ever while in a confined place. So I took my tongue out of her and started licking her clit while I massaged her inner thighs with my hands. Her clit was a little bigger than normal and it stood erect against my tongue. The counterclockwise direction really got her going as I licked her pussy until I almost became dizzy. My mouth was covered with her scent and juice. Finally, I felt what seemed like a shock of an electrical volt jolted her body up from the chair as Tammy grabbed my head tightly and started shaking until her orgasm took her breath away. It was a night to remember and I'll never look at the Fox Theatre the same way again.

Those excited, spontaneous moments became a routine part of our relationship as Tammy and I started seeing more of each other. While we enjoyed spending time with each other, we also found out we had similar goals in life. Tammy was passionate about having a family some day, and she wanted it to be with a man that would understand that she wanted to have a career as well. After completing her MBA, Tammy had planned to work for a couple of years before establishing her import/export company. She wanted to import and export goods from China and the Caribbean to America. It was a sound enough plan and I knew she'd do it one day, successfully. Our relationship was clearly defined as casual, but with each visit, I could sense Tammy's feelings growing for me. I was feeling her as well, but not the same kind of emotions that I had developed for Tina, at least not yet.

While visiting me one weekend in New York, I took Tammy to the 40/40 Club in Manhattan. There seems to be this fascination with Jay Z's new club and most visitors in New York want to experience it just once. I decided to fulfill her curiosity. The first thing I noticed as we walked through the door was that the club was truly a hip-hop spot. There was no dress code as many club goers were wearing baggy jeans, Timb boots and other urban apparel. I felt a little overdressed even though I wore casual pants, a button–down, striped shirt and shoes. Tammy was totally glamorous like she was gonna meet Jay Z, the man himself. She looked good and maybe in the back of her mind she thought she could give Beyonce a little competition. With her elongated legs hovering four-inch black stilettos and a little black dress that barely made it down her thighs and flawless make-up, all eyes were on Tammy as we walked in the club. I can't say that I didn't receive a few glances myself.

While we were in the club having a good time, I decided to check out the sports room while Tammy walked around to check out the rest of the place with one of the hostesses as her tour guide. Everyone who patronized the club was offered a free tour by one of the hostesses. I had been there before and there was no reason for me to repeat the tour. Besides, the Mayweather/De La Hoya fight was on, and I didn't want to miss that. I couldn't wait for the golden boy to get his ass kicked by the pretty boy or vice versa. Either way, it was a highly anticipated fight by two great fighters. I felt like De La Hoya had lost his edge while Mayweather was gaining an edge. I really wanted De La Hoya to walk away with a draw because it would've left a glimpse of hope in great boxing. The days of Sugar Ray Leonard, Marvin Hagler and Roberto Durand were long gone. Mayweather sat atop of the boxing world without a real challenger in sight. I was sitting there chatting with a few brothers about the boxing world when this gorgeous lady came and sat next to me. The place was crowded and this guy had given up his seat to her. She was leaning a little bit on me when Tammy walked in and that's when I saw the questionable side of her.

"No this heifer is not just leaning all over my man," Tammy screamed out with a feisty attitude loud enough for the whole room to come to a complete halt with full attention towards her. The Mayweather/De La Hoya fight was no longer the focal point of the room; everyone turned their attention to the new anticipated fight between Tammy and the woman. "You're not gonna call me out my name, bitch," the other woman answered with an even feistier attitude and a Bronx accent. Tammy may have been tough, but I questioned whether or not she would've had a chance against the Bronx bombshell. The remainder of Tammy's Sex on the Beach drink left the bottom of her glass and found its way to the lady's face in less than a New York second. There was no time to bob and weave or dodge the wet bullet flying her way full steam, with the jealousy of a tigress. Everyone jumped to their feet to watch the live show, but to their dismay, security responded quickly and effectively. The swift movement of Tammy's drink smashing against the woman's face was the only action to be seen that night.

Tammy was escorted to the front door with my ass in tow making sure the bouncers didn't act too aggressively. I'm not saying that I would have fought two big ass bouncers if they got out of line, but I wouldn't stand around and watch them beat Tammy down either. After all, it was me that she became jealous over. Once we were out the club, the banter started, "That trick was lucky security came and broke us up, I would've beaten her ass down," she said angrily. I had no idea where all that anger and jealousy were coming from. Tammy had no reason to feel threatened by that woman at all. I wasn't sure if I ever wanted to see that side of her again. That situation created a dent in the way that I viewed Tammy. I honestly thought that she was or could be a basket case a la Glen Close from *Fatal Attraction*. That was definitely something that I didn't have room for in my life.

The drive back home was a bit more apologetic after Tammy calmed down. I didn't buy the explanation that she felt "disrespected" by the woman. If the woman had any intention of flirting or getting with me, I didn't notice it. I thought that the room was so crowded that she got a little too close to me by accident. After that little incident, I didn't know if I wanted to bring Tammy out to a club ever again.

She never displayed that behavior in Atlanta and there was no sign that she could carry that kind of attitude. From then on, I was being cautious with her. However, that caution only applied until I saw her naked body in front of me, then all caution was thrown to the wind. She was bad.

CHAPTER 21

My Brother's Crazy World

My vacation in Atlanta came and went and I had a great time with Terrence the rest of the time. I also made sure that my brother dropped Marla like a bad habit. Cassandra ended up going to the benefit gala with him, and he had to take out a restraining order against Marla. Well actually, he had to deal with a lot more drama than that. She was so pissed that my brother didn't take her to the gala, she came by the house and smashed his windshield and more, then wanted to fuck his brains out afterwards to keep him from pressing charges. However, it didn't just stop there. Marla's money faucet was about to be shut off and she didn't know how to handle it. I damned near had to whoop her ass before I left. That crazy ass chick came by the house calling me all kinds of names without finding out who I was first. "You fucking this big titty bitch? Is that why you can't return my calls," she screamed at the top of her lungs, when my brother opened the door after she rang the bell. "You also took this bitch to the gala with you on Saturday, didn't you?" she questioned. "If I get one more bitch outta you, I will mop the floor with yo ass," I said to her. "Come on then. Let's get it on. You wanna fight over some dick, we can fight," she yelled. It was the wrong neighborhood for her to be acting like that. She got her exclusive pass revoked by showing her ass out like that.

"Look, you're not gonna come here and disrespect my sister like that," my brother said to her. "She's your sister?" she asked shockingly in a monotone. "I'm sorry. I didn't mean to be disrespectful," she said, trying to save face, but it was a few minutes too late and she had confirmed my suspicions that she was a chickenhead to begin with. I didn't have to convince my brother that she had to go anymore. She was too hyper and he advised her to go home. He wanted to tell her that he wasn't going to see her anymore, but the timing was wrong. Lord knows what that chick would have done if my brother told her then that he didn't want to see her anymore. So it was the right call at the time.

I was a little too anxious to see my brother rid himself of that headache and I wanted it to happen before I left. An hour after she left, she called my brother back and I knew it was her on the phone because of his facial expressions. My brother had a hard time letting people down, but he sure as hell could knock the daylights out of an opponent. I gritted my teeth and told him that he had better tell that girl that it was over between them before things got way out of hands. "Marla, I can't see you no more. It's over." Click. All she heard was a dial tone as he hung up the phone quickly in her ear. His soft heart couldn't let her have it the way she deserved it. I was disappointed, but happy that he did it.

Marla wasn't going to let my brother off the hook that easily. Who was going to finance her ghetto fabulous lifestyle now? She wasn't having that. The wrath of a woman scorned was about to hit my brother in the worse way. Marla claimed to have left a few things at my brother's house and wanted to pick them up. My brother agreed to leave the garage door open so she could pick a box of miscellaneous items that he gathered from the house. It was the biggest mistake that he ever made. He gave her total access to that Cadillac Escalade truck he loved so much. He opted to drive his brand new Mercedes Benz to practice that day. Having a bag full of golf clubs hanging on the wall didn't help either. Marla took out one of the golf clubs and smashed out the windshield of his truck, then proceeded to smash all the rest of the windows out as well after impatiently waiting for my brother to show up. As if that wasn't enough, she found his toolbox and took out a screwdriver and poked holes in all four of his tires. She was going mad. She found some spray paints and spray painted his whole garage. So much for a secluded home in an exclusive community. She ransacked his car and the garage until she was completely satisfied before going home.

When my brother arrived home to find a complete disarray of his garage, he went nuts. He called Marla and told her that he was going to snap her neck for destroying his home. He had no idea that she was recording the conversation. She never mentioned anything about destroying his property; she only allowed him to rant about killing her then hung up the phone. My brother was heated when he called me to tell me about the events. I wanted to go back to Atlanta to kick Marla's ass myself. The first thing I told my brother was to call the police and report it as a crime. I also told him to take pictures of it in case it ever ended up in court. I tried as much as I could to console him, but while we were on the phone, Terrence called on the other line. I knew my brother needed to vent so I chose not to answer the call. Will continued to express his anger for another twenty minutes before my phone started ringing again and it was Terrence, again. He told me to go ahead and pick up the phone and that he would call me later.

CHAPTER 22

Getting To Know Terrence

"Hi,baby!" he said excitedly. "How was your day?" he then asked. I proceeded to tell him about my day and my brother's situation. Terrence informed me to advise my brother to file a lawsuit against Marla for defacing and destruction of his property. "Chickenheads like that are able to get away with their malicious and ghetto behaviors because men are not willing to make them pay for their crime. They always feel that pussy is a good enough reward. That's why I don't mess with chickenheads, and I never will," he said unapologetically. I could understand where Terrence was coming from, so I didn't respond to his comment. "Enough about chickenheads, how's my stud doing?" I asked playfully. "I could be doing better if you were down here with me," he said. "And why is that, may I ask?" "Because you make me feel whole and happy. I've been looking for a person like you all my life," he said. He was starting to butter me up and I was all bread.

I can honestly say that I felt connected to Terrence on many levels, but the one thing that bothered me was his lifestyle. It was a little questionable to me. While I was in Atlanta, I visited his office and I noticed that traffic was light to say the least. How he lived so grand with so few clients, I didn't understand. He had couple of clients who were probably third or fourth string players on the bench, but nobody notable enough to earn him the kind of money that he lavishly lived by. Having been a practicing attorney in the past, I figured he must've had some high profile cases where he earned beaucoup money to sustain his lifestyle. However,

I'm nosey. I needed proof. I was not the kind of girl to be fooled by good looks, good dick and what appeared to be a great lifestyle. I wanted to check the layers underneath before getting sprung.

For the next few days, Terrence and I talked regularly and he even flew to New York a couple of times to see me. While he was New York, we went everywhere from the Empire State building to Ellis Island to the Brooklyn Museum. But the most memorable place we went to was Central Park. The cast of an evening shadow was just dawning on us and the cool breeze of winter rendered our bodies in a tight embrace underneath a tree away from the walking trail. It was there that Terrence planted a big, wet juicy kiss on my lips telling me he loved me. I didn't quite arrive emotionally there with him yet, so I simply nodded. "That's all I get after I told you that I love you, a nod?" he said. "Terrence, I just came out of a long term relationship and I'm just watching my heart for now," I told him. "I see," he said in an uncertain tone. I didn't know whether or not Terrence truly loved, but I thought it was a little too soon for him to be springing that love shit on me.

"How about we just go with the flow and see where it leads us," I suggested. "All right, no pressure. Just know that I love you and I want to do everything in my power to make you happy. I'm patient. I'm not going anywhere," he said. He didn't sound completely confident, but it was an honest enough effort. I wish I could reciprocate his feelings, but I couldn't at the time. I enjoyed his company and more importantly his dick and being so close to his minty fresh breath was making me horny. I wanted to settle the mood down a little, so I reached in for a kiss from Terrence. He obliged. It was sweet and tasteful. I could feel his taste buds intertwining with mine and I was breathless. Terrence was a daredevil who decided to bury his face in my chest. I soon found myself leaning against a big tree with my arms wrapped around Terrence and one my tities in his mouth. I was charged up through the suction of his tongue on my breasts. My hands wandered around his chest underneath his winter coat. The temperature was perfectly cool for the beginning of winter, and I was so hot, it didn't really matter whether or not it was cold outside.

In a situation like this, it would have served me better to wear a mini skirt for easy access, but I had no intention of fucking Terrence at the park before I left the house. With one eye focused on the lookout for oncoming intruders, I reluctantly pulled off my pants exposing my bare ass under my trench coat in the middle of Central Park. I didn't wear any underwear before I left the house because I knew that Terrence and I would be going at it when we made it back to my house, but my plans came sooner rather than later. I was standing there in my boots with just a shirt on with my breasts hanging out my bra and Terrence buried between them. It gave the illusion that I might've been wearing a mini skirt or something in case the cops pulled up. My pants lay on the ground nearby and before I knew it, Terrence had made his way down my pussy, eating the hell out me with my legs spread apart. "Oh my God," I kept whispering to myself as he ate my pussy like a carnivore eating his favorite t-bone steak. The tree was my only source of balance and support as Terrence wrapped his tongue around my clit forcing a nut out of me, unexpectedly.

It was getting dark and I knew that there was no way anybody could see us even from the walkway. His hard dick was thrusting against my thigh through his pants and I wanted to taste him orally. I slowly eased my way down to his crotch and I pulled out his ten inches of pleasure and took it in my mouth. My tongue made circles around his dick like a merry-go-round, and Terrence kept humming in pleasure. I licked the head then slowly made my way down to his balls, licking them one at a time. His dick seemed even bigger from the bottom of his nuts. I started jerking him with my hands while I juggled his nuts in my mouth. Terrence was losing control, but I wanted to get fucked before he even thought about busting a nut. "I want you to fuck me," I said to him. With his pants now down to his knees, he bent down to reach for his wallet to grab a condom. I felt like riding his dick raw, but I didn't know him like that, and I didn't want to take the chance with all those down-low brothers coming out of Atlanta. I eagerly grabbed the condom out his hand and wrapped it around his dick, swiftly inserting it in my pussy from the back.

I soon found out that the most orgasmic position for me was atop a hill while a well- endowed man smashed it from behind. Terrence was working it and I was cumming a mile a minute. My juices were running down my leg as Terrence fucked the hell outta me while I wrapped myself around a tree. "Ooh, I want this pussy to be mine. That's some good pussy you got there," he said. His nasty talk only increased my consumption for the dick. "Give it all to me, daddy," I whispered. "Keep grinding that ass, baby. Ooh, that ass is so good. I want this pussy all the time," he whimpered like he was about to cum. I pulled away slowly to give him a chance to regain control of his dick. I wanted to take my time enjoying the dick. There's no way in the fucking world that I went through the trouble of taking off my pants in a public park for a fucking quickie. I wanted Terrence to fuck me for a while.

He turned me around and held me up in his arms against the tree while he pummeled my pussy. We were covered in sweat fifteen minutes later as Terrence had one of my legs up against his shoulder with my pussy giving a clear path to all of his ten and a half inches. I enjoyed watching him go in and out of my pussy. He was stroking and stroking and stroking until I felt something overtake my body; it was my nut coming down. I tightened the muscles around my pussy to make Terrence cum along with me, and that he did. He held me tight against the tree as he stroked harder than he ever had to get his nut off. By the time we were done, we were exhausted. Terrence had once again demonstrated that he was a master with his dick and I loved every minute of it.

The trips back and forth between New York and Atlanta continued for a while and we even went to Foxwoods Casinos in Connecticut one weekend and had a blast. We saw a well-known comic who was very funny, we danced the night away, but most important of all, we fucked our brains out that weekend. I knew I wasn't losing myself in Terrence yet because I still thought about Darren. The intimacy that I shared with Darren couldn't be erased from my mind, at least not yet anyway. Terrence was fun and I enjoyed him, but something about him made me a little uneasy and uncomfortable with his lifestyle that just couldn't go away. I felt like I knew Darren like the back of my hands and I was confident about everything that I knew about him. Terrence, on the other hand, had the swagger of a hustler even though he was a lawyer. I saw his degree and I called his school to verify that he had indeed attended, but something about him was slick.

My daddy always says that the truth comes out in time, so I was willing to wait and see what happened. Thinking about my daddy made me want to give him a call, but I didn't want to be rude to my company. Besides, I worked with my mother and father everyday. I wanted to give Terrence my undivided attention for the whole weekend while he was with me. As I was walking down the hall to my bedroom, I could hear Terrence in the bathroom whispering on the phone to someone about a money transfer that needed to happen very soon. At first, I thought it was kind of odd for him to be conducting business during the weekend, but then I thought about it and realized that my daddy did the same thing, sometimes. I didn't want to stand by the door to eavesdrop on his conversation, so I took my ass to my room and minded my own business.

Another thing that bothered me about Terrence was that everything had to be top notch all the time. He wanted to live in a top-notch world. He had to have the best wines when we went out, nothing less than VIP was suitable, only designer name brands mattered, and he didn't hide the fact that he was paid. However, I wondered how he was getting paid so well. The house that Terrence owned easily cost millions and his lifestyle cost even millions more. What really raised my suspicions was the fact that he was willing to visit me in New York during the week so often. No busy businessman would make himself as accessible to me the way that Terrence did. It was too soon to question him, so I decided to play it by ear, but with my guard up. Meanwhile, I had no objection to his long strokes. A girl couldn't simply give up her guilty pleasures.

CHAPTER 23

Surprise!

It had been a while since I talked to Darren and I was genuinely concerned about his well-being. I wanted to know how he was doing and what was going on in his life. I came home from work and wanted to wind down a little to some of my favorite jazz CDs. While I was in the living room relaxing, I started reminiscing about the good times that Darren and I shared. It was joyous for the most part, but something kept pulling us apart. I wanted to hear his voice, so I picked up the phone and called him. I thought he could've been away on business in some hotel room somewhere being bored to death, but what I got was a little shocking. "Hello," he said almost out of breath. I knew exactly what he was doing. He had picked up the phone a few times like that while he and I were in the same position when we were together. All I could do was imagine that chick riding his dick and getting something that should've been mine. I quickly hung up the phone.

My plan was to tell him that my phone dialed his number by accident if I ever talked to him again. I already knew that he knew who called because my number showed up on his caller ID. His stupid ass took forever to call me back and that only confirmed the fact that he was fucking his new girl. I remember when Darren used to fuck me for hours and I never got tired of him stroking, smacking, and rubbing my ass down with that big dick of his. I imagined he was the same way with his new girlfriend for hours at a time. He didn't call me back until the next day and by then I just ignored his call because I was too angry to talk to him. All I could think about was the time that it rained for a whole weekend and Darren and I spent the entire time in his house without stepping foot outside for anything. His fridge was stocked up and we made the best use of the Chinese and pizza delivery services in his area.

I can vividly remember that weekend. I went straight home to pack my bag after work. It was the lightest that I ever packed in my life. I simply brought lingerie and a jogging suit to wear back home on Sunday evening. The forecast was rain all weekend and Darren and I planned on lounging around his house all weekend long, watching movies and fucking all day and night. We did more fucking than watching movies. I brought some of my favorites, *Waiting To Exhale, How Stella Got Her Groove Back, Soul Food, Love Jones,* and a couple more chick flicks because I knew that Darren was going to have me watch Kung Fu and porno flicks all weekend long. As much as I enjoyed watching *Soul Food* over and over, Darren didn't quite feel the same way about it. All I remember while sitting on the couch was that one of my breasts was in Darren's mouth soon after the movie started. He had taken my attention away from the television and before I knew it, my bra was coming off and I was in my underwear lying across his couch with his twelve-inch dick standing as hard as a support beam for a building in front of my face.

Darren stood in front of me and I couldn't resist. My lips were wrapped around his super sized beef in no time while Darren stood before me butt naked with his sexy six-pack stomach and chiseled chest as I worked my mouth into an orgasm for him. He purposely stood in front of me blocking my view from the television. I ended up having to rewind the movie over and over because each time our session ended, a new one started minutes later. As my hand went up and down his washboard stomach, his dick was like a delicacy that I never grew tired of in my mouth. His huge head had my mouth wide open as I sucked his dick like the champ that I was. There was something about Darren that made me want him all the time. Maybe it was the way he caressed my hair while I was sucking his dick. He made me feel like he cared about me. "I don't just love you because you can suck a mean dick," he would joke, and make me gag. Darren would make sure that I got off before he got off, each and every single time.

We soon found ourselves in the sixty-nine position on the couch. I was on the bottom, he was on top. Darren ate my pussy better when I was on my back. With his knee planted on the couch to support his weight, his dick was at a perfect angle in my mouth. He licked my clit up and down while finger fucking me. Darren enjoyed the smell of my pussy, the shape of my pussy and even my soft hair when I allowed it to grow. "You have the best pussy in the world," he told me with sincerity. That just fueled my need to please him even more. His dick became my bad habit. I wanted it all the time. With Darren's fingers moving upward towards the wall of my g-spot and the flick of his tongue on my clit, there was no controlling my orgasm. He held me tight and steady as I shook into a trance enjoying his perfect talent. Moments later I was kneeling on the couch facing the wall as Darren penetrated me gently from behind. My pussy grew accustomed to his oversized dick. The throbbing sensation between my legs could only be soothed by his thrusting. Slowly, he started stroking me while rubbing my ass. His hands felt good, but his dick felt even better. I was grinding slowly, enjoying his pelvic thrust that had taken me to the heights of heaven so many times in the past. "Ooh, baby. Yes, Darren," I said, confirming that his performance and talent were appreciated.

Darren reached for my breasts with his hands while the thrusting of his dick inside me continued. I was being pleasured from all angles simultaneously. The top of the couch was my comfort as Darren softly plunged his dick in my pussy with cadence. I didn't have to tighten my muscles around his big dick because it felt like I was virgin tight. The deeper he went, the more orgasmic I became. As I was about to cum, Darren brought his lips to mine and started to fiercely French kiss me until we both climaxed together. If I were a smoker, I would've smoked a blunt after that session because a cigarette would've been too weak.

Thinking about Darren's delicious dick, Da'ron, threw me off course. A feeling of jealousy overtook me as I continued to imagine Darren fucking that girl. Not only that, she was gorgeous and sexy. I gave credit where credit was due; by no means did I feel threatened by her. I knew I shouldn't have allowed Darren to occupy even a minute space in my mind, but I felt like I still loved him. Terrence was great in a lot of ways, but Darren was irreplaceable.

CHAPTER 24

My Mind's Playing Tricks On Me

Just when I thought that I was getting over Tina, she had to call and remind me that she still existed. I can't say that she didn't cross my mind a time or two, but I was trying to focus on Tammy. I tried as much as I could to immerse myself in my work and Tammy so that I could forget about Tina, but it must not have been working that well because one telephone call from Tina had me tripping. I was actually glad that she called. At the very least, I knew that she didn't completely forget about me. She probably thought I was having sex with some woman when she called, but the reality was that I was trying to do my last set of push-ups and I didn't want to stop in the middle of it. I got one last good one before I picked up the phone all out of breath and everything. When I was away on business trips I tried as much as I could to exercise either at the hotel's gym facility or in my room. Push ups and sit ups kept my body looking tight and I never had to miss a beat.

A part of me was glad that Tina called, but another part of me wished she hadn't. I knew it was going to be hard getting over Tina because we knew each other so well and I didn't have to put up a front for her. I enjoyed being myself around her. She was my comfort zone and I liked that. After a while, I wasn't bothered too much by the fact that Tina was all over that pretty boy the night I saw her in Atlanta. Something about him seemed so phony and I knew Tina's nosey ass would find out what it was sooner or later. I wasn't trying to be cocky or anything, but I knew that I would always have Tina's heart and vice versa. She was my first love and I would never forget her, but she was a little too demanding with the sex. I felt like everything was starting to become routine and I needed a break from it.

I had to admit to myself that she was looking sexy as hell when I saw her that night, and if Tammy wasn't with me, I probably would've tried to take her home with me. Tina was my kryptonite. Tammy's beauty and my urge to see her naked later that night kept me strong. Tammy was nice and all, but after that stunt she pulled at the club, I was trying to keep a little distance between us. I needed to get to know her slowly. I must've been drawn to people with drama because Tina brought more drama than I thought I could ever handle. Tina's drama was a little different, however, because I knew the type of person she was. Now this new drama that I was faced with, I had no idea where it would lead. I wasn't sure I wanted to find out.

I was a little angry that Tina didn't pick up the phone when I called. That pretty boy was probably all over my favorite goodies and enjoying every minute of it. I knew Tina's overactive libido was probably trying to get fucked as much as she could by that pretty boy. I tried not to think much about them together, but I couldn't help thinking that I might've made a mistake by letting Tina go. Tammy was something new and exciting, but I was starting to wonder what the hell I was going to do when the novelty started to wear off. I thought about how exciting it was between Tina and me when we first met, and how we couldn't keep our hands off each other for the first year of our relationship. I started to question whether or not that was the only thing that Tammy had going for her at the time.

Meanwhile, I kept the same regular routine with Tammy. We talked to each other every night while I figured out a proper time to discuss the poor behavior she displayed at the club. For some reason I had a hard time bringing up the conversation with Tammy. She also made it seem like what she did was normal. Oddly enough, she felt that I was supposed to be happy and proud that she was getting jealous over me. I didn't think I knew her long enough for her to feel that she had the right to be going overboard for something she perceived wrongly. I didn't know what kind of men she dated in the past, but I damn sure wasn't the type to get flattered about silly shit. I expected a woman to act like a lady, dignified and with manners in public. Tina might've been a lot of things, but she was always a lady in the company of other people. I never had to worry about her embarrassing me.

I could be blamed for not saying anything to Tammy about the incident, but I also felt that she needed to apologize to me for embarrassing me in public and getting me kicked out of the club in front of a whole bunch of people. She never even said anything about it. I wasn't raised like that and that shit was bothering me. I wasn't going to feel right until I said something to her about it, but I also feared that I might cut off my pussy supply. Not only that, I was mesmerized by Tammy's beauty and I knew that every man who saw her with me wished they could have her on their arms. I was caught between a rock and a hard place. On one hand, I could just act like the incident never happened as she did and continue to enjoy the benefits of her company, or I could let it all boil inside me and one day explode for no reason. I wasn't ready to do either, so I just rolled with the flow in the meantime.

CHAPTER 25

Marla Gone Crazy

I hadn't talked to Will in almost a week and I wanted to know what transpired with the Marla situation. I was worried that Marla might've gone overboard with her antics. I didn't want my brother to suffer as a result, so I was willing to do whatever needed to be done to help him get rid of that chick. I understood that she was desperate and probably would have gone to great lengths to restore her meal ticket. This was a woman who was from the projects, getting thousands of dollars at will from a wealthy man. Women like that are the most dangerous because they have no idea how hard a person has to work to be successful. By the luck of the draw, her pussy was good enough to get whatever the hell she wanted out of my brother, so I could understand her plight after she realized that her ATM card had been cancelled. That shit was enough to make anybody in that situation go nuts.

The phone rang a couple of times before Will picked it up. I figured he wanted to make sure he checked the caller ID before picking his phone up from then on. I didn't call his cell because he often ignored his calls. It was always easier to get him at home as only a few people had his home number and that included my parents and me. "What's up, sis?" he said, sounding a little perturbed. I could sense right away that something was not right. "Will, is everything all right?" I asked. "Not really. That crazy ass chick Marla keeps coming by here causing a scene for no reason and my neighbors are starting to complain. Not only that, she's also been following me around, slashed my tires a few times and found out who Cassandra is." It was some serious shit and I was getting mad that this woman could just decide to wreck my brother's livelihood. I wasn't having it. "Did you get a restraining order against her?" I asked. "I wanted to, but she recorded a threatening conversation that I had with her. She threatened to take the tape to the media if I seek any injunction against her. If this shit ever gets out, it can be the end of my career as a football player," he said sadly. Will sounded a little defeated on the phone, and I knew my brother was not the type to let people walk all over him.

I wanted to go down to Atlanta on the next flight to wring the girl's neck. I knew from the start she was not good for my brother. "Will, you have to be smart about this. You can't stoop to her level because you have everything to lose. I'll come to Atlanta and figure out a way to handle her. As a matter of fact, I'm gonna bring mom with me." I knew that Will didn't want our mother in his business, but he had no choice. My mom grew up in Marcy Projects in Brooklyn and worked hard along with my father to make sure that we didn't have to deal with the same struggle and bullshit that she had to face. So I had a hunch that she would be able to help me out with the situation. "T, I don't want mom in my business. I'm a grown ass man. I need to handle this on my own," he said firmly. "Will, listen to me, nobody's saying that you're not a grown man, but because of your position and status in life, you can't deal with this situation on your own. This woman can ruin you, and it's me and mom's job to make sure this doesn't happen." "T, I also don't want you and mom to get in trouble for this. I'll figure out a way to handle it. I'll just move to a new home," he said. "Fuck that! You're not gonna let this chickenhead push you out of your own home. Did you hear yourself? We're gonna take care of her and make sure she doesn't come near you," I said angrily.

115

"T, this woman almost had her crew jump Cassandra. And the bad thing about it is that Cassandra has no idea that I used to see her. I'm afraid if she finds out that I used to sleep with this crazy ass woman she might not want anything to do with me anymore. Cassandra was scared out of her pants, and I don't want that shit to happen again," he said. "How do you know that she did that?" I asked. "She called me after it happened and told me it was just the beginning. What made it worst was that Cassandra wasn't able to identify any of the assailants because they wore bandanas over their faces." Goddamn! This chick must've thought she had bigger balls than Superman. If she thought the projects at Bankhead Homes was hard, she was about to meet some folks from the Marcy Projects in Brooklyn.

"Will, let me call you back. Don't worry yourself about this chick anymore. Your problem will soon go away," I assured him. "T, I wanna get rid of this chick just as much as you do, but I don't want my freedom or yours jeopardized because of this lunatic chick. And I know if you bring mama into this, it's gonna get crazy," he said. "Will, sometimes you got to fight fire with fire, or crazy with crazy. We're not gonna sit by and watch this woman destroy you. We're a family and this is going to be solved as a family. I don't think daddy needs to hear about your problems, though, for now. You know how he gets. I'll talk to you later. I love you." "Thanks, T. I love you, too," he said before hanging up the phone.

CHAPTER 26

A Plan of Action

I only saw Marla once, but I knew I wanted to kick her ass. How dare she try to blackmail my brother? I immediately got on the phone with my mother to tell her about the whole situation. My mother wanted to get on the next flight to Atlanta. She even wanted to pack my father's gun on the plane, but I had to quickly tell her it was an easy one-way ticket to jail. My mother was feistier than the most ghetto chicks I ever met in my life. It took a lot to bring that side out in her, but when it came out, she was like an angry bull chasing a matador. I had to explain to my mother that Will didn't feel comfortable having us meddling in his business. Whatever was going to take place had to stay between us. However, I made sure she understood the severity of the situation.

Every detail of this woman's life was soon to be found out through our investigation. My mother made a few calls to some cousins who still had their feet planted in the Marcy Projects back in Brooklyn. My second cousin, Ray Ray, was a hot head who represented Brooklyn to the fullest, and his pack of wolves were always hungry for some action. His crew included males and females. Though we didn't see that side of the family often, we got together during funerals, weddings and family reunions like most black families do. Ray Ray and Will spent a lot of time together when they were younger, but Ray Ray was more interested in fighting the guys around his neighborhood more than anything. They were different in that aspect. Nevertheless, they were cousins and were down for each other. Also, the fact that my parents moved to Long Island created distance between the family members.

Ray Ray was just too happy to have the opportunity to go to Atlanta with his friends and lounge for a few weeks, all expenses paid, courtesy of my mother. A plan was devised and he brought a couple of his boys and three of the toughest women he knew in the projects to help him take care of Marla. The men were brought just in case he needed extra muscle because women like Marla probably knew a lot of men and many of them would risk their freedom or even their lives for pussy. My job was to simply point out Marla and the rest was up to them. I really didn't care whether she lived or died because she was pestering my brother for no reason. However, I did state firmly that I only wanted her to get a beatdown that would scare the mess out of her, so she could leave my brother alone. I also told them to make sure that they seized the tape with my brother's threats on it.

When I pulled up in the projects, my cousin, Ray Ray, was sitting at his usual spot on the bench watching his crew looking for potential customers. With one eye out for the cops and the other on his money, he looked like the typical hustler. What appears to be a forty-ounce in a brown paper bag in one hand, and the other hand free in case he had to pull out and buck somebody, Ray Ray embodied the street life. My dad tried to give him a job with the company, but he complained about the commute and he didn't like the required hours. He noticed me the minute I got out of my car. At six feet, two inches and two hundred and forty pounds, Ray Ray looked very intimidating. With his pants sagging down his ass and white t-shirt big enough to cover a king size mattress, he headed toward me full speed. "What's up, cuz?" he greeted me with a hug. "What's up, Ray Ray?" I hugged him back. "Y'all know y'all should never have a problem coming to me when it comes to Will because that's my favorite cousin," he said. "I know Ray Ray, but I don't want you going to jail for this shit either. So you're gonna have to follow my mother's plan," I said to him. "No doubt," he answered.

As hard and street as Ray Ray was, he told me he was afraid of flying. As much as he'd run in the hood, jumping from building to building when he's being chased by the cops, one would think that he would be comfortable on a plane. Ray Ray walked me to his corner office, which was an alley behind one of the buildings, to discuss the plan that my mother had devised. After giving him every detail of the plan that he needed in order to take care of Marla, I handed him an envelope with ten thousand dollars. It was probably the biggest payday that Ray Ray ever saw, given that he was sitting on the block all day hustling rocks. He would get another ten thousand dollars when he returned from Atlanta. Ray Ray and his crew decided to ride down to Atlanta in a brand new Chevy Suburban, rented courtesy of some chick he was boning at Avis, he told me. I opted to take the quick way on a plane down to Atlanta. Besides, I knew exactly what was going to happen during that fourteen-hour drive from New York City to Atlanta. As much as Ray Ray's friends seemed to have been addicted to blunts, it was probably going to be a smoke fest with all kinds of weapons loaded up in the car. I did not want any part of that. My mother decided not to go with me to Atlanta because she did not want my dad to grow suspicious.

CHAPTER 27

Tammy's Tripping

It was one thing when Tammy got all angry for no reason with the chick at the 40/40 Club, but she was starting to piss me off thinking that I was looking at every woman who walked by me. We were on our way to a Broadway play in Manhattan when this Puerto Rican woman walked by. Her resemblance to J-Lo was uncanny. Even the tourists were taking pictures of her. Body, face and the whole nine was J-Lo, walking down the streets of Manhattan. I was being an admirer just like everybody else. I wasn't thinking, *I want to fuck the hell out of her*. It was more like a "wow" effect. Out of nowhere, I felt Tammy's stinging hand on the back of my head, followed by, "Don't be disrespecting me, Darren. Don't be looking at some woman like you wanna fuck her while you're with me." I was like, "What?" This chick was out of her fucking mind. There was no way that I even thought about that woman in that way. Not only did she hit me, she also got all loud out on the street like she wanted people to know that she controlled me. My first impulse was to snatch her up and wake her ass out of whatever dream she was having, but I had never put my hand on a woman and she wasn't going to make me start.

"You need to calm down and control your impulses and emotions, Tammy," I said to her. "Why the fuck should I calm down? You're the one looking at the skeezer, but you wanna tell me to calm down. No, you keep your eyes where they belong, on me, and I won't have to act a fool on you," she screamed out. I was thinking to myself, *Was this chick serious? Was she a schizophrenic of some sort?* "You can't be serious, right? What the fuck happened to the nice young lady I met at the airport a couple months ago? Yo, you're a little too controlling for me. I'm not into jealous or controlling women like that. We might have to dead this relationship," I said to her. "You know what? I'm not surprised, Darren. You're just like most men...you just wanna get what you want from a woman then do whatever the hell you please, without thinking about how she's affected. That's okay because you're the last motherfucker that I will ever allow to fuck me so quickly in a relationship, ever again," she said angrily. I had no fucking idea that this woman had me in a relationship with her so soon. We never even discussed it.

"I don't think I want to see a Broadway show anymore. You need to take me home so I can grab my belongings and go about my way," she insisted. I did not want Tammy to leave my house because she had come to New York specifically to visit me and there was no way I was going to throw her out. "Tammy, look, you're a little upset now and I understand completely why you may not want to stay with me tonight, but I'm not gonna let you leave unless I know for sure that you have a place to go and you're gonna be safe." I wanted to make my position clear to her and it was up to her whether or not she was going to stay under the conditions and circumstances. "I don't need you worrying about my safety. I'm a grown ass, independent woman who made a grown ass decision to come to New York to see you. I can take care of myself. I don't need a daddy," she said irritably. I knew the drive home was going to a bitch. I braced myself for complete silence and peace as we hopped in my car for the long drive to my apartment.

What I hoped for was peace and silence, but it would never come. Tammy kept on from the time we got in the car until we arrived at my house. She called me all kinds of stupid names, and it got to the point where I didn't give a fuck if

121

she got kidnapped, shot or even raped in New York. I gave her a hundred dollars for a cab then called it a night. All that fineness that I used to see went out the window. She was never going to hear from me again. "You'll never meet a woman as good as me in your life again, Darren. Goodbye," were her last words to me before she walked out the door. It was more like good riddance for me. I was just hoping that chick got out of New York safe because I didn't want to be blamed if anything happened to her. With that flip mouth of hers in New York, anything was possible. To be honest, I didn't get much sleep that night because I worried about Tammy all night. I wished that her claim as an independent and grown ass woman wasn't a bluff. All I could do was pray that she got back to Atlanta in one piece.

CHAPTER 28

Terrence's Secret

This time when I got to Atlanta, I didn't even let my brother know that I was in town. I tricked him into telling me Marla's last name and address for Ray Ray. Just like I assumed, she lived in the Bankhead Homes Projects. I was only in town for a couple of days, so I made arrangements to point her out to Ray Ray and his crew before I left, but the rest of the time I had planned to ride Terrence's sweet dick. The excitement of being with Terrence took over from the time I boarded my flight at John F. Kennedy airport in New York. My imagination was running wild as I began to think about the many ways I was gonna fuck Terrence around his house. The stainless steel washing machine was one of my first choices for a quickie on the spin cycle. I wanted to see if technology and time had changed the way a washing machine operated. My next stop was the bear skin rug in the formal living room. I saw myself rolling around on it and gripping the soft rug as Terrence penetrated me from behind. Then it was off to the Jacuzzi where all the magic would happen. I would sit on Terrence facing the opposite direction while the pressure from the jetted water hit my clit. It was going to be fun.

At least those were the thoughts I had when I was on the plane. First of all, when I got to Terrence's house I was shocked. He must've let his guard down because he had fucked me a few times too many. I noticed condom wrappers all in his trash bin in the bathroom located in the master bedroom, alerting me that that he was fucking somebody. It wasn't just a couple of condoms, there were many wrappers.

The scents of a woman or women were all over his house. The house smelled like bad pussy. I could also smell bad body oil in the aroma as well. It almost smelled like the cheap oils the strippers like to use. I was turned off right away and my pussy got dry. *The nerve of him*, I thought. He could've at least tried to conceal whatever the hell he was doing. Since it was his house and he and I weren't in an exclusive relationship, I had no right to say anything. However, I became a little distant when he tried to playfully plant a kiss on my lips. All that playing with his dick in the car on the way from the airport had him thinking that I was gonna drop my drawers the minute I set foot in the house. And I was going to, until I saw that shit in the master bedroom when I went to use the bathroom to freshen up.

He was walking around with a hard dick because I could see it through his pants, but my pussy was dry as hell and I didn't want to be touched. I didn't even know if he changed the sheets after he fucked the last chick in his room. That nasty bastard wasn't gonna get any pussy from me. All of a sudden, he didn't seem as dreamy as he did in the beginning. I was starting to see a player, and I didn't like players. I used to be one. We watched television in the family room; I talked about what had been going on with me and the situation with my brother without giving him any clue that I was in town to help take care of it. My brother's problem with Marla was the opportune situation that I needed to avoid having sex with Terrence that night. He probably didn't mind the fact that we weren't gonna have sex anyway because he had gotten some prior to picking me up. It couldn't have been that long since he fucked someone because the washcloth that he wiped his dick with was still wet in the hamper. I checked it to make sure and it smelled like pussy with a bad yeast infection-like odor.

Around ten o'clock, after watching a rerun of *The Jamie Fox Show* on BET, I decided to head to bed. "Do you have some sheets that I can put on the bed?" I asked. "Why you wanna change my sheets?" he questioned in a defensive tone. "I just like to sleep on fresh sheets when I go over people's house. I don't know who's been sleeping in the bed with you," I said sarcastically. He didn't even see my sarcasm. "Look in the linen closet down the hall from the bedroom, you should find some clean sheets in there," he said. He obviously wasn't going to follow me to the bedroom and I was glad. After changing the sheets, I lay in bed talking on the phone with my mom letting her know that I made it safely to Atlanta. Terrence stayed downstairs in the family room watching television while I was upstairs. I was just lying in the bed with my eyes open because I couldn't sleep.

Fifteen minutes into my gazing at the mirrored ceiling in Terrence's room, I heard his phone ring. He was talking in a low tone, but I could make out what he was saying. "Just bring the money tomorrow and I'll write you a check that you can take to the bank and deposit on Monday. We're making so much money now, we're gonna have to start spending a little more. I can't clean all that money as fast as we're bringing it in," he said to the person on the other line.

I wasn't sure, but it sounded like Terrence was laundering dirty money with a partner through his business. "Look, come by early tomorrow cause I got a little sexy bitch from New York visiting for the weekend. You know how we do… we got hoes in every area code. That's what ballers do," he said before hanging up the phone. I was just some hoe to him. His stupid ass couldn't even come up with his own original line; he had to steal one from Ludacris. Since he thought I was a hoe, my hoe ass was about to surprisingly get my period the next morning. I wanted to make sure he stayed away from me. I was gonna teach his ass not to fuck with me. One of the girls I met back in college used to tell me how she used to carry a Kotex pad with her all the time. In case she didn't want to have sex with a man, she would put on the pad and act like she was on her period. However, this chick was crazy and took it one step further. She would use a safety pin to stick herself on her finger to get some blood to put on the pad to make it believable in case the guy wanted proof. A lot of men are hipped to the pad game, so they sometimes wouldn't take the woman's word for it.

I contrived my plans as Terrence's ass snored all night. Before, I never noticed his loud ass snores, but that shit was bothering me all night that night and I could not fall asleep. I even nudged him a couple of times hoping he would wake up so I could quickly fall asleep before his ass started snoring again like an hibernating bear. To no avail, I was destined to stay up all night without any sleep. I didn't even take a nap on the plane because my ass was too busy thinking about how I was gonna fuck his brains out. Since I couldn't sleep, my mind was working a mile a minute and I came up with the best possible plan to avoid having sex with Terrence. My plan wasn't one hundred percent fool proof because a lot of men have no problems having sex with a woman on her period. But I was laughing at myself because Terrence was going to find an unpleasant surprise when he woke up the next day. I had planned to milk it for all it was worth, too.

Since I only carried one pad with me, I needed to make sure that I made the best use of it. Terrence woke up the next day with a hard dick ready to shove it in my pussy. He went to the bathroom to brush his teeth and that's when he found the unpleasant surprise. In plain view was a Kotex pad with bloodstains confirming him that my friend, Little Red Riding Hood, had come for her monthly visit. I figured the best way to tell Terrence that I had my period was for him to discover it on his own. I didn't even bother folding the pad. While he was sleeping, I snuck into the bathroom, poked my finger with a safety pin that I carried in my purse and I let the blood just drip all over the pad. I left the pad in the wastebasket in plain view, where he could see it from any angle when he entered the bathroom. I then rolled up some tissue and filled up my underwear with it in case more blood was coming down from my "fake" period. I even stained the tissue with the blood from my finger a little in case he questioned the authenticity of my period. I could hear his reaction to the blood in the bathroom, and I knew then that I had just bought myself an "I can't have sex with you this weekend" pass.

When Terrence got back in the bed, I could hear him mumbling his disappointment with me. "You didn't tell me you were on your period," he said. "It just came last night. It's not supposed to come till next week. That's why I came down this weekend," I lied. "Can you do me a favor? Can you please fold your pads or just keep them out of the wastebasket in the bathroom altogether? I don't want to have to wake up to that shit again, please," he begged. I wanted to tell his stupid ass to keep his condoms out of my sight because I didn't want to be greeted by them when I walked in the bathroom as well. "Okay," I said. "Thank you," he replied sarcastically. "Terrence, I'm gonna need you to run me to the store after we get up because I need to go get some more pads. I used the last one I had last night. Or you can just go to the store yourself to get me some." I was trying to work his nerves. "I'll just take you to the store. You won't catch me buying no pads at nobody's store," he said firmly. It wasn't like I had a lot of blood on the pad, I barely got a few drips to fool his ass, but he was tripping.

That was done. I didn't have to worry about Terrence bothering me for sex for the whole weekend. He was grossed out by the sight of blood. I was just hoping the weekend went by fast enough so I could leave his house. I may have been a nympho without standards in the past, but my therapist helped me regain my self-esteem and self-worth. I wasn't going to let Terrence walk all over me because of some good dick. Sunday couldn't come soon enough so I could pack my belongings and leave his house. Hell, the next day couldn't come soon enough.

The next morning, I woke up with a funky attitude and a funky mood. I didn't even want to be around Terrence anymore, but I had to stay with him in case I needed an alibi. I could've easily packed my things and checked into a hotel, but I wasn't sure what Ray Ray was planning to do and I didn't want my name anywhere near it. After taking a shower, I went downstairs to get some orange juice out of the fridge. When I stepped into the kitchen, I could hear Terrence and somebody else; they were having a conversation. "That's about half a mil in those two bags in large bills. I got about four more bags I'm gonna be dropping off later," the man with the deep voice said. "I'll write you a check for five hundred thousand for now. Don't deposit this check until Monday because I have to go to the bank and talk to my boy to make sure everything is clear," Terrence said. My suspicions were confirmed. Terrence was a money launderer and a shady businessman who was cleaning up dirty money. "That's why you're my favorite cousin and we're in business together. This drug money is so easy once you get past all the street hustling and getting the right connects. I'm glad you put me on to those Columbians. Now you don't have to get your hands dirty anymore," the man said. Terrence was in business with his cousin and using his office as a front to launder money. I knew that bastard was a crook. He had about ten b-list clients who were barely making the minimum salary offered by the NFL. They' could've negotiated their own contracts, they made so little money.

I was messing around with a drug dealer and money launderer. I had never been fond of street hustlers and I damn sure wasn't about to start. I heard all that I needed to hear to know that I didn't want to mess with Terrence anymore. I tiptoed back upstairs without being noticed. I didn't even bother getting the orange juice. I was thirsty and hungry as hell and orange juice was a morning routine for me. I decided to announce myself before making my way back to the kitchen as if it was my first time down. "Terrence! Terrence!" I screamed like I was looking for him. I wanted to give him heads up so he could wrap up his little illegal meeting. "What!" he yelled back. "Do you have any orange juice?" I asked. "Look in the fridge, there should be some in there," he responded. I went downstairs wearing boy shorts and a matching top. I wanted to torture Terrence for calling me out my name. I wanted him to see what he couldn't have, but even better, I wanted his cousin to drool over me, too. After pouring myself some orange juice in a glass, I walked into the living room to find this guy, who looked so obvious as a drug dealer that it wasn't even funny, standing there flashing his diamond grill like I was supposed to be impressed. He wore a velour brand name sweat suit with a matching pair of Air Jordans and enough platinum and diamonds to have his own jewelry section at department store. He typified a flashy hustler to the max.

"Hi, I'm Antwan," he said, trying to flirt with me in front of Terrence like it was nothing. He grabbed my hand for a kiss while flashing his ugly ass diamond grill. I could've thrown up right there. He wasn't the most attractive guy that I had ever seen. "I'm Tina," I said abruptly. I really didn't want to say anything more to him. I started to turn and walk back upstairs, then I heard, "Dat's a fine bitch right thur," coming out of his country mouth. Terrence wanted to front like he didn't condone the man's reference to me as a bitch. "Don't call her a bitch, man," he suggested. "Oops, I'm sorry. She gotta ass on her, though," he commented. Before I went crazy on his stupid country ass, I decided to go back upstairs. Because he knew I was upstairs awake, he started talking all loud about the kind of cars he had, the houses and the money he was making like I gave a fuck. His ugly ass couldn't have me even if he was the last man on earth. Even then I would've opted for my dildo. These fucking drug dealers always think that every black woman is interested in their dirty money. These fools have these chickenheads lying to them and sometimes they believe all the bullshit they hear.

I jumped in the shower and got dressed very quickly. I needed to go see my cousin about Marla, so I asked Terrence if I could take one of the cars to the store to go get some tampons. I knew he would honor my request because he looked like he needed to have a private meeting with his drug dealing partner. "Go ahead, take the Benz. If I'm not here when you get back, just come in through the garage. I have a garage opener in the car," he said. With hesitation and bad judgment, I decided to drive one of Terrence's cars. I knew the risk that I was taking by doing that, but I needed to see my cousin. There was no way in the world that Terrence could possibly think that he was getting away with laundering all that money. I saw the two huge bags filled with money sitting in the living room. I didn't know if it was greed or his desire to live a luxurious life, but to me Terrence was no better than the scumbags on the street who plague the black community with their drugs. *How can a man who sacrificed seven years of his life to earn a degree in law risk it all for dirty money and the fast life?* I wondered. There wasn't an ounce of respect for Terrence left in me.

Before leaving the garage, I searched his car throughout to make sure that there were no drugs or guns inside. The last thing I wanted was to get pulled over by the cops and get arrested for some shit that I played no part in; I didn't want that. As I backed out of the driveway, I noticed a red convertible Bentley sitting on the side of the driveway. I assumed it was Antwan's flashy car because everything else about him was flashy. My heart was beating a mile a minute as I drove to the hotel to go meet with Ray Ray. There I was, sitting on my high horse judging Terrence, but I was about to contribute to the beatdown of a woman who was

130

blackmailing my brother. I was no better than Terrence, but I felt better about what I was doing because I was defending my brother. I kept looking in the rearview mirror for undercover federal agents following me because of paranoia. I sighed a deep breath of relief when I finally made it safely to Ray Ray's. I think I watch too many movies.

CHAPTER 29

Identifying Marla

Ray Ray and his crew took up three adjacent hotel rooms so they could all walk back and forth to each other's room as they all unlocked the doors that separated the rooms to allow access. The room had all kinds of gadgets. Those people were some of the roughest looking people that I had ever seen. Even the women looked rough. I felt sorry for Marla because she was about to deal with Brooklyn's worse. Ray Ray called for the whole gang to get up and get ready to ride out to Bankhead Homes. Shit, I was scared driving Terrence's car on my way to Ray Ray's, but this time I was triple scared that if we got pulled over that I was going to jail for certain. The hunger for violence seemed to have permeated the seven-passenger Chevy Suburban my cousin and his goons were driving. They all piled into the back as I sat up front with my cousin while he drove. I didn't want to leave any trace or connection to Bankhead Homes, so I pulled the directions to Marla's house from Terrence's navigational system in the Benz. I quickly wrote everything down on a piece of paper, and it led us right to Marla's front door. My job was to simply confirm who she was.

When we got to Marla's apartment, one of my cousin's friends got out of the car and went to ring her doorbell. We knew she was home because there was a brand new Benz CLK convertible with vanity plates that read her name "MARLA." *My brother's money probably paid for that car,* I thought. After my cousin's friend knocked on her door, she appeared wearing a muumuu with her head wrapped in a

132

bandanna and a little girl standing by her side. All the glitz and beauty that my brother talked about were absent. My cousin's friend turned around to look at me and I shook my head to confirm it was her. I didn't know what he said to her, but she stepped out of the house and started pointing like she was giving him directions to a place. We drove down the block to pick him up because we didn't want to link the car to him. My cousin didn't need me anymore. He had all the information that he needed in order to do what he wanted to do. His friend revealed when he came back to the car that he acted like he was looking for someone in the projects and couldn't find the address. She was trying to point him to the right address as she flirted with him.

After witnessing the little girl next to Marla, I had a request that needed to be honored. I did not want anything too severe to happen to her because I didn't know if that little girl depended on her. I simply wanted them to get the tape and scare that woman into leaving my brother alone. However, my cousin's friend, Trey, quickly told me that it wasn't her daughter. He asked her when he knocked on the door. I didn't want to say anything to incriminating to Ray Ray's friends, anyway. She was babysitting someone's child for the day. I was relieved that this woman was not a parent. A schemer like that didn't need to bring any children into this world. Women like Marla make it very difficult for the good women of the world to find suited husbands. I didn't really care to know what my cousin and his friends planned on doing to Marla; I just wanted to get back to the car so I could leave.

After we got back to the hotel, I expressed my discomfort about staying with Terrence to my cousin. I also told him about the illegal dealings that Terrence was involved in. I didn't want to become a victim of circumstance. However, when I mentioned the money that his cousin, Antwan, brought to the house, my cousin's eyes lit up. He mentioned nonchalantly that he wouldn't mind robbing Terrence for calling me out my name. I knew my cousin cared about me, but robbing Terrence had nothing to do with me. He wanted to do that because that's who he was. My cousin was a hustler just like Terrence and Antwan, and he saw an opportunity that he couldn't pass up. I was totally against it because I didn't want to get involved. My cousin wanted some details about the house, but I didn't give it to him. I hopped in the car and drove straight to Terrence's house.

CHAPTER 30

The Ugly

When I got back to the house, I noticed the Bentley was still sitting in the driveway, but Terrence's Range Rover was gone. I walked in through the garage and found his cousin sitting on the couch with a big grin across his face. Terrence was gone, and so were the bags of money. I really didn't know why Antwan was in the house by himself. "Terrence done went to take care of some bidnis. He be right back," he said. I didn't say anything to him as I walked upstairs to go to the bedroom. I was in the bedroom for no longer than five minutes watching television and lounging with my clothes on when Antwan barged through the door. "How dem boys in Nu Yok treating you?" he asked with a country accent. I had no idea what he was trying to get at, but I didn't want to be bothered. I knew that he was smart enough not to try anything because Terrence knew that my family was aware of my whereabouts. "I'm trying to watch television. Can you please leave me alone?" I said to him. "You stuck up Nu Yok hoes think you all dat. Fuck you den, bitch," he said, before walking out. I shut the door behind him and locked it. Moments later, I heard him in the driveway peeling off like he was on a racetrack. I figured Terrence probably told him to try and see if he could get some from me. There was no other reason for him to be waiting at the house for me, alone.

Antwan was very disrespectful and I knew just the right person to teach him a lesson while he gained something in the process. I had overheard him tell Terrence that he would be bringing a couple more bags of money to the house the following day, so it was my opportunity to teach his ass a lesson. My flight was scheduled to leave at nine o'clock in the morning and I wanted to make sure that Terrence and Antwan never called another woman a bitch or hoe and get away with it for the rest of their lives. Terrence wasn't fooling me when he tried to check his cousin for calling me a bitch. He had done it himself. If he showed disrespect, why would his cousin show respect? I knew a hungry bunch of people from New York who were interested in more opportunities than the reason they initially came in Atlanta for. I wanted my cousin to rob them.

I called my cousin and told him that I would help set up Terrence for the robbery, but my involvement would be minimal. I told him about Antwan's plan to bring about half a million dollars in cash the next day at Terrence's house, and he was more than happy to plan a robbery. The plan was simple; Ray Ray and his gang needed to get into Terrence's complex and I would leave the basement door open for him to enter the house. I only promised to leave the basement door open and nothing else. I told him the address of the house and the distinctive look of the house so that he would not make any mistake as far as which house to target. I told him to go around the back under the deck and he would find the basement door unlocked. I wasn't worried about Terrence calling the police because it was illegal money, and I knew that he didn't want the cops involved.

I was even a little excited plotting to teach Terrence and his cousin a lesson. Those bastards had no respect for me or women in general and that had always been one of my pet peeves. I never would've thought that Terrence was that kind of person. I never thought he had an ugly side. The package he was wrapped in when I first met him was so deceitful until it was unwrapped.

CHAPTER 31

Get Your Freak On

I sat around all day waiting for Terrence to come back to the house so we could go out and do something together, but he never showed. It was his suggestion. I really didn't care to be around him, but I was hungry and wanted some food. After I got tired of waiting, I jumped in his car and went to get something to eat at Gladys Knight's restaurant on Peachtree. I sat there alone and ate as everyone stared at me strangely like it was so odd for me to be eating alone. The food was good and I enjoyed spending time by myself. However, while I was in the restaurant, Terrence's phone dialed my number. I said, "Hello," but he didn't answer and I could hear him fucking not one, but two women in the background. His phone must've dialed my number by accident. "Suck it, baby. I wanna eat your pussy while she sucks my dick," he told one woman. This visit was getting stranger for me by the hour. I was now sitting in a restaurant listening to Terrence fuck a couple of women while he left me to be alone at his house.

At first, I thought about hanging up the phone, but my curiosity got the best off me. I paid the bill for my food then headed to the car in the parking lot in the back with the phone to my ear and the mute button on. I sat in the car listening to every detail of Terrence's sexual encounter with those women. I figured these women had to be comfortable enough with each other to partake in a threesome with Terrence. "Look at that flawless skin. I wanna fuck that ass all night," he told the other woman. "She has no blemishes on her skin whatsoever," one of the stupid women said out

137

loud. "Terrence, your dick is so long. I hope you don't hurt me with it," the other women tried to stroke his ego.

It appeared as if all the discomfort between them was removed because I started hearing some juicy stuff from all three of them. My nosey ass definitely wasn't going to hang up the phone then. The compliments on everybody's bodies went on for a little while as Terrence played with the women's breasts and asses. One of the women sounded like she had been fucking Terrence for a long time, while the other one seemed to have been new. I could hear the heavy breathing as Terrence started kissing the woman that he was least familiar with. His hands were either on the other woman's breasts or clit because there was no reason for all that moaning without any banging. I could hear the other woman finally tried to catch some air as she instructed the girlfriend to caress both of their bodies. She sounded dippy like Chrissy from *Three's Company*.

"Damn that dick is hard," the new woman said. I could only imagine the grin flashing across Terrence's face because like most men, he probably thought these women were with him for his good looks and game but not his high profile lifestyle. I probably would've done a threesome with Darren back when I was in college, when I thought about it. I was a little angry that Terrence left me in the house all alone to go fuck not one, but two women at the same time. Minutes later, I could hear one of the women taking Terrence's dick in her mouth. She was loud as she licked his dick and tried to act sexy simultaneously. They had to be on the couch because I could hear Terrence ordering the other woman to come sit on his face while he had his head propped up to eat her. "I wanna watch her suck your dick," she said, taking her time before honoring his request. "Suck that dick, trick. Let him know that you're the shit!" she screamed at the other woman. The smacking of tongue against Terrence's dick became louder. "Oh yeah, suck it like the champ you are," he said. I

138

wasn't grossed out just yet. I wondered if these chicks were putting on an act for Terrence or for each other. It was too much talking taking place between them when they should've been fucking a lot more.

The other woman must've sat on Terrence's face because I heard moaning coming from her while the pussy licking and the dick sucking lingered on. "You got some nice tities. I can never get enough of them," Terrence mumbled in between suction and licks. "Let me suck the left nipple because it looks like it's getting jealous of the right," he said, trying to use humor in the middle of a threesome. Terrence was the ultimate player. Suddenly, there were two people moaning at the same time. "Ooh, rub my clit, daddy," the dumber of the two said as she moaned. Terrence must've been having a good ole time. He had tities in his mouth and clit on his fingers, what else could a man want? "Lie down on the couch, and you can sit on top of the couch. I want her to suck my dick while I eat your pussy," he said. It was nothing but moaning and groaning for a good five minutes. "Oh my God! That tongue is so good. You're making me cum!" she screamed. She wasn't lying. Terrence was great with his tongue. He was able to make me cum at will. "Damn that bastard!" I screamed to myself quietly.

His girlfriend, the one he seemed familiar with, must've been sucking his dick well because she got all excited when he told her she's gonna make him cum. "Don't I always make you cum when I suck your dick?" she asked teasingly, trying to show off for the other woman. Shit, I used to make that mu'fucka cum myself, but only when he wanted to. The other woman was about to bust an intense nut when Terrence slowed down his licking. "Why the fuck did you slow down? I was about to bust a nut," she told him disappointingly. "We got all night, why you gotta rush your nuts?" he asked. He had all night my ass. If his ass didn't show up at the house by midnight, I was gonna take his car and head out to the club.

"I know what I'm doing. I want this memory to last for a lifetime. I'm gonna get you there again, but I want you both to suck my dick at the same time," he ordered. That dumb chick ignored her own nut and went down and started sucking on Terrence's dick along with the other chick. "Yeah, that's what I'm talking about," he said in a happy tone. "Yeah, suck the skin off that dick like it's your last meal," he said, talking shit. "My mouth is tired. I wanna take a break," one of them said. "Why don't you sit at the top of the couch so I can eat you, baby," he said to the obvious girlfriend. I hated the fact that Terrence had so much dick control. That man could receive head for hours without cumming, not unless he was ready to.

"Oh yeah, eat that pussy, baby," she yelled, to show off for the other woman. That chick was overacting. "Smack! Smack!" "Yeah, smack that ass while you eat my pussy," she said. I wanted to reach through the phone to tell them to shut the fuck up. I was torturing myself for no reason, but I wanted to hear it through the end. I had already made up my mind that I was never going to sleep with Terrence again, the least I could do was to allow myself to be entertained. "Oh shit, Terrence, I'm cumming. Yes, I'm cumming!" one of them started screaming. That chick was fronting for the other chick. "I want you to fuck me," she then said. She wanted him to fuck her because she didn't cum. That lying ass trick had Terrence fooled.

A feeling of nostalgia overcame me as I listened on. I started remembering how the threesomes that I had when I was in college were the bomb. That boy was hung like a horse and knew exactly how to use that big ass dick of his. I'll never forget Bobby. He knew how to put it down in the bedroom. I had yet to meet a man who was as skillful as Bobby. I can still remember the night he fucked the hell out my girlfriend and me. My girlfriend would not stop talking about that night. She even tried to see if she could find him once while she was visiting the Baltimore/DC area. That's where Bobby was living at the time. The only reason why I was thinking about Bobby was because I was trying to find solace in the whole situation. Listening to Terrence fuck the hell out of two women was painful even though I didn't want to be with him. The fact that he never really cared about me or respected me was what hurt the most. I thought he was different when I met him. I was starting to believe that there was no man on this planet as perfect as Darren for me. Suddenly, I was thinking about him and missing him again.

However, I continued to listen in on the threesome. Shit, it was better than calling a sex hotline. This show was free and I couldn't wait to see how Terrence was going to act when he saw me later. I needed to know how good of an actor he could be or men in general when they get caught in a lie. "Ride the dick, baby. Ride it. I want you to eat her pussy while she's riding me," he instructed. Somebody was doubling her pleasure because all I heard was "Ooh! Ah! Yes! Give it to me, daddy. Eat that pussy, bitch!" By then I was jealous because I wanted to be in her place. I wanted my pussy licked while I was being banged. "I want you to pull my dick out and rub it up and down her clit, slowly," he instructed. "When am I gonna get some of this dick?" said one woman, who seemingly started to get bored because nobody was fucking her. "Let her get a turn, Bev," said Terrence. It was the first time he called his girlfriend by her name. I assumed her full name was Beverly. "You gotta learn how sit on the dick right, Marla," said Beverly. "I know I didn't just hear the girl call out somebody named Marla," was all I could say to myself. I was hoping it wasn't the same Marla who had my brother sprung over her pussy. "Trick, ride that dick and represent for Bankhead Homes," said Beverly. My suspicions were confirmed. Marla was the same stank skeezer that my brother was having problem with.

"Oh shit, this bitch knows how to work her pussy. I'm cumming. Get up, I'm cumming. I want it splattered on both of your faces," said Terrence. That motherfucker was fucking two stank hoes and didn't even bother to wear a condom. I was heated. He wasn't just fucking with his life; he was fucking with mine as well. I saw the reluctance in him to wear a condom when we first got together, but I made sure he wore one. "Damn that shit was good. We're gonna have to do this again real soon, ladies. I have to run because I have some business to take care, but I'll call you later, Bev," Terrence shouted. "Terrence! You forgot to leave me the five thousand dollars that we talked about to get my car fixed," Bev yelled out. "My bad. There's a little extra in there so you and your friend can go out tonight and have a good time," he said. He must've handed her an envelope with money because I could hear these tricks screaming like they just won the lottery. The door was slammed and Terrence walked out the door. His phone must've fallen on the floor because I could still hear the two scheming hoes talking about his dumb ass after he left.

CHAPTER 32

You Talk Too Much

"Bev, I see you got some game. We gotta let these mu'fuckas know that the pussy ain't free," said Marla. "Did you really bust a nut?" asked Bev. "Hell yeah I bust a nut. I ain't gonna let the mu'fucka have all the fun. I ain't cum as many times as he thought, but I bust my nut when he was eating me," said Marla. "For some reason, this mu'fucka doesn't do it for me. I hear women talk about him like he's some god, but the mu'fucka just can't fuck to me. If he wasn't paid, he wouldn't be getting this pussy. I admit he eat pussy aight, but he ain't great at it." I was thinking, *Damn... who the hell has this trick been fucking*? I thought Terrence had skills. Maybe I just haven't been fucking the best men out there. She was talking about Terrence like his dick was trash. I was starting to believe what she was saying; then I thought about it, she was trying to downplay Terrence's skill so her girl wouldn't go after him. And that other trick lied because she didn't want Bev to know that Terrence fucked her so well that she probably came ten or twenty times. I'm a woman and I knew these tricks both came numerous times. I wasn't a fan of Terrence, but I had to give the brother his props in the bedroom. Shit...if I continued to fuck with him he would've had me sprung. That mu'fucka banged those chicks for almost two hours straight and he only busted one nut. That was some fucking energy and dick control there.

I started to hang up the phone until Marla decided to start running her mouth. "I got this mu'fucka that I was fucking with who's paid. He plays for the Falcons. He's the one who practically paid for my Benz. He must've gotten some new pussy 'cause he's been acting funny lately, trying to cut me off and shit. I ain't find a replacement for him yet. Does Terrence have any baller friends?" she asked Beverly. I knew this was about to be a whole new conversation and I couldn't wait for the details. "How you gonna try to hook up with a baller and your ass still live in the projects? Ain't no real baller coming to no projects to see your ass," said Bev. Her statement made me wonder if Will ever went by her house. I got her address from him when he was trying to have all her shit mailed to her house. She decided she was gonna come pick everything up and that's how the whole mess with him and her started. He should've cut that chickenhead off from a distance. If she never had access to his house, she wouldn't have been able to cause all the damage she caused. I still wanted to hear what Marla had to say about living in the projects and driving a Benz from scheming on men.

"I ain't leaving them projects. These cats be acting up and you never know when they gonna cut you off, just like that sucka cut me off. I ain't paying but a hun'ed dollars a month for that apartment. My grandmamma died and left me that apartment. I ain't giving it up even after I'm married. Where I'ma creep at?" Marla said. That chick was something else. "Besides, if I'm fucking with a baller, why he need to come to my house anyway? I can go to his." I knew there was a reason why I couldn't stand this chick. Women like her and her friend gave women a bad name. "Bitch, you know you crazy, but I like yo' style, though. I'ma hook you up with Antwan 'cause he be balling out of control," said Bev. Yeah Antwan would be a good match for her country ass. "What he look like? Is he at least presentable?" asked Marla. "Girl, what you worried about? He's paid," said Bev. I couldn't believe "Mr. I Don't Talk To Chickenheads" was fucking two of them and acted like he was too classy for those types of women. "Girl, you ain't never lied. I usually don't care about what they look like as long they paid. The football guy I told you about was cute, though. I got that mu'fucka thinking I got him recorded on tape threatening to kill me. I'ma use that to get all the money I can from his stupid ass." That was it right there, I wanted to jump through the phone and smack that trick right in her mouth.

While they were in there giggling and planning their next scheme, a knock was heard at the door. "Who is it?" asked Bev. I couldn't make out the other voice from the outside, but after she opened the door, I could hear clearly who it was. "You see my phone?" asked Terrence, after walking in the house. My eavesdropping was coming to an end, but I was happy that I at least found out that chick was bluffing. "I think I left it here. Can one of y'all call it on your phone for me?" Terrence asked of the ladies. I could hear Marla jumping to her feet to get to her phone so she could get Terrence's number to call his phone. That trick was about to go behind Bev's back to get Terrence. "What's the number?" she asked. Terrence yelled out the number and before he could catch me on the phone, I hung up so he could hear it ring. I had no idea what happened after that, but I heard what I needed to hear.

CHAPTER 33

Leaving the Liar's Den

I rushed back to the house after hanging up the phone. I didn't want to give Terrence any reason to act suspicious when he got home. I just wanted to see his Oscar worthy performance. But first, I had to take care of something that was a lot more important to me before Terrence got home. At this point, I felt there was no need to stay at Terrence's any longer. I could just go to a hotel until the next day or call my brother to pick me up. Calling my brother was out of the question because I would have too much explaining to do. My second option was to have my cousin pick me up and take me to a hotel, but I was too lazy to pack my belonging that night and I didn't want anybody to see my cousin near Terrence's home. I decided to just spend the night and act like everything was normal. If Terrence was going to be an actor, I needed to be an even better actress and act like I didn't know about what he'd just done. I needed to get on the phone before he got home because I didn't want him in my business.

After learning that Marla was only bluffing, I was relieved and happy that Ray Ray and his friends didn't have to do what they came down to Atlanta to do anymore. Everyone could just go back home and live their happy lives, at least that's what I thought until I spoke to Ray Ray. The phone rang twice before Ray Ray picked it up. "Who this?" he growled through the phone like he was DMX or something. "You need to look at your caller ID so you'd know who's calling you, fool," I said to him. My cousin was silly like that, sometimes. He never paid attention when he needed to.

"What it be, cuz?" he replied. "Ray Ray, you can abort the plan. I found out that Marla was only bluffing. You all can go back home. Everything's gonna be all right," I told him. "What about old boy? You know I ain't tryna leave without sticking him," he said. All sympathy for Terrence was out the door and I really didn't care if my cousin robbed him. "I don't want you getting locked up while you're down here, you need to go back home. At least you have family in New York. If something happens down here, you can't call anybody to help you," I reminded him. "You must be trippin'. I got my cousin Will down here. He won't let his favorite cousin rot in jail," he reminded me. I completely forgot that he and Will were close at one time, but I didn't want Will's name involved in any bullshit that Ray Ray was about to get himself into.

"Look, Ray, I know you're gonna do what you want to do, but I'm telling you that all I'm gonna do is leave the door unlocked for you and nothing more. I don't know why you're doing this stupid shit, anyway. I don't even know why you're acting like a thug and don't want to leave the streets alone. We don't even have any more family in the projects. You're the only one who's still hanging out with the bad crowd. You already served four years in jail. I don't want to see you spend the rest of your life there." I went off on him. However, Ray Ray had an even better comeback for me. "Oh, now I'm acting like a thug and hanging with a bad crowd, but when your ass needed me to come down here and take care of this shit for my cousin, you didn't care about me being a thug. I know y'all want me to be like y'all because we're family, but I'ma come up the way I wanna come up. I ain't choose the game, the game chose me," he said like he was reciting a verse from one of those corny ass rap songs he listened to all the time. Ray Ray had a point, though. His thuggish ways were convenient when I needed him, and now I was calling him out of his name because I didn't want him to do something. "You're right, Ray. I'm sorry. I'm gonna leave the door unlocked for you, but be careful down here. You know you're still my favorite thug cousin," I said through laughter. "Somebody gotta be a thug in the family. We can't have everybody acting all straight laced except for my aunt and me. You know your mother's the truth when it comes to thugging," he said laughing. He was right. My mother used to be one of those down ass chicks back in the day. That was one of the things I liked about my cousin, he kept it real.

I realized that I had to allow Ray Ray to be himself. As much as I wanted him to walk a straight and narrow path, that was not his thing, and I needed to understand that. It's not like he had ever called us to ask for money or anything. Ray Ray had always wanted to make it on his terms. While my brother chose sports, he chose the streets. Even though we didn't like his lifestyle, we still loved him because he was family. We all knew that Ray Ray lived in the moment, so we just got used to the idea that he was gonna become this big drug lord who was gonna end up spending the rest of his life in jail after he made it or worse, dead. It was something hard to get used to, but as they say, "You can only lead a horse to water, but you can't make him drink." Ray Ray was that horse that we all wished we could beat over the head and force him to a better life instead of the hustling life.

It was understood that Ray Ray wasn't going to do anything to Marla anymore. We agreed that she didn't have to get hurt and that I would get my brother to go to court and get a restraining order out on her. I just wanted that woman as far away from my brother as possible. All the scheming and harassing was about to stop and I was happy that I discovered the truth, and a way out of this mess for him.

Anyway, I decided to spend the night at Terrence's house for better or worse. I had just gotten off the phone with my cousin and was in the bedroom watching television when

Terrence came in. I didn't really care to find out where he was coming from because I already knew, but the guilt that he felt had him singing to me like a little bitch. I didn't even say anything to the man, I just stayed in bed and continued to do what I was doing before he came in. "Why you look like you got an attitude?" he asked. I know I didn't have an attitude because if I did, he would have heard it from me the minute he walked through the door. At that point, I didn't care about Terrence anymore. He was just providing me with shelter for the night and a ride to the airport in the morning. I purposely had my Aunt Jemima head scarf on my head making it clear to him that I didn't want to be bothered. I didn't even bother answering his question. "Did you hear me say something to you?" he asked again. "I heard you, but I don't have to answer you," I said. "Why it gotta be like that? I'm just tryna make sure you're all right," he said. "Look, man, I'm tired. It's midnight and I have to get up early tomorrow to catch my flight; just leave me alone," I told him. Maybe I had just a little attitude.

"Okay. I know you're mad that I took so long to get back, but I was with one of my clients and I had to go over some paperwork with him. You know how these rookies are, they're always looking for endorsements they can't have. But I think this one is gonna come through, though. I'm sorry for getting back so late," he said. "You don't have to be sorry. You're a grown ass man and this is your house, so you owe me no apology. Just do you, player," I said sarcastically. I was trying to avoid an argument at all cost because I didn't want to be thrown out of the house, but Terrence was pushing my buttons with all his lies. "I know I don't have to apologize to you, but I want to," he said, trying to flash his fake ass smile my way. "Look, can I just get some sleep and we'll talk about this in the morning on the way to the airport?" I suggested. "Fine, I'll be sleeping in the guest room tonight. I'll see you in the morning." He finally decided to follow my directions. "Goodnight, Terrence," I said to him with an attitude.

I knew this dude didn't think that he could just come home and bullshit his way out of leaving me to be by myself the whole day so he could go get his freak on. I didn't want to hear his poor excuses, especially since I knew his no good ass was lying, anyway. I set the alarm on my cell phone so I could wake a couple of hours before my flight. I flopped my head on the pillow and off to sleep I went very quickly. I was either very tired or completely disgusted with Terrence because by the time I opened my eyes again, my alarm was ringing like a school bell. I made all kinds of noise after I got up to make sure Terrence woke up.

By the time I got out of the shower, he was up and ready to take me to the airport. He didn't even bother coming to the room to try to sweet talk me. It was either his guilt or he felt what we had was done and over with. After packing my things, I walked downstairs wearing my skin tight jeans, a white shirt and a nice pair of brown suede boots that matched my brown suede jacket. I even threw on my sunglasses for more of a diva effect. Even my Louis Vuitton luggage matched my outfit. I knew I was looking good, and I also knew that Terrence was going to try to sweet talk his way back into my pants. He was the type of man who liked high maintenance looking women, even though I didn't consider myself to be high maintenance. Everything I did was simple, it just came off as high maintenance, but that's exactly what I was going for that morning. I wanted Terrence to see something that he was never, ever going to get in his life again.

I sat on the sofa in the family room while Terrence was upstairs washing his face and brushing his teeth. I noticed two big duffle bags sitting on the corner. They were different than the ones I had seen earlier. My curiosity got the best of

150

me and I walked over to take a look. I couldn't believe my eyes; one bag was filled with money while the other one was filled with pure white powder cocaine. Terrence was a full fledge drug dealer. It was time for me to get the hell out of there. "Terrence, hurry up!" I yelled out. "What?" he yelled back. "You need to hurry 'cause I don't want to miss my flight." I had plenty of time to make my flight; it was getting busted in a house full of drugs and dirty money by the police, FBI, DEA or whoever the hell was watching him I was worried about. "Hold your horses, I'll be right down," he said. He came downstairs trying his best to look dapper wearing a blue velour sweat suit, blue and white sneakers and an all white Nike cap. I didn't even see his beauty anymore; all I saw was a lying monster. I wanted to get home right away.

The ride to the airport would've been a lot more enjoyable if Terrence didn't keep apologizing to me. And when that didn't work, he offered to take me on a trip to Hawaii like I could be bought. He didn't realize he was talking to the wrong woman. I could care less about his illegal money. If I wanted to go to Hawaii, I had plenty of money to buy my own way there. He kept piling lies on top of lies and I just couldn't take it anymore. I was happy when he finally pulled up in front of the Delta doorway at the airport. He got out of the car to retrieve my luggage from the trunk then tried to sneak in a kiss. I pulled back and said, "You might want to save that kiss for those tricks you were with last night. Have a good life, Terrence." I was proud of myself as I sashayed my way inside the airport leaving him standing there with what I assumed was a bewildered look on his face. I never looked back, so I couldn't confirm his facial expression

CHAPTER 34

Tell Me Have You Seen Her?

After that brief tumultuous experience with Tammy, I didn't want to think about meeting another woman for a while. The only thing that bothered me initially was the fact she left my house so late that evening and I had no idea where she went. I was relieved when she called me a week later to tell me she was back in Atlanta and she was okay. I didn't think I got any sleep that whole week because I worried about Tammy so much. She refused to answer my calls and I had no other way to get in touch with her. I tried calling her job, but because she was a flight attendant, I was never able to confirm whether she was still alive or not. The people at her job wouldn't reveal any information about her to me. New York City was not the best place for a woman to exercise her feminist rights at night. The criminals in New York City can care less whether or not a woman is a feminist. Rape, murders and other atrocities are the norm in New York, and when Tammy left late that night, I was worried. I didn't want her to end up on the wrong side of town or with the wrong people because she didn't want to spend the night at my house. I was conscionably responsible for her because she flew from Atlanta to New York to see me. In turn, my conscience wouldn't allow me to get any sleep until I knew she was all right.

I had never met a woman so jealous in my life. I couldn't say that I wouldn't miss that sweet pussy and that bad ass body, but I could do without the jealousy and the crazy attitude. The more I thought about Tammy, the more I realized that there was no such thing as the perfect woman. On the

152

surface, Tammy was every man's fantasy. She wasn't even a dream because dreams can be attained. She was a fantasy for the simple fact that she had beauty, brains, and great conversation. I never said anything to her, but I took notice when the men were drooling over her whenever we went anywhere. I remember we once went to this event that was being held at a museum in New York. It was a black tie affair and the lights were bright as can be. When Tammy and I stepped in the room, it seemed as if the lights got even brighter and everyone parted the floor to make way for Tammy and me to walk through. I knew they weren't looking at me. I knew that I was easy on the eye, but Tammy was like Princess Diana, but ten times more beautiful without all the elegance. She was admired for her beauty everywhere we went. That was one of the reasons I couldn't understand why she was so jealous. Men of all ages, races and status would stare at her beyond belief and I knew that most of them wondered what the hell she was doing with an average Joe like me, especially the rich men.

Unfortunately, I had to let Tammy go. Her beauty and brains didn't outweigh her jealousy for me. I didn't want to be with a woman who couldn't control her emotions. Even though she finally returned my calls a week later, we still ended up arguing about the same things we argued about previously and I knew that there was no way that I could put up with Tammy. I had to completely erase her out of my life. She could've been great, but she was a little too demented.

After Tammy and I stopped talking, I found myself looking back to a familiar territory. I hadn't talked to Tina in a while and I found myself thinking about her and missing her. Tina and I had our problems, but they were nothing that couldn't be worked out. I realized that after we broke up. She wanted to have sex all the time, so what? I was having crazy sex with Tammy all the time, anyway. I started to see my fault in our break up and I realized that all Tina wanted from me was some love and affection. I wish I could've grabbed the phone to call her, but my foolish pride once again got in the way. I even went through my phone to check the last time that Tina and I had spoken, but there was no trace of any calls because it had been so long. I wanted to believe that she was no longer seeing that pretty bastard that I saw her with in Atlanta, but deep inside I knew it was just a wish.

I was wondering what the hell was I going to do with my life without Tina. She was the only woman that I ever loved and I didn't know how to overcome that. I felt like I made the biggest mistake of my life when I let her go. Most men would kill to have a woman like Tina in their lives. She wasn't just like any woman, she was the best woman. We could kick it like we were friends, we could chill like we were lovers and we could even hang like she was one of my boys. Where the hell was I going to find another woman like that? To me, Tina was one in a million and I didn't want to go search a million times to find another one like her. I wanted the original. I was yearning to see her so much, I started humming the melody to this tune, but I couldn't quite remember the lyrics. The tune stayed in my head, but the lyrics never came to me until one day when I went to the mall to shop for a new computer.

Things didn't get any easier for me. It seemed like everywhere I went I was listening to the instrumental version of the song that was in my head. Then one day while walking through Best Buy, the lyrics to the song were revealed to me. It was "Have You Seen Her" by the Chi-Lites. It was playing on the overhead speakers attached to the intercom at the store. When I heard the lyrics blasting over the speakers all I could do was think about Tina. I ended up leaving the store without my new laptop computer. After the song ended, I wanted to leave the store. I couldn't believe how much I was missing Tina. I managed to push her out of my life because I was being selfish. I didn't think about her feelings. As much as I wanted to blame her for our break-up, I realized it was me who should be blamed for it. All she ever wanted was to spend time with me and make love to me, but I didn't appreciate it. Instead, I ran to another woman, a crazy woman who almost drove me insane because of her jealousy. I wanted to hear Tina's voice, I wanted to see her. So I called her mom and asked, "Have you seen her?"

CHAPTER 35

Ray Ray

I always felt that my family thought I was good for one thing and one thing only, thugging. They couldn't be more wrong about me. When I was a kid living in the Marcy Projects, I hated it. I had to fight for my life everyday and the drug dealers there thought they ruled the world. It was either be down or get down. No one but my mother knew that I was a straight A student. Shoot, I wanted to make something of my life, but I had to act a certain way in order to get respect from these fools. I wasn't looking for the kind of respect that people die for on the street everyday; I was looking to be left alone, actually. I was tired of fighting them, but whipping an ass or two gave me the respect they were willing to give. My mother decided to move to Laurelton, a section in Queens, New York, during my junior year in high school. I didn't want to leave my high school in Brooklyn and start all over again with new friends at a new high school. I decided to take the long commute back to Brooklyn everyday for school. I was too comfortable in my setting to change it, plus, I didn't want my grades affected in any way, and my mother agreed.

I was never really the thug that my family believed I was. My mother could attest to that. I had to get in where I fit in. Those bastards in the projects weren't the nicest people as far as bullying all of the kids into selling drugs, but I refused. I acted like I was down with the crews, but selling drugs was out of the question. My real name is Raymond Barkley, but the nickname Ray Ray was affectionately given to me by my Aunty Gail, Tina's mom. Somehow, the name stuck and I was known throughout the projects as Ray Ray. With a name like Ray Ray, deviant behaviors were always attached to me even though I was not a devious child. I did what most children would do. I got into fistfights every now and then because I had to stand up for myself. I was an only child. My mother had a hard enough time raising one child by herself, there was no way she was going to have a second one. After my father left us, my mother never even bothered to take him to court for child support. He just up and left us like we never mattered to him. I sort of became the man of the house at five years old. My Aunty Gail tried to look out as much as she could for us, but she had her own family, and they were trying to build a business.

My mother and Aunty Gail are sisters. Aunty Gail is the older of the two. I think she was also the smartest. Not that I'm saying my mom was not smart, but she didn't use good judgment when it came to men. Look at me, I never had a daddy. Aunty Gail was smart enough to date a man who wanted to marry her before she even had children by him. I remember when Uncle Allen married her. It was the first time that our family had gotten together in a long while. Everybody seemed to be happy for her that day. I was maybe five or six years old, but I remember the day like it was yesterday. I think Will was about my age, and Tina was a couple of years younger. See, what happened was that Aunty Gail got pregnant and Uncle Allen took her to the Justice of the Peace and married her before the baby was born. That's all he could afford at the time because he was just starting his company.   However, five years later when he started earning some good money, he decided to have real wedding because he could afford it. I admired that about my uncle and I respected my Aunty Gail for hooking up with the right man. Anyway, I've said enough about Aunty Gail.

Since my best friend, Jamal, lived in Marcy Projects, I would hang out there after school and would leave to go home before it got dark. Jamal and I were determined to keep our friendship and make something out of our lives. Both of us were the only children of our single mothers, so that created a bond from the instant we met in first grade. We fought the bullies in our neighborhood together and we resisted the temptation of selling drugs together as well. By the time we got to high school, we had beaten up so many guys who tested us. They decided to just be cool with us instead of antagonizing us. We never liked those bastards, but we acted like we were cool with them. We didn't like the fact that they were corrupting their own community with drugs and prostitution. We wished we could do something to clean up the neighborhood. All of that was wishful thinking. Jamal and I wanted to go to college so we could become police officers and lock away the bad elements in our neighborhood. The projects would have been a nice place to live if all the bad elements weren't there, we thought. We wanted to be the saviors of our hood.

It wouldn't be until our junior year in high school that Jamal and I would find out that we could have the opportunity to change our neighborhoods. It was career day at the high school and many people from different professions came to speak with us. There were doctors, lawyers, police officers, firemen, engineers, nurses, businessmen and even positive rappers who came out to inspire us. The one person who stood out to us was this FBI agent named David Williams. David was the first black agent that we had ever seen. He told us about a junior agent program that the Bureau had and Jamal and I wanted to sign up. The FBI agent decided to become our mentor and we met with him away from our neighborhood. He prepped us for a future in law enforcement and told us the steps we needed to take in order to join the FBI.

Jamal and I worked diligently and by the time we graduated from high school, we knew we wanted to study criminal justice in college so we could join the FBI. Our interest was always to go back to our community to help clean it up, but David made it clear to us that there was no assignment guarantee with the FBI. We could end up anywhere in the world. However, he told us that most FBI agents worked undercover and if for some reason we did end up being assigned in New York, our identities as agents had to be kept a secret. We both decided to go away to school in Massachusetts at North Adams State College. It was a small school in the most western part of the state. The name of the school was later changed to Massachusetts College of Liberal Arts. We excelled academically and the four years went by pretty quickly. While there, we also took self-defense classes to get ready to join the FBI. By the time we graduated from college neither of us had reasons to go back to Marcy Projects. Jamal's mom had moved out during his freshman year, and we spent the whole four years in North Adams during our academic years up there. We never even went home during the breaks. We didn't want to expose ourselves to any possible threat that would keep us from joining the FBI.

After graduating from college, we were ready to apply to the academy for acceptance. Jamal and I both scored high on their exams and we were both accepted with the help of Agent David Williams. He wrote a recommendation letter on our behalf and the Bureau was happy to have us. After graduating from the academy, I got my wish of being assigned to New York while Jamal was shipped to the West Coast. I never even told my family what I was doing. Only my mom knew that I even graduated from college, but I swore her to secrecy after my graduation because I didn't want to place her life at risk. My mom was the only person at my college graduation as well as the graduation ceremony at the academy. She was so proud of me; the tears kept falling from her eyes. I couldn't do any of the things I did without my mom's help. I love that woman.

When an assignment for a major drug gang operating out of Marcy Projects became available, I came highly recommended because I was already familiar with the area and the people. What made it even more attractive to me was the fact that I was going to be taking down an enemy that I despised since I was a child. This guy named Killer Ken was the one who kept trying to get Jamal and me to sell drugs, and every time we turned down his offers, he would send his wolves after us to beat us up. We never backed down, though, and because of that he respected us; but we hated him and he hated us because he felt that we thought we were better them. That's how I became known as Ray Ray "the hustler" on the street. Oh yes, one more thing, everybody in the hood thought I went to the federal pen to do a bid during my four years in college. I had the rap sheet and all to prove it. The FBI is good with what they do and they checked the background of every person in Killer Ken's gang to make sure that none of them ever had connection to the federal pen that I claimed to have been locked up in.

CHAPTER 36

Start Spreading the News

I was so excited about calling Will. I couldn't wait to tell him the good news. I knew Will was going to be happy to hear that Marla really had no evidence of him threatening her on tape. He picked up the phone on the first ring, "What's up, sis?" "How's my big brother doing?" I asked. "I'm doing fine, but I'm disappointed that we're not gonna make the playoffs this year. We got our ass kicked by the Giants and the loss automatically kept us from being playoff contenders. We only lost by one point, though, on offense; but the defense wore our guys down. The offensive squad gotta stop relying on Michael Vick to make all the plays. Some of these players gotta start earning their paychecks. Other than that, I'm great," he vented. "Sorry to hear that your team is not going to the playoffs, but I got some good news," I told him. "I can use some good news right now," he said. "Well, I just saved a bunch of money by switching to...No, I'm only kidding." I had to lighten the moment because my brother was a little upset about his not making the playoff. "Will, I found out that Marla was fronting about having you on tape threatening to beat her ass. I have a connect who told me that she told her she was going to use that to extort you and exploit the situation," I said excitedly. "Tina, what connect and how do you know this person's not lying?" he questioned. "Trust me on this, Will. My connect wouldn't lie to me. I think you need to take a proactive approach to this and go down to the courthouse to get a restraining order against her," I suggested.

I knew Will was a grown ass man, but I wanted him to protect himself. I didn't want that crazy, loony chick to take advantage of him. "Cassandra and I have discussed it and we didn't know which way to go about handling it, but if your information is correct, I can be down at the courthouse tomorrow filing that order. I have evidence that she destroyed my property. Are you certain about your connect?" he asked skeptically. "Will, on mom, I swear to you that my info is correct," I said definitively. My brother knew I wouldn't swear on my family unless I was absolutely certain about something. "Word! I'ma have to go out and celebrate tonight with Cassandra. This chick had me worried for a minute. I didn't know if I was gonna have to deal with the press about all this. The other black athletes have not been presenting a good image for the NFL lately, and I damn sure didn't want to add to that," Will said with relief in his voice. I was glad that I could comfort my brother.

"Enough about crazy ass Marla…how are you and that pretty boy doing?" he asked curiously with excitement. It was my turn to unload my bucket of sadness on him. "He's an asshole, Will. He's just like many other men out there; he was a player and his true colors started to show. I don't want to talk about him," I said sadly. I really didn't want to mess up my good mood. I realized I was happy that my brother's spirit was lifted and I wanted to stay on the positive course with the conversation. "We don't have to talk about it, but you know I've got your back. All you have to do is say the word and I'll get on him, if he hurt you. I knew I caught a bad vibe from that cat the very first time I met him, but I didn't want to mess up your groove and…" I cut him off, "And act like the big brother you've always been to me? I'll be fine, Will; we all get played at least once in the game of life. Anyway, tell me about Ms. Cassandra. How has she been treating you?" "Cassandra is it. She's the perfect woman for me. This woman can cook, she knows how to iron, she's clean and she's the bomb in the bedroom, you know what I am saying?" he said, sounding all happy. It was a little too much info, but my brother and I had that kind of a relationship. He felt that he could tell me anything. "I'm glad that you've finally found the one, Will. I'm happy for you," I told him cheerfully. "Tina, how many sisters out there got it going on like Cassandra? On top of all that I said she does, she's also a successful attorney working at one of the top firms in Atlanta. Lucky? That I am," he said resolutely.

"You sound very serious, Will." "I am," he responded. "Does that mean that she's gonna be meeting mom and dad soon?" I asked cautiously. "Real soon. I think I want to spend the rest of my life with her. She's the best I think that's available out there and I'm snatching her up," he said. Will was beyond sprung. He was whipped. At least this time it wasn't a chickenhead trying to suck him dry. I liked Cassandra and I felt she was the orderly type who would contribute positively to Will's life. Not only that, she was also gorgeous. I didn't have to worry about having bucktooth nephews and nieces. "Will, I'm happy for you. I gotta go, but don't forget to go down to the courthouse tomorrow to get that restraining order," I reminded him before hanging up the phone.

CHAPTER 37

I Miss Him

Talking to Will got me thinking about Darren. I wondered how he was doing and what he'd been up to. I hadn't talked to him in so long because I thought I was going to find a new boyfriend in Terrence. Men ain't shit! Darren, however, was no ordinary man. Darren was that knight in shining armor that I was looking for, everywhere else. He had always been, but I was too selfish to recognize it. So what he was too tired to have sex with me all the time, we still had sex every other day. I should've understood that he was a lot more tired than I was when he got home because his job was more demanding. He traveled most of the time and jet lag was something more serious than I cared to admit at the time. My sweet Darren was probably wrapped up in that chick's arm giving her all the love that belonged to me. Boy did that man know how to love. I even miss his smile and the way he used to make me laugh all the time. He had a weird sense of humor that only I understood. Darren and I connected on many different levels. He was sweet, gentle and loving and I missed him.

That high maintenance looking chick probably had no idea what he was really like. She had gotten herself a gem of a man. Darren was a simple man whose simplistic needs were minute. He didn't care for a lot of things that this high maintenance looking chick was probably into. I went wrong in so many directions. I wished I could change everything back. My Darren was gone and I was left with nothing but the memories that we shared together. If that chick was any smarter than me, she'd hold on to him because I knew too many women who were looking for a guy like Darren. Shit, I was even willing to apologize to him for behaving like a spoiled brat who needed his attention twenty-four hours a day.

Sleeping around with a bunch of men was a thing of the past for me. I yearned for that monogamous relationship with one man, but I wanted to be loved by him and I wanted to be the center of his world. I realized that one man was Darren. Guys like Terrence who could lie so easily couldn't provide the kind of love and relationship that I wanted. Guys like him are usually too busy using their pretty looks, success, and their swagger to get as many women as possible to spread their legs open to them. Not just that, I lost total respect for Terrence when I found out he was involved in drug money laundering. The fact that I found evidence that he was probably a drug dealer as well completely turned me off. Even if he just condoned it, he might as well have been one himself. It was all about the easy money, the fly cars, big house and the pretty women. Well, he got all that and he could keep having it for all I cared. I didn't plan on ever calling him again. I wouldn't even answer his calls. I refused to play one of his "area code hoes."

I knew Darren wasn't perfect, but he showed me respect and he was a dignified man who wanted to obtain success the right way, and the legal way. He wasn't driven by greed and quick money. In his field, it was so easy for him to be deceitful. As an accountant he had a lot of power and access to money that could've made him a millionaire instantly if he was a crook, but my Darren didn't have a crooked bone in his body. He had the qualities that I wanted passed on to my children. My Darren, oh boy did I miss my Darren.

CHAPTER 38

The Underworld

To live in the underworld, a person has to develop a certain swagger and characteristics that are not easily comprehensible to the masses. I was living in that world and I knew that at any moment's notice that my life could be taken away from me. I wasn't worried about my freedom because I worked on the side of the law as an FBI agent, but I worried about getting caught slipping because of my mother. Because I was an FBI agent I had to go the extra mile, most of the time, to prove to my fellow gang bangers and drug dealers that I was a disciple. If these street cats read the bible, they would've known that Judas was a traitor who betrayed all the other disciples, including Jesus, and I played the role of Judas in a good way. It was easy for me to betray Killer Ken and his gang because he was no Jesus. To me the worst scums of the earth were those people who didn't care about turning their mother or sister into a crackhead for a quick buck. I despised these guys to the umpteenth power, and I wanted to rid the streets of them. Too many of my mother's friends fell victim to crack when I was a child; I wanted to do something about it. Most of the people that I used to call aunt and uncle while growing up in the projects were now on the street begging to suck my dick for a hit. It was sad.

Killer Ken, aka Kenneth Smith, looked like a typical drug dealer. He drove around in a Benz with enough accessories that even a plane in the sky could spot his custom painted, light blue Mercedes Benz. He was probably the darkest black man I ever met, with the reddest eyes. He stood about six feet tall, very slim and toned. If I had to guess his weight, I'd say he weighed about a buck fifty. He didn't look bad even with red eyes, but the expressions he wore on his face all the time and the gold fronts made him deadly. Killer Ken usually wore what he called designer suits everyday for no reason. To me they were more like the pimp suits that you'd find guys in Snoop Dog's entourage, like Don "Magic" Juan wearing. Pop was totally opposite of Killer Ken. He was a show-off who led by brute force. Standing at only five feet, six inches tall with a muscular build that he developed while serving time in a state prison, he looked very intimidating. Even at his height, he was able to walk around carrying about a buck ninety in body weight. He looked strong, mean and deadly. As a matter of fact, he was deadly. Pop wasn't the best looking gangster out there either. It was commonly known that most people referred to him as crooked eye Pop behind his back, but no one dared call him that to his face. He was a brown-skinned man with a broad nose and chapped, dry lips like Malik Yoba. Pop's government ID identified him as Erick Black, as noted on his birth certificate.

I infiltrated Killer Ken's gang a year after I graduated from the academy. I had to be trained to play my part in the underworld of organized crime perfectly. The lingo used on the streets for hustling, the body language, the prices, weight and everything else associated with drugs, I had to learn. It was easy for Killer Ken to allow me in because I came back to the projects looking like a crackhead. It took a lot of work, but the FBI could get a black person to look Chinese if they wanted to when it came to undercover work. So looking like a crackhead was an easy task. "Oh shit, if it ain't Mr. Almighty from back in the day. I know you ain't done turned into a crackhead," said Killer Ken when he first saw me. "Suki suki now." He called one of his boys over. "Yo', that's little Ray Ray. Remember the dude we was always fighting trying to get him down with us?" He was trying to help the others recollect who I was. "You mean dude that fought us almost everyday?" one of them said with shaken certainty. "Yeah, I believe he might've whipped your ass once or twice," Killer Ken said laughing. It wasn't a good joke at the time because that guy was easily provoked and I didn't want to get my ass whipped my first day on the street. "I ain't never whipped his ass," I said, while scratching myself like a crackhead in my dirty clothes looking at the ground. "C'mon now, even the crackhead remember that he couldn't whip my ass," I heard Pop say, who I later found out was Killer Ken's right hand man. The nickname Pop was given to him because he would pop anybody, anywhere, sometimes for absolutely no reason. Word on the street was that he had shot and killed at least thirty people. He was the most feared member of Killer Ken's gang, beside Killer Ken himself.

Playing the role of a crackhead, I had to show respect. I couldn't go up to Killer Ken or Pop to ask them for drugs. I had to go to their little flunkies on the street to purchase small amount of drugs for my "supposed" high. As luck would have it, one day Killer Ken pulled me to the side and told me that he remembered how fierce I was as a kid and that I could be a good soldier in his army, but I had to get myself cleaned up. It was the opportunity that I was waiting for; I was invited to become a member of Killer Ken's organization. It took about a couple of months to act like I was going to rehab everyday. Day by day and week by week, I started showing up looking less high, cleaner and smelling better, thanks to the great make up artists at the Bureau. The Bureau made sure that my safety was never compromised, but I still worried. I needed to become a gangster and drug dealer. The story about me being in the pen for stabbing a guy during a bank robbery in the Midwest was bought by these dumb fools who never bothered to read a paper. However, the Bureau made available my rap sheet online and a few bogus articles about the robbery, just in case. As far as they knew, I was legit. I didn't worry about being found out.

Jamal and I kept in contact while he was on the West Coast and when I told him about my assignment, he was a little jealous. I knew sooner or later I was gonna have to prove my loyalty to Killer Ken and there was no one better to help me pull it off than Jamal. It was gonna be one of those random acts of violence because I was so fucked up in the head that I could kill somebody for no reason. I couldn't front, I had to sell the drugs that I despised for almost three months to gain Killer Ken's trust. I avoided direct hand-to-hand exchanges of drugs and money by having the crackheads hand the money to these other peddlers who worked for Killer Ken. Nevertheless, I felt like I was dealing drugs. A fake confrontation with Jamal and me was set up by the FBI near the projects where I hustled my drugs. I was walking with the crew one night and Jamal came out of nowhere and said, "You scums need to leave the neighborhood alone. You are destroying your own people. Killer Ken's top man, Pop, was amongst the group and he recognized Jamal right away. I could see the hatred he harbored for Jamal because Jamal was actually the one who whipped his ass when we were little.

The FBI was watching the whole thing from a nearby van in case the plan didn't go accordingly. I saw Pop reaching for his gun and I quickly intervened and said, "I got this." The rest of the crew stood around to see what I was about to do. "What did you say, chump?" I said to Jamal with authority in my voice. "I said that you punks need to leave people in the neighborhood alone and stop selling your filth here," he repeated. "Ray Ray, is that you? Did they turn you into a scumbag, too?" he questioned. "Shut the fuck up. The only scumbag I see is about to die in a minute if you don't shut the fuck up," I said. "Fuck you, Ray Ray. I knew your stupid ass was a follower," he said with fake anger in his voice. I was the only one who knew that Jamal was only acting. I knew Jamal was wearing his bullet proof vest just in case, but without saying another word, I quickly pulled out my gun and shot four blanks right through his chest. The FBI exploded the fake blood patches tied to his body with a remote control and Jamal fell down to the ground covered in fake blood.

The whole crew scrambled, but I stood over Jamal and shot four more times as they ran. I needed to be the hardest gangster in that gang if I was ever going to get near Killer Ken. That was the day that I was embraced by Killer Ken's gang. The FBI even held a fake funeral for Jamal to make the gang believe that the killing was real. Jamal and I would talk about the great lengths that we had to go through to protect our community. Often times, we would laugh about certain events, but most of the time, it was really sad. He couldn't come back to New York until I cracked my case, but I went out to California to hang out with him when I was on vacation. It was hard sometimes because hustlers don't really take vacations. They usually on their hustle 24/7, but I managed to lie to the gang about lying low to avoid jail because of some of the things that they were doing on the street. I tried as much as I could to keep people from getting killed, but a few people in the game were expendable. That's the thing about the drug game, everyone is a potential victim.

When my cousin told me about this chick who was trying to extort money from Will, I called a couple of favors in Atlanta. By then, I had guys working for me on the block so I could get away if I wanted to. I also had to check out a new contact down in Atlanta for Killer Ken, so I took this other guy who was part of the gang with me. Initially, Killer Ken wanted to send an army to Atlanta to show strength, but we got halfway through New Jersey when he called me back and ordered the wolves back on the streets. He didn't want to lose out on the money these guys were making on the street everyday. I found out the one guy that ended up going down to Atlanta with me was an undercover DEA agent after I called the Bureau and to report to them who was selected to go down to Atlanta with me. It was a calculated choice because he was the most trusted guy under Pop's command. Pop trusted him with his life and for the first time I felt that I had an ally within the gang. His name was Bobo on the street, but his real name was Kevin Thompson. Kevin and I kicked it on the drive to Atlanta about our undercover work and when we got there, we hooked up with a few other agents who were assigned to the extortion case as well as another drug case under investigation in Atlanta. All the agents looked like weed smoking thugs. I thought they even fooled my cousin. She looked frightened when she saw them for the first time at the hotel. I needed my cousin to identify the woman so the FBI could watch her. I was glad they came to me with their problem because if they had gone to anybody else, someone could've gotten hurt and they could've possibly gone to jail for soliciting a beatdown on behalf of Will. Life works in mysterious ways. I'm glad I've been able to fool my family into thinking that I've been nothing but a hustler and a thug who would do anything to protect them, however illegal I appeared to be. I'm also glad that I found out from Tina that they didn't really want me out there hustling on the streets, it demonstrated love. I knew they cared because Uncle Allen offered me a job every time I saw him.

CHAPTER 39

Cousin Ray Ray

I was worried about my cousin, Ray Ray. I needed to make sure he didn't go to jail for trying to rob Terrence, even though deep down inside I felt Terrence needed to be taught a lesson. I also thought about what he said about the family leaning on him whenever some street shit was about to pop off. He was right. We encouraged the bad boy, hustling qualities, and he felt like he had to walk around carrying that with him all the time. I started to see my cousin in a different light. I remember he fought hard to avoid becoming a hustler when he was a kid. One time he even brought Will down to the projects to intimidate some of the guys who were trying to bully him. At thirteen years old, my brother was already standing over six feet tall and weighed over two hundred pounds. Half of those guys were intimidated by his mere presence. This was when guns weren't so prevalent in the hood. Not to say that shootings didn't happen, but people weren't shooting each other at the drop of a dime like they do now. Honestly, I couldn't recall when the transition from stand-up guy to thug and hustler took place with Ray Ray. All I knew was that Ray Ray had developed a reputation in the projects as one of the toughest drug dealers out there. I learned all that stuff from my mother. She still kept phone contact with some of her friends from back in the day. Every now and then she would assist them with their rent and other household utilities, and they would give her the scoop on what was going on.

I needed to speak with Ray Ray in order for my mind to be at peace. It had been a couple of weeks and I didn't hear from him. I skeptically dialed his number hoping and wishing for the best. "Who this?" he said in his signature manner and voice. "Ray Ray, it's me Tina. Is everything all right?" I asked. "Yeah everything's all right. Why you ask?" he said. "Well, I was worried about you and I wanted to make sure you didn't get locked up for doing something stupid down in Atlanta. I hope you know that the family loves you and we would do anything to help you change your life whenever you're ready," I told him. "Cuz, don't worry about me. I'm all right. When I'm ready to leave this game, I will do it on my own," he said. "Ray, you don't understand; we want you to leave while you're still alive, in one piece," I sadly said to him. "These streets love me, I ain't worried about it," he said. From his tone, I could tell that he was showing off for somebody. There had to be somebody near him for him to be talking like that. "What happened with the Terrence situation?" I enquired. "Oh, we gonna take care of ole boy. They didn't bring that money like they said they would, but I got my people watching to see when they bring the bags in," he said.

As long as he wasn't involved with it, I was cool. "When are you coming back to New York?" I asked. "I already came back. Tell your mom I'll have the rest of that dough to her, too. We didn't really use a lot of it. Remember, whenever y'all are dealing with something like this, you should always call me first. Cousin Ray Ray is connected to the streets, baby." Ray Ray was something else. He embodied what a street hustler was supposed to be. He was always on the move and always had his ears out for anything that went down in the projects. We wanted him to be careful because the gang he ran with was starting to become overly violent and we didn't want him getting caught in that shit. Lord only knew that the family prayed for Ray Ray everyday. There wasn't really much we could do to change him, so we just allowed him to be who he was. Every family has a hustler, and ours was no exception.

My father always thought that Ray Ray was too bright to be wasting his life on the streets. He tried as much as he could to convince him to take a job with our company, but Ray Ray used the commute to Long Island as an excuse. My father even offered to get him an apartment near the job, but Ray Ray declined his offer saying that Long Island was dead and that there wasn't enough action out there for him. His infectious personality couldn't be denied. Whenever Ray Ray was around, there was bound to be laughter. He was the comedian of the family. If there was a wake or a wedding, often time that was when our family got together, Ray Ray would be the center of attention as well as the entertainment. We continued to hope that he would someday realize that life was not about hustling on the streets. My dad loved that guy. He saw a lot of himself in Ray Ray. He was just as rebellious as a young man and he didn't take crap from anybody. I guess that's why he and my mother were a match made in heaven.

CHAPTER 40

When I Reminisce Over You

I remember how her voice was soothing, especially when I had a long day at work. Not only that, Tina was a master when it came to sexual healing. Marvin Gaye must've been in love with a woman like Tina when he wrote that song. I remember coming home one day after doing a long audit for this company in Manhattan; Tina treated me like a king. I left the house around seven o'clock in the morning and I didn't make it home until eleven o'clock that night. It was one of those audits with a deadline and I had to expedite everything that day. I was tired as hell when I got home. All I wanted to do was jump in the bed and go to sleep. I didn't even eat well that day. I opened the door to my apartment to find Tina standing there butt naked, in high heels, lip glossed and a bottle of massage oil in her hand. I also smelled Creole shrimp, stir fried vegetables and wild rice warming up in the oven in the kitchen.

She took my briefcase away from me and pulled me towards her. She then went on to pull off my jacket, shirt, and pants. I lay across the couch on my stomach as she sat on the back of my legs to give me a deep tissue massage. Her hands were sensual and felt good all over my body. The heating oil felt great against my skin coupled with her touch. I no longer felt the aches and pain and the stress of a long day. I was relaxed. She took away the tension around my neck and shoulders as she massaged me with her slow hands. By the time I turned around for her to work on my chest, I felt a burst of energy. My manhood was standing straight up through my underwear, but Tina wouldn't let me have her, at least not until after she fed me her delicious food, spoon by spoon until my hunger was gone.

I wanted her and from the look in her eyes, I knew she wanted me, too. But Tina wanted to make the night special for us. She led me to the bathroom where she ran me a nice warm bubble bath. She washed my whole body with this special sponge she bought from Bath & Body Works. I was in heaven. She treated me so well that night. I wanted to make love to her, but she knew that I needed my energy to get up for work the next day. After drying me off with a towel, I couldn't resist the sight of her standing before me looking so sexy in her high heels. I wanted to take a bite, a light one. Tina stopped me short of penetrating her with voracity. I knew I was looking for a quickie because I didn't have the energy for our usual marathon sessions. She started kissing me and I kissed her back. She tasted especially good that night. It was something about loving her that night that felt oh so good. My dick was saying one thing, while my mind was saying something else.

"Let me lick you. I wanna eat you," I begged. "It's all about you tonight, daddy. Don't worry about me," she said. It was time for me to sit back and relax and let her do what she did best, love me. She started licking me from my chest, down to my navel, and didn't stop until she had all of me in her mouth. Tina had blown my mind with her oral skills in the past, but that night it was different; it was especially good. As she ran her soft tongue up and down my dick, I could feel her taste buds tingling my skin. It was nice and slow and very sensual. Her soft moans increased the fiery passion attached to her lips. My dick had never felt better. "Ooh, baby, yes. I appreciate you," I groaned. "Just relax, mommy's gonna take you there," she assured. I loved when Tina treated me like a baby, sometimes, especially while we were making love. She always knew when I needed to be pampered.

Her lips were wrapped around the head of my penis as she moved her tongue slowly to my most sensitive area. I started grabbing the sheets as a necessity. I was losing control and I didn't want to explode too soon. It was too enjoyable to let the moment pass so quickly. I closed my eyes to enjoy the moment. Tina's engaging eyes were my weakness. I could never stand looking at her when she's sucking me. Her sexy stares always forced me to succumb to her oral prowess. The sheets were being pulled from the bed from end to end as I moaned in ecstasy while my dick savored the touch of Tina's tongue. The tightening of my body was no match for her skills. I could feel the rush and there was nothing I could do to stop it. I just gave in to her. It was more than one squirt, but I didn't get a chance to see any of it because the warm release of my protein disappeared in the back of Tina's throat. The head of my penis immediately became sensitive afterwards. I was begging for mercy. After one last lick, she took my dick out of her mouth and released it as a prisoner from her warm mouth.

No excuses were necessary that night. I was given a free pass to drift off to sleep. I imagined Tina looking over me as I slept the night away in complete tranquility. Tina was a very special woman who knew how to give me that special treatment when I needed it, and for those reasons and many others, I could never stop loving her.

CHAPTER 41

When I Think of You

Darren was no ordinary man, he was my Superman. I don't know why I thought there was a better superhero out there than my Superman. His heroics were different than what people expect of heroes. When I was almost implicated in that murder with that crazy ass white boy, Darren swallowed his pride and welcomed me back in his life. Most men would have run for the hills, especially after it was revealed that I slept with so many men. Darren was an understanding and forgiving man and that's all that any woman could ask of any man. More importantly, though, Darren was loving and caring. He left me with so many great memories. When I thought of him most of the time, I either smiled or got completely moist. I didn't get moist because of Darren's sexual prowess in the bedroom, I got moist because his kindheartedness, sweetness and overall gentleness.

I'll never forget the time when Darren showed up to my office with a picnic basket and a dozen roses because my father and I clashed about something earlier in the day. It was after hours, and I decided to work a little later that day to get my mind off my father. It was winter, so he came in wearing a pair of cowboy boots, long trench coat and a cowboy hat. I guess he was trying to bring a smile to my face, and it worked. It was the first time that I had ever seen a black cowboy live. In the basket, Darren had dinner that he picked up from one of my favorite local restaurants and a bottle of wine. He also brought a blanket that we spread out on the floor in my office to add more of a picnic vibe to the occasion. We sat there, ate and talked for what seemed like hours. Darren never took off his coat, which made me a little uncomfortably warm. I didn't question his motive for keeping his coat on, but he mentioned that he was a little chilly, so he got away with keeping it on while we ate.

After dinner, we started drinking the wine and enjoying the moment. I had a little boom box radio in my office and we turned it to Magic for some soft music. Darren and I danced in the middle of my office, talked, and enjoyed the moment altogether. I was having a lot of fun and he took away all the stress that I had been feeling all day. Just when I thought it couldn't get any better, Darren dropped his coat to reveal himself in the buff wearing a cowboy hat and boots. He was looking hot, too. My temperature started rising as I stared at Da'ron. He started teasing me by doing a slow dance in front of me. I was sitting on the floor, so his dick was at face level to me. "Do you want to ride the cowboy?" he teasingly asked. I returned a flirtatious smile revealing that I was hot for him. Darren continued to dance in front of me, pulling all kind of western silly stunts. He acted as if he was on a horse and started shouting, "Giddy up, giddy up," while moving his body side to side. I was overly turned on. I wanted to pull him near me and take him in my mouth. But Darren had other plans for me.

He became the dancing cowboy trying to emulate the moves of Jessica Beal from the movie *Flashdance*. It was when he jumped to his knees that his lips met my lips gently and I knew I wanted him to just tear me up. I took his tongue in my mouth and I slowly caressed it with mine. Our lips never parted as he reached for one of my breasts with one of his hands. My nipples immediately became erect as Darren kissed me gently while fondling my breasts. The tingling feeling inside of me started surfacing. I wanted him. No, I needed him. "I want you so bad right now, baby," I whispered softly, while quickly pulling my lips away from his. We connected again, but this time he pulled and sucked on my lips, fueling my desire for him. "I want to love you forever," he mumbled quickly, not wanting to let our lips part ways. He kissed me harder while holding the back of my head.

He slowly towered over me and had me lying on the floor without breaking his concentration through our long passionate kiss. The direction of his mouth was descending slowly south towards my chest. The kisses were slow from my neck down to my back. Then the ascension was even sweeter with his wet tongue riding my back up my shoulders while he caressed my breasts with his hands. I could feel my need to climax rising and I started losing control. Darren was the only man who had ever made me cum while only kissing me. His kisses resumed from the back of my neck to my lips while he held me from behind. I could feel his twelve-inch dick standing hard against my back, but I wanted it inside me. My hands somehow found it, and I started stroking his dick back and forth as our kiss sauntered. "Baby, you taste so good; I can kiss you all night long," he told me. I could've kissed him all night as well, but his delicious dick kept calling my name. While he kneeled in front of me, I got on my stomach and took him in my mouth. I wanted to taste him badly. The head was big, so I licked it all around slowly without putting it all in my mouth. I could see him tilting his head back confirming the joy I was physically bringing to him. "Yes, baby. I like that," he said, as I blew on the tip of his dick slowly. The frigid air from my mouth was blissful as he started making weird faces and trembling.

He sat on the floor as I continued to work my magic on his dick. Being on my stomach exposed the whole circumference of my ass to him. He teasingly smacked my ass as I tried to deep throat all of him in my mouth. Then he slowly inserted a finger inside of me from the back and then two. I was grinding on it and it felt good. "I wanna taste you," he said as he took the fingers in his mouth. He lay down flat on the floor as I turned my body around to place my pussy in his face. We were in the sixty-nine position, but it was more like sixty-eight because I wanted to just sit there and let Darren eat my pussy. I owed him one and it would come in due time. "I like the way you taste." He quickly pulled away to tell me. "I love the way you eat my pussy," I confirmed. Darren knew how eat pussy well, but I couldn't just lay there on his stomach staring at his juicy dick. I reached for it slowly and took it in my mouth. We were both having a great sixty-nine moment when Darren did something with his tongue that I had never experienced before. He stuck his tongue in my ass and I lost control. "Oh, shit!" I came against my will. It was one of those good surprise nuts. I placed my face between his thighs and gripped his leg as I shook off my nut. My body was relaxed, but I wanted Darren to fuck me.

I lay flat on the floor on my stomach as Darren straddled me from behind. I could feel him penetrating me slowly. About six inches in, my pussy started getting tighter around his dick. He stroked me slowly while inching his way in. I could feel my walls collapsing to his love stick. "Fuck me! Fuck me, baby!" I screamed. Darren started stroking me harder. "You know you turn me on even more when you tell me to fuck you," he said. That was my plan. I wanted to get fucked. Darren continued to stroke me while he caressed my ass with his hands. He was enjoying my ass and my pussy while I enjoyed his dick. He had never tried a double penetration before, but the surprise was pleasant as he inserted his thumb in my ass while rhythmically fucking me to the beat of our hearts. Sweat was pouring down on our bodies, but we didn't care. Darren dropped his whole body on top of me while holding his weight with hands that were grounded to the floor. The strokes were faster and longer and even more pleasurable. I knew that I was about to cum again and so was he. I arched my ass up so I could take all twelve of his inches. "I'm about to cum, baby," I warned him. "Me, too," he replied. With just the right timing, Darren stroked me to ecstasy while I helped him with his own release. I could've smoked a whole pack of cigarettes that night if I were a smoker.

Darren was an extraordinary man in many ways. He catered to my every need and that's one of the reasons that I knew that it would take me another lifetime to meet a man like him. Someway, somehow, he always knew how to make my days better. I didn't have to ask or say anything. He simply knew.

CHAPTER 42

Talk It Out

The way I saw it, I could sit around and mope all day about missing Tina or I could just pick up the phone to let her know that I had been thinking about her and was even missing her. I knew that I needed to swallow my pride to do this, but I was willing to take that chance. I only hoped that it wasn't too late. I honestly didn't want to interrupt her relationship if it had gotten serious with that pretty boy. Something about him seemed slimy, but I couldn't pinpoint exactly what it was. I told myself that I would be supportive and I would just accept it as closure if she had decided to get serious with the dude. My hands were trembling as I dialed Tina's number. I didn't know where that nervousness came from. I needed something to calm my nerves. I pressed about eight digits before I decided to get a drink to relax a bit before I called her. A shot of Courvoisier always did the trick, even though I wasn't much of a drinker. I was one of those guys who only drank socially. I didn't like sitting at home drinking for no reason at all, but in situations like these, the limited liquor in my cabinet came in handy.

After relaxing a bit, I worked up the nerve to dial Tina's number this time without any hesitation. I couldn't wait to hear her sweet voice on the other line. As the phone was about to start ringing, I received another call on the other line. I didn't even check the number when I answered the call, and to my surprise, it was my sweet princess. "Hi, Darren," she said, after I greeted her with my usual hello. I had no idea who it was on the other line, so my greeting didn't come out as special as I wanted it to be. Had I known it was Tina calling me, my demeanor and tone would've been a lot more pleasant. I didn't want to seem too eager, but I was happy to hear her voice. Hopefully, my number didn't show up on her phone when I dialed her number. I might need to use this moment in the future against Tina. I have always been the first to call whenever we had a disagreement in the past. Tina has had more control than me, but I always knew that she was just waiting by the phone for me to call. The difference between Tina and me, however, was the fact that I always used an excuse to call her. Tina was very straightforward with her intent.

"Look, Darren, I'm not gonna beat around the bush. I'm calling you because I miss you and I realize that you're the only man that I want to be with, forever," she said. Forward was not even a strong enough word to describe her approach, but I wanted to say the same thing, except I wouldn't have had the courage to allow that statement to be the first thing out of my mouth. I felt like Tina wanted to take control of the situation, well, she actually did. "I realize you're the only woman I want to be with as well," I said sounding like a punk. "I'm glad to hear that, Darren, because I'm getting older and I don't have time to be on nobody's market. A convertible Bentley doesn't stay on the market. People have to place special orders for convertible Bentleys because they are limited. That's what I am, Darren, a convertible Bentley. I only want one special owner and that's you," she said bluntly. The metaphor worked and I got it. I didn't really care to know what happened with her little boy toy at that point. I was happy that Tina realized I was the man for her. I was intoxicated by her. She was my good drug and I needed a relapse, but I didn't want therapy for my drug of choice. Tina was my good drug.

"Baby, you know that I love you and we both were angry when we made the hasty decision that we made. I'm willing to let bygones be bygones so we can move on with our happy lives," I told her in my most genuine tone. Since Tina was showing courage, I figured I might as well show courage in the line of passion as well. The shot of Courvoisier put me at ease and on an even plane with Tina, and I felt just as confident as she did. It was pretty much a done deal, nothing too complicated. We were two people in love and we made a mistake when we broke up. All that needed to happen was for us to recognize our mistake then move on.

I know I learned a valuable lesson when Tina and I broke up. I realized that no matter what, there's never going to be anybody out there that's a perfect package. Even man made items are not made to perfection. The most expensive luxury cars are sometimes recalled because of some malfunctions and imperfections. I knew what I'd learned from the experience, but I didn't know if Tina walked away with the same lesson. I was sure she and I would be talking about this situation sometime in the future, but I didn't want to ruin the moment. "Baby, we should go out tomorrow night and celebrate our reunion," I suggested. "Sure, we can go to the very first nice restaurant you took me to when we first started dating," she said. "Baby, that restaurant is closed," I told her. I opened the door to a whole new argument. I thought that the first time Tina and I had ever gone out to eat we went to the Motown Café, which was once located in Manhattan, but she named some other restaurant that I didn't even remember or knew existed. Since women seem to be better at remembering sentimental stuff like that, I agreed to go to the Thai food place where she insisted our first date took place. We could both be wrong, but it didn't even matter to me.

"You know I'm really happy to have you back in my life, right?" I told her. "I'm happy as well. I wanted to put it all on the line and I'm glad I did. I love you so much, Darren," she said, sulking. The only thing I could say was, "I love you, too." I could've asked Tina to come over right away so we could make up while we were in the moment, but the moment had to be special. I couldn't treat her like some booty call. Besides, I wanted to go to bed with a big ass Kool-Aid smile across my face. We must've said "I love you" a thousand times before we got off the phone. I felt all giddy inside after talking to Tina. Suddenly, the next day at work wasn't going to be a drag anymore.

CHAPTER 43

Bad Boy Watcha Gonna Do

I wasn't lying when I told my cousin, Tina, that Terrence was being watched. The FBI had been on his case for a while, but they never got the break they needed to plant a bug in his house. We didn't care about his little five hundred thousand dollars; we wanted to take down the whole organization, including his cousin Antwan who was one of the biggest drug traffickers in the South. Antwan was brash and flashy. Kevin and I were down in Atlanta to connect with him and Terrence on some new deal they were about to broker with Killer Ken. It was a coincidence that Antwan and Terrence were related and working together. This Antwan guy, I found out after meeting him, was slick. The feds had been on him for a while, but he managed to evade them and avoid getting caught on numerous occasions. His drug empire was colossal compared to Killer Ken's chump change operation in New York. However, Killer Ken's case took precedence because of all the murders that his gang had committed. A lot of innocent people's lives were taken because he wanted to make examples out of them. His right hand man, Pop, would be lucky if he saw another day on the street once the case was solved.

I witnessed many murders committed by these two cowards during my fours years working as an undercover agent, and I was eager to bring these guys to justice, every single one of them. They were so proud of me when they thought I had taken Jamal's life for no reason. My action was celebrated at a strip club in the Bronx in the VIP room with five strippers. These assholes supposedly took a life then went out to celebrate their crime. That shit became routine, but the people dying weren't important enough for us to move in on Killer Ken just yet. I guess you can charge it to the game. Not everyone's life is important to law enforcement. We wanted to catch a bigger fish along with Killer Ken and his gang. He had been dealing with some Dominicans in the Bronx who supplied him with his drugs every four weeks, but we couldn't get video surveillance of the exchange. I refused to wear a wire because the risk was just too high. Every time I caught a break in the case, my back-ups were nowhere close to make the bust. Then I discovered Killer Ken's plan to use a new supplier in Atlanta so he could force the Dominicans' hands to drop their prices.

The FBI didn't want the assignment to end just yet. I was given the order to take the lead role in the new deal. By then, Killer Ken thought I was down for his cause and my devotion to him seemed solid. He started trusting me more and more and even tried once to reminisce about our upbringing, like we had anything in common. The only thing we had in common was the fact that we both lived in the projects, nothing more. I ended up working the case for another six months. Killer Ken allowed me to be the middle man between him and Antwan in Atlanta. I saw more drugs than I ever saw before and more crackheads were sprouting around the neighborhood everyday. I didn't like what I was seeing and I wanted to put a stop to it before the whole damn community turned to a bunch of zombies walking around high all day scaring people away.

I called, David, my mentor. I expressed my disdain with the case and I wanted to bring in Antwan and Killer Ken. They may not have had any murders directly connected to Antwan, but we had plenty of evidence for drug trafficking and indirect connections to a few homicides. Antwan was slick, but he wasn't that slick. I also found out that Terrence was the brain behind the whole drug empire. He had his law degree all right, but he always intended on selling drugs. He started selling reefer when he was a freshman in college, and it was there that his zeal and desire to become rich and powerful developed. He turned over control of the street operation to his cousin Antwan after he took the bar exam and passed with flying colors. It was then that he decided he was going to become a sports agent, and because he had access to some of the athletes in Atlanta, he was able to get a couple of bench warmers to sign on with him as clients.

Terrence was a smart man who loved the celebrity lifestyle. He was at every function that involved professional athletes. He didn't mind forking over thousands of dollars to mingle with the real celebrities. He even started to become known to the club owners as one of the high rollers in Atlanta, Vegas, LA, Miami and a few other cities. Terrence was setting the stage to take his drug money and turn legit, but greed got the best of him because he couldn't find any high profile clients to help maintain his lifestyle. Rosenblaum, the well-known Jewish agent, snatched every potential high profile player from the time they started playing Pee Wee basketball or Pop Warner football. Terrence didn't stand a chance against him.

It was another coincidence that my cousin happened to be dating this guy, Terrence. I couldn't let her in on my secret of being an agent because a lot of women tend to run their mouth when they're at the receiving end of some good loving. I didn't want to risk blowing my cover. The rest of my family probably will never find out about my job, because I don't want to jeopardize their safety and compromise mine. They can think whatever they want about me until I'm reassigned out of New York, I won't be telling them a damn thing about my job. The only person who needed to know was my mama, and I kept her quiet by telling her that I could die any day if she opened her mouth to the rest of the family. I had to keep mama in check because she was proud of me.

CHAPTER 44

My Boyfriend's Back

I was glad I drank a couple of shots of Tequila before I called Darren; doing it sober was out of the question. I couldn't work up the nerve to talk to him like that sober. I really didn't expect to get the reaction I got from him. I've always known Darren to be sweet and welcoming with me, but I figured his little hoochie mama would have had his nose open by now. I guess I was wrong, or was I? I didn't even bother to ask about her. I just assumed that I was going to be able to call him and win him back, which I'm glad I did. The events that led to that phone call had me thinking about life in general. Most of us seem to be on an endless journey for the perfect mate, and that journey sometimes can drive us insane. While it's true that it's natural for human beings to try to bond, sometimes we take the word bonding to the extreme. All of the requirements attached to it tend to take away the true meaning of the word.

I know through this brief experience with Terrence I learned many lessons, and one of them was to never judge a book by its cover. Yes, I know it's cliché and unoriginal, but that's what Terrence taught me. I remember how impressed I was when I first met him. I even said to myself that he was a better man than Darren. A handsome, driven attorney with aspirations beyond what most of us expect from a man; hell yeah I was impressed. That's what I grew up believing. Society has taught us to believe that highly educated and successful people are the best of the bunch. However, while setting up the standards and making up the rules, they never once took into consideration that a lot of highly educated and successful people can be dishonest, hateful, deceitful, selfish, greedy, careless and most of all evil. I'm not associating all those characteristics with Terrence, but from the small amount of time I spent with him, I discovered that he possessed at least three of those qualities.

Everything happens in time and everything is also discovered in time. Twenty years ago we had to call the operator to interrupt the phone line during an emergency if we needed to reach a loved one. Now people can communicate with each other from every part of the world without any wires or cords attached to their cell phone. That discovery happened with time. It's the same thing with people; time allows us to get to know each other. It can only do one or two things: bring people together or push them apart. Terrence's scheming ways and the choice he's made with his life forced me to make the decision to stay away from him. Simultaneously, that period of time was sufficient for me to realize that I needed to get closer to Darren. The endless search for the perfect mate will always end up being just that, a long search. We have to realize as humans we are flawed and we also have to accept these flaws from other people in order for us to create that bond that most of us yearn for.

Darren has always been sweet to me and I knew this, but it took Terrence to make me realize that fact. Sometimes we allow our egos to get in the way of making the right decisions for ourselves and in our lives, and that can prevent this "special bond" to develop with that special someone. All of the standards, prerequisites, expectations and responsibility we place on other people and ourselves sometimes can force us to be complete strangers even to ourselves. Most people would be quick to say that they have to look at the man in the mirror, but even then they lie to themselves in the mirror because of the standards that society wants them to live by. In reality, I didn't need any truth serum to gain courage to talk to Darren the way I did. I had to convince myself I did because of all the standards and expectations and responsibilities that I placed on myself as well as Darren. Our love for each was never questionable, but the thirst to find better compatibility, higher standards and expectation caused us to fall apart.

I was lucky too that Darren accepted me back in his life without any reservation, but many people never get that chance because of the so called standards. Those standards get in the way of true feelings and commonsense. Our bruised egos sometimes force us to go elsewhere to look for something that we already have. Darren and I could've gotten all bent out of shape about the fact that we both left our great relationship to explore other people, and that would've ruined the chance for us to ever have a solid bond. Most people don't believe in second chances because their standards leave very little room for compromise. I truly feel that life is about lessons and I try my best to learn a new one everyday.

I couldn't wait to see Darren for our date. If he was near me, I probably would have jumped his bones and made up for all the time we'd lost. Darren may not have been the perfect man in every aspect of his life, but I realized that he was perfect enough for me. He was my perfect man and that's all that mattered. I couldn't wait to see my man and ride that dick that I loved so much. I pulled out my favorite little black dress, which was also his favorite, of course, and I decided that I was going to let myself go and just allow myself to love Darren and Darren to love me. I smiled as I flopped my head down onto the pillow that night after we talked. It had been a while since I had a long dreamy night.

CHAPTER 45

The Takedown

Terrence and Antwan walked into Justin's restaurant in Buckhead like they were partners with P Diddy. Confident, brash and abrasive was their demeanor. While Terrence looked conservative and professional in a two-piece tailor made suit, his cousin's attempt to wear a blazer, slacks and a dress shirt wasn't exactly a success with all that metal in his mouth. His platinum and diamond grill was a turn-off to many of the women in the joint. Antwan couldn't keep from advertising his baller status to the world. His big ass diamond encrusted platinum chain was long enough for the projects kids, where he sold his filth, to play double dutch with. His wrist was damn near blinding half the people who stood within a few feet from him. It was bling bling everywhere.

I chose to meet with them in a public place in case they decided to change the plans. I didn't know who the hell I was going to be dealing with, and I didn't want to risk getting robbed of a million dollars of Killer Ken's money. Kevin and I took a cue from Antwan's personal stylist. We decided to dress like big ballers to emulate the role to perfection. My crisp, white Air Jordans sat under my sagging Sean John jeans with my Coogie sweater over my white tee, and enough bling bling to make Terrence believe that I had more money than he was worth, courtesy of the Bureau's jewelry confiscating department. As I moved up the ranks within Killer Ken's organization, I needed to start showing them that I was actually living the life of a drug dealer. The Bureau made every piece of scrap diamond they confiscated available to me. I was always careful not to wear too many pieces that looked better than what Killer Ken and Pop wore. I wanted to show things gradually, but at the same time, I needed to look hungry like I wanted to make this money. Kevin wasn't as flashy as me, but he was also in street gear and looking like he was on the come up. He wore a fresh pair of Timberland boots, sagging Roc-A-Wear jeans, a button–down, striped shirt, Yankee baseball cap, and the usual bling he sported in New York around the gang. His diamond bezel Rolex watch confirmed that he was one of the top men in Killer Ken's organization along with the diamond medallion with the words "Get Money" inscribed on it.

Killer Ken must've given over half of his stash to me for this deal in Atlanta. Kevin was supposed to be Pop's trusted eye, while Killer Ken trusted me to make the deal. For some reason, Killer Ken thought I was more intelligent than most of his honchos and I played the role to a tee. Their stupid asses didn't know half the shit I knew, so of course I was the smartest amongst them. We all recognized each other right away after stepping into the restaurant. Terrence and Antwan had gotten there before we did, so we walked up to the bar to find them each with a bottle of Dom Perignon in hand. Terrence was less obvious than Antwan. His bottle sat on the bar counter, while Antwan held his bottle with a grip so tight, one would think that the bottle was trying to run away from him. It was one of those typical "hood rich" moves to let the other patrons know that he was paid. We exchanged greetings while patting each other down for weapons in an inconspicuous manner. I didn't want to risk a shoot-out at a public crowded place. And the place was crowded. Antwan was the bigger of the two, so I figured I'd be the one to take him down in case something went abnormally wrong. Kevin was slightly smaller than me standing at an even six feet tall and weighing about two hundred pounds, but he seemed to be in great physical shape and he looked like he could handle himself. At that point, I knew that he'd better known how to handle himself. That night was going to be Terrence and

Antwan's last night of freedom and the FBI wanted to humiliate them publicly just like they'd humiliated so many families.

Meanwhile, there were no knock search warrants issued for Terrence and Antwan's homes waiting to be executed on my word. While they both had many residences, they made the biggest mistake when they started bringing shit to the place where they lay their heads. The money and drugs were coming so fast, they started getting paranoid. They couldn't trust leaving their money and drugs in places where they couldn't protect it. Mind you, there were millions of dollars stashed in every residence they owned. I found this out because all of the homes were raided minutes after the DEA and FBI discovered evidence of drugs and money at their primary homes that evening.

In New York, the FBI and DEA were making plans to round up all the members of Killer Ken's crew. An around the clock, forty-eight hour surveillance by the FBI confirmed that all the members of the gang were converging for a meeting headed by Pop in the absence of Killer Ken. Killer Ken couldn't get comfortable with the idea that a million dollars of his money was in the hands of two men who were in the same game as he was. Everyone knows the saying that "there's no honor amongst thieves," but I also found out that there's no honor amongst drugs dealers either. Killer Ken wanted to be there and make the deal himself. Pop was planning to ambush the Dominican suppliers as they delivered their last shipment to the gang. The situation was becoming more violent by the day and everyone wanted to show their strength. However, none of them realized the strongest people and the spoilers were the FBI and the DEA.

FBI and DEA agents were positioned throughout the whole restaurant waiting for my signal to move in on Terrence in case the plan went sour. And there were even more agents outside in the parking lot working as parking attendants waiting for the exchange to take place. Killer Ken was kept abreast of every move we made and every meeting that was set up via telephone. We expected him to stay back in New York to formulate his plan to rob the Dominicans, so we were surprised when he changed his plans to be part of the deal going down. He showed up in a stretched limo at the restaurant looking as dapper as a drug dealer could look - gator shoes, diamond cufflinks, wool slacks, virgin wool sweater, diamond bracelets, diamond pinky ring, a huge diamond stud in his left ear and a big platinum chain and diamond emblem with the words "Killer Ken" inscribed in the center. He had no idea that the limo that picked him up from the airport was being driven by an FBI agent. As smart as Killer Ken believed he was, the FBI and DEA were even smarter. They knew his every move because everything he owned was bugged, down to his toilet paper holder.

One of the FBI agents who was sitting in the restaurant, signaled for me to meet him in the bathroom to give me the heads on Killer Ken joining us unexpectedly. I guzzled down the champagne that Terrence had poured in a glass for me while I used an excuse to go to the bathroom. "Man, I gotta take a piss. I been holding this shit since we left the hotel 'cause I didn't want to get here all late and shit." It was believable enough. After meeting with the agent and being briefed on the situation, I returned to the bar to continue my meeting with the two drug lords. At that point, Kevin knew something was wrong and he needed to follow my lead. The plan was changed and Killer Ken was going to be handing the money to Terrence and Antwan. There were two briefcases full of money in the trunk of my car, and two sample bricks of cocaine in the trunk of Terrence's car as well. We wanted them to hand us a brick each so we could get them both for distribution. The plan was for them to also give us a key to a storage place where we would find the rest of the drugs.

The events went almost as perfect as we planned it. The only thing that happened differently was the fact that Killer Ken took charge when he arrived because he wanted to flex his muscle and show off to his new partners. Kevin and I also took our role as subordinates in his presence. After drinking at the bar, eating dinner at the restaurant and making sure that they were comfortable with us, Terrence invited us to go outside to make the exchange. Most of the workers at the restaurant, except for the full-time employees, were agents. I was confident that these guys weren't packing any heat on them, so my comfort level was very high while we were inside the restaurant. However, when we got outside, it was a different story. As long as I had been working undercover in the underworld, I could never recall a situation where a drug dealer came to do a drug deal without bringing any guns for security. I was not armed and neither was Kevin. We needed to make sure these guys didn't go in their cars to retrieve their guns before handing us the drugs. As they headed to the car, I said, "Hold up, fellas. It's not that I don't trust y'all, but I'd rather you guys just get the shit out of the trunk before you go in the car, and we'll do the same. I don't know what y'all got inside that car just like you don't know what we got. So let's make this simple." I took a chance and it paid off, but Killer Ken almost fucked up the whole plan when he said, "Yeah, you country mu'fuckas down here can be slick. Ain't nobody going inside no car," he said, like he was in a position to give orders. That motherfucker needed to keep his mouth shut. "That's fair," the levelheaded Terrence replied without acknowledging stupid ass Killer Ken's comments.

The first thing Kevin and I did was hand one of the briefcases to Killer Ken. Since he wanted to be the boss, he snatched both briefcases from us. Terrence and Antwan shook their heads wondering why that fool was tripping. It was overkill with the New York shit while we were inside the restaurant whenever he opened his mouth, but when we got outside I wanted the shit to end so I could put that bastard in handcuffs already. After handing a briefcase each to Terrence and Antwan, they handed him a package containing the drugs, and then agents swarmed them. Everyone came out the restaurant when they heard the commotion. Some of the women who gave their numbers to Terrence and Antwan felt ashamed. "I'll be out in an hour," Killer Ken yelled out to the agents. "And that rat bastard is dead," he said referring to me. Terrence just shook his head because he knew he was gonna go to jail for a long time. Antwan said nothing as they cuffed him and placed him in the back of the car. Killer Ken was a different story; no one could shut him up. "I will have your jobs when this shit is over. I'm from New York, bitch. Ain't nobody can keep me locked up. I got more money than fucking Trump; you motherfuckers are gonna regret this," he blabbed and blabbed and blabbed. Then finally Kevin and I both had enough of his motor mouth. I connected with a left hook on one side of his jaw while Kevin connected with a right. He got knocked the fuck out.

I later found out the Dominican supplier, Pop and the gang were all taken down in New York by the FBI and DEA minutes before we arrested Killer Ken in Atlanta. During the raids on the other homes that Terrence owned, they found Marla living it up with her girlfriend, Beverly. They were engaged in what appeared to be some kind of sexual bondage experiment in a house full of drugs and illegal money. Beverly was tied up to the bed with handcuffs while Marla wore a dominatrix outfit screaming out orders. "From now on, I run this show. Everything I say goes, including first rights over Terrence and how he spends his money on us." There were lines of cocaine on the coffee table signaling that they had been getting high. Marla was charged with conspiracy and faced twenty years in prison. Terrence, Antwan, Killer Ken, Pop, the Dominicans and the rest of the gang members involved all received maximum time in the federal penitentiary. The major players had to kiss their freedom goodbye for the rest of their natural lives while the flunkies in the group received the minimum of twenty years each. Many of them turned snitches to help lighten their sentences, while strengthening the prosecutor's case. Marla was also charged with extortion in connection with the case involving my cousin. Even Beverly became a witness for the prosecution as she explained in details how Marla was planning to extort money from Will. She received three years probation for her cooperation while Marla was sentenced to an additional five years for extortion. I was glad that this case was finally over because it was starting to take a toll on me.

CHAPTER 46

It's Been a Long Time

I left work as soon as I could after I completed this project for a new home that my daddy assigned to me. He was trying to give me more responsibility and this project proved more difficult than I originally thought. He and I had been going at it and I knew that I needed to act professionally even though he was my dad. He deserved that respect in the work place because I was still one of his employees. I didn't own the company just yet. He hadn't signed the papers and handed them to Will and me yet. I needed to acknowledge and follow through with my assignment. It was also my daddy's way of teaching work ethic, discipline as well responsibility in the business. He was setting me up to excel. Even my mother backed him on it.

It was the most excited that I had been in a while. I was going to be in Darren's arms once again and this time I wanted to hold onto him forever. I knew I couldn't let him get away from me ever again. As soon as I got home, I kicked off my shoes and headed straight to the shower. I wanted to be fresh and clean for my man. I washed and scrubbed every inch of my body like I was trying to rid myself of Terrence's touch and scent, even though it had been a few months since I had been with him. My little black dress with the spaghetti straps was laid out on the bed and my open toe stilettos were brought out to max out my sex appeal. After rubbing lotion all over my body with my favorite raspberry scented lotion from Victoria's Secret, I eased into my thong and slipped into my perfect little black dress. My hair was looking great in drop curls over my shoulders. I rubbed extra lotion on my heels, toes and elbows in case Mr. Ashy decided to show up for an unannounced visit. I slid on my shoes and voila! It was me at my best, perfect the way God intended me to be. Perfection to me was my own sense of comfort and acceptability. I accepted who I was and what I looked like. However, I did enhance my natural beauty with a tad bit of eyeliner and lipstick that evening. A lady couldn't go out there leaving her face completely naked, could she?

I was feeling so vulnerable that evening as I sat around waiting for Darren to pick me up. My vulnerability was because I was ready to let go and just focus on my relationship with Darren. I wanted to envelop myself in his love. I wasn't nervous at all. This was the kind of moment that I always wanted to get excited over. No man has ever brought that kind of excitement out in me. Darren had that special "je ne sais quoi" about him that I was still attracted to. He made me yearn for him and his responsible ways made him sexy to me. I didn't have enough words to describe my feelings for this man. Yes, some people might call me wishy-washy because I stepped out and started messing with Terrence, but deep down inside I knew that my heart belonged to Darren. Just as I was sitting there waiting impatiently, the doorbell rang. Darren was a stickler for promptness and I knew it wouldn't take long for him to show up.

He was looking dapper in his tan single-breasted suit, white collared shirt, brown belt and brown shoes. He smelled good, too. He was wearing his and also my favorite new cologne, BLV by Bulgari. I could've eaten him alive. "Are you ready?" he asked, while handing me a bouquet of flowers. With my purse in hand and a little giggle across my face like a little girl, I was more than ready. I quickly gave him a light peck on the lips as I wanted to conserve the fresh look of my lipstick, and I didn't want to rub it all over his lips. I really could've just stayed home with Darren and I would've been happy. After closing the door behind me, Darren held the door open for me to get in the car. We talked on the way to the restaurant and I found out that Darren had been missing me just as much as I missed him. He was very candid when he said, "We need to develop a better way of communicating. We can't allow our lack of communication to destroy what we have. I have been miserable without you for the last few months and I don't want to ever have to experience that again." How much more sincere can a man get? My panties were getting wet as he poured out his heart to me. I wanted to reach over and give him a big kiss.

"I know, baby. It was my fault, I shouldn't have been such a pest to you," I told him. "Don't blame yourself. The responsibility falls on both of us. I carry half the blame," he said trying to comfort me. We agreed that we wouldn't talk about the past anymore. It was time for us to look to the future. We finally got to the restaurant a little after nine o'clock that night. It was crowded and for some reason it seemed like all eyes were on the couple in love. We made people smile as we stood there holding each other's hands affectionately and playing with each other. I felt secure on Darren's arm. He started telling his corny jokes again and I was laughing hard. He was cracking jokes when my stomach started growling because I hadn't eaten anything all day. I wanted my stomach to stay flat so I could look good in my dress for him. "I can't believe how women can just starve themselves just to fit into a dress. No man on this earth would keep from eating just so they can wear a suit. We'd be at the store like, 'Do you have a bigger size?' We're not gonna starve ourselves because we want to look good in some damn clothes. But we do some stupid shit for some pussy, though," he joked quietly. I was laughing my ass off; then he went on with his best imitation of a flamboyant store clerk and said, "You know women are digging those yellow shoes," and guys be like, "Gimme three pairs and everything else you got in yellow." I knew that his sense of humor was weird, but I loved it.

We were able to get a table fifteen minutes later by the window. Darren and I sat there and cracked on every person that walked by. We realized that New York has some of the weirdest people on this planet. I was in the mood for something different, so I ordered the Panang duck while Darren ordered the Seafood Delight. We fed each other and played footsie under the table. Darren even dropped his napkin on the floor so he could take a peek between my legs, and I spread 'em open wide so he could see what he was gonna have later for dessert. After taking a peek at my crotch, Darren hurriedly ate his food and I did the same. I could feel the growth of his manhood with my foot under the table. We needed to hurry and get the hell out of there for some lovin' at home. A handsome tip was left for the waitress after he paid for our meal. We ran to the car holding each other's hand. Darren even stopped to lift me off the ground and planted a big wet kiss on my lips. I wanted to wrap my legs around him and have him penetrate me right there, but we were on the street and all eyes were on us. A lot of people believe that New Yorkers don't mind other people's business, but I'm here to tell you that's a lie. Everybody was watching us. Maybe it was because we looked like a couple of crazy kids in love.

The drive home was excruciatingly painful to me. I wanted Darren so badly I couldn't wait for him to make it back to my house. As we entered the Midtown tunnel to head to the Long Island Expressway, I rolled up my dress to expose my thighs, teasing Darren as he drove. With a finger in my mouth and my other hand rubbing my inner thighs, Darren warned me, "You're gonna make me crash this car." I actually wanted him to pull over on the side of the road so I could have a quickie with him. Darren must've been clairvoyant because it was as if he read my mind when he slowed down and pulled over on the side of the road. With his hazard lights flashing signaling we had sexual tension emergency, we both moved to the backseat. Since Darren's car was very spacious, I was able to get on my knees, unzipp his pants pull out Da'ron and started sucking. Oh my God, that dick looked good. It had been so long since I tasted it, I acted like a hungry child. No one could tell what was going on as Darren kept an eye out for the cops. He was enjoying my lips service. He tried holding the back of my head so he could fuck my mouth briefly. I tightened the grip around his dick with my mouth to make it feel like a hot, tight pussy. He was going for broke and started humping back and forth. I tightened the back of my throat like he was hitting my vaginal wall. I could feel that Darren was about to cum as his humping accelerated. I tasted his thickness as he released what seemed like three tablespoons of semen down my throat. I sucked him gently, extracting every single drop left in that nut.

The cars kept going by full speed. There was no worry about people seeing us. I came up and sat next to Darren as he took a deep breath and said, "I needed that, but you also need this," as he spread my legs open and kneeled to the floor. Darren pulled my thong to the side and started eating my pussy like he really, really missed it. I had my legs spread across the backseat while I enjoyed his cunnilingus treatment. He was tugging on my underwear as he stuck his tongue in and out of my pussy, and sucked my pussy lips gently. My juices were flowing and it was hard to keep my eyes open on the lookout for the cops. "Oh shit, I missed that tongue," I said to him. "My tongue missed your pussy, too," he said. I could feel one of his fingers penetrating my pussy as he moved his tongue up to my clit. "You eat me so good, baby," I told him. "I love eating cause your pussy taste so good," he convinced me. "Eat my pussy until I cum. I wanna cum, baby," I begged. "I'm gonna make you cum," he assured me. The velocity of his tongue slowed down as his finger picked up speed. My clit was bursting in pleasure while my g-spot was screaming in ecstasy. Darren's finger hit the right spot while his tongue held my clit hostage. I felt the bursting energy of a compressed nut and I just had to let it go with a loud scream. "I'm cumming! I'm fucking cumming! I'm cumming, Darren." The outburst was followed by shakes and movements of all types. It was one of the best nuts I busted in a long time. After satisfying our sexual appetite with a quickie, Darren jumped back in the driver's seat and me back to the front passenger seat and drove to my house.

I played with his dick the whole ride home. The center consul in his car kept me from riding the whole way home with his dick in my mouth. Only God knew how much I wanted him in my mouth. I resorted to stroking his hard, stiff dick with my hand all the way to my front door. I pressed the extra automatic garage door opener that I kept in my purse in case of an emergency; the door went up and Darren pulled his car into the garage next to mine. He stepped out of the car with his dick ripping through his pants and my mouth and pussy watered over it. After closing the garage door behind us, I pulled Darren towards me before he got a chance to step inside the house. The hood of his car was still warm, so we made our way over to mine. He sat on the hood of my car with his pants halfway down his legs and his dick reaching for the ceiling. I did what any woman in love would do; I took his dick in my mouth. Darren leaned back towards the windshield and placed his hands under his head while I sucked his dick just right. He was a marathon man, so I knew his second nut wouldn't come until his dick was wrapped tight inside my pussy. Since the head was my favorite part, I sucked it like my favorite ice cream that never melted. I ran my tongue around it, sucked it lightly, blew on it softly and then finally I just took it down my throat and held it prisoner in my mouth while Darren moaned and groaned in pleasure.

His dick was delicious, but Darren had his sight set on my dripping pussy.

It was like we were making our own porno flick as Darren got off the car and went around behind me while I placed my hand on the hood as if I was about to get patted down for criminal possession of a firearm or something. There definitely was fire and I was about to strong arm Darren's dick right into my pussy. I stuck one finger in my pussy and then stuck it in his mouth. A second finger followed while he palmed my breast with his free hand. He reached over and kissed me. I was in heat like a dog and I wanted his dick inside of me. Darren wanted to free himself from the restrictions that his pants imposed around his ankles, so he took off his pants and underwear completely. By now his right hand was moving my thong to the side as he used his left hand to insert his dick slowly inside my wet pussy. I could feel the head of his dick spreading my pussy hole open wide and it felt good. Even with a dripping wet pussy, my hole still felt tight around Darren's dick. He held onto my thong as he stroked me slowly, allowing me to enjoy every single thrust. It was amazing how his dick could just make me feel so good. I started winding and grinding on his dick and the feeling was just sensational. We went at it for about fifteen minutes until Darren decided that he wanted to carry me inside the house while holding me up against his crotch with his dick inside me.

I could feel every single inch of him up against my sugar walls as he walked slowly into the house, through the kitchen door, and placed me on the breakfast table. Darren held my legs wide open with his hands as he glided in and out of me. If there ever was a heaven, Darren's dick was it. "Fuck me hard," I begged. The movement of his pelvis shifted to a higher speed and he brought my pussy closer to his crotch so he could punish me. I begged even more and he fucked me even harder. He leaned his head down into my body and I

206

could tell that his second nut was soon on the way. I grabbed the back of his neck to help maximize his pleasure, but my own climax couldn't be controlled. "Oh shit, I'm cumming again," I warned. Darren stroked me harder and his mouth found mine and we started kissing each other hard as the last drop of our love came down. "Oh, yes! Yes!" he yelled. I couldn't speak because my nut was just feeling too good. Tears welled up in my eyes as I looked up at Darren. I realized that I could be with this man for the rest of my life.

After that long session in the kitchen, Darren and I decided to move to the bedroom for a much needed rest. While I went in the bathroom to brush my teeth and wrap my hair, Darren was making plans of his own. I came back in the room to find him on one knee butt naked with a two-carat, princess cut, engagement, diamond ring in his hand as he popped the question. 'Tina, will you spend the rest of your life with me?" The tears quickly came back as I jumped up joyously and said, "Yes! Yes! I will marry you." It was the most memorable night of my life.

CHAPTER 47

Don't Worry, Be Happy

I finally did it; I asked Tina to marry me. It was a decision that I had been contemplating before Tina and I even broke up. I wasn't the player type and I didn't want to go out there looking for ass every single night at some club or single's bar. I wanted to be with one woman and one woman only, and Tina was that woman. Not that I was shopping for anyone else because in the back of my mind, I always knew that I was going to end up marrying Tina. Even with all her flaws, my mother loved Tina while she was rude to every other woman that I ever brought home. There must've been something special about Tina that captivated not just my mother but my father as well. I remember when she was going through her trials and tribulation with that nutty white boy; a lot of people were passing judgment. Not once did either of my parents say anything bad about Tina. I always knew that my parents were loving, open minded and forgiving, but I didn't know they could be that forgiving. It was my dad who saw the pain in my face when it was revealed that Tina had been very promiscuous in college and during our break-up when she came back home from school. My father only asked me one question, "Do you love her?" I didn't hesitate to give him my answer. "Yes," I said. "Well then, it shouldn't matter what anybody else thinks. You're the only person who has to forgive her and you're the only person who can be happy with her because right now you look miserable," the old wise man told me. My decision to give our love another try was an easy one because I never could build enough hatred in my heart for Tina to leave her alone.

I knew that it was usually women who got all excited about getting married to the person they love and want to cherish for the rest of their lives, but I was the exception to that rule. Since I never had too many friends, there weren't too many people to call to spread my good news. My mom had been asking about Tina forever and I avoided giving an answer to her. I didn't want to lie to her. So naturally, she was the first person I called. "Hi, mom, guess what?" I didn't even give her a chance to guess. "I'm getting married!" I hollered through the phone. "Is your mind right, boy? How are you getting married, you're not even engaged?" she said in a peculiar tone. "Mom, Tina and I got engaged last night and we're gonna get married," I told her. "Well, it ain't no news to me. I always knew you were gonna end up marrying her. You couldn't get a better woman even if you had Michael Jordan's money. That Tina is strong and independent. She reminds me of the way that I wanted to be, but you know back in dem days, I couldn't be like that, and your daddy wouldn't have married me. I'm happy for you, baby," my mama said. "Thanks mama. Is pops home?" I asked. "Yeah, he's sitting over there with a big smile on his face. I think he was eavesdropping on our conversation. Do you want to talk to him?" she asked. I told her yes and she handed my father the phone. "My boy is finally growing up, huh?" he said with pride. "I'm sure you heard, pop. Tina and I are gonna get married and I feel like the luckiest man alive," I told him. "Well, you sort of have to be. You got a woman who's smart, pretty and she cooks, cleans and has hips that look like she can bear me some grandchildren. I'd say you're a lucky man," my father said approvingly.

I already knew I was lucky, and I wanted to share my happiness with the whole world. I was calling family members that I hadn't talked to in years to tell them about my engagement. My cousin, Joe, whom I spent much of my childhood playing with, wanted to take me out and celebrate my engagement. I hadn't seen him in so long; I had no idea what was going on in his life. Joe and I were close until my parents left Queens and moved to Long Island. Like most typical families, we saw each other on special occasions at family gatherings and it was always love. Joe got married a year after he graduated from college, a decision he regrets till this day. He didn't want his kid to grow up without a dad because he resented his father for leaving him and his mom. But due to the pregnancy, Joe decided to get married. He was in love at the time, but at twenty-two years old, when a man is getting pussy regularly, why wouldn't he be in love?

Joe never got to enjoy life as a single man because he and his girl had been together since high school. The marriage didn't stop him, though. He had more girlfriends than the most eligible bachelors I knew. He was always looking for an excuse to get out the house, so my engagement was the perfect excuse. I knew I was in for drama when I agreed to go out with Joe. He was like a kid trying to eat as much candy as he could while he was out because he didn't know when he was ever going to get candy again. We made plans to go to this club in Manhattan that was jumping every Saturday. I knew I hadn't seen Joe in a long time, but when we hooked up it was like we were never apart. That boy had me cracking up all night and I genuinely had a good time with him. I also noticed that he was no longer the Joe of old. He had changed for the better. He started to realize how important his family was to him and he decided to stop cheating completely. I didn't even see him try to holler at any women that night. I was proud of him.

Now that Joe and I were both going to be married men, our friendship and the bond we once shared was going to be rekindled. I liked being around him because he was funny and didn't give a damn about anything or anyone but his family. Joe also cautioned me about telling too many family members about my wedding. "You how our family is...half of them people are gonna come to your wedding empty handed, and half of them are gonna leave with their bags full," he said. Joe was brutally honest. "Please, whatever you do, don't invite that negro Teetee. Last time I was around him, my wallet went missing for three hours. When I asked Teetee if he saw it, he pulled it out of his coat pocket and told me he found it on the floor; yes the floor of my house," he said in a serious but comical tone. I was laughing my ass off because cousin Teetee was really like that. He was a slick cat who was always trying to outsmart people out of their money. Then Joe got all serious on me. "You know what, Darren, marriage is a beautiful thing. I know that my wife and me had a lot of problems with my cheating in the past, but I realized I was being selfish. Marriage is a give and take situation; you can't give it all or take it all or your spouse is gonna get fed up with you. You know how I grew up in a broken home. That's probably why I did some of the things that I did to my wife. But you, you had a better foundation and grew up with both parents, which is why your life probably turned out better than mine and that's what you should want for your children; a better life than yours," he said.

It was the first time Joe had ever gotten serious with me. He was always a joker looking for a laugh, but cousin Joe was maturing. He was becoming a man. "Don't take your wife for granted, Darren 'cause if you do, you might lose her. And that's all I'm gonna say about that," he said, trying to imitate Forrest Gump. I just sat there and listened to my cousin, a man who had come a long way. He was inspiring to me. That night we both left feeling reconnected with each other and my cousin stayed in touch with me like he used to when we were younger. We talked on the phone almost every other day, and we even made plans to hang out again at a basketball and a football game. He was a Knicks fan, and so was I. It was toss up between the Giants and the Jets when it came to football. I was glad to have my cousin back in my life.

CHAPTER 48

The Family

"I'm gonna be a brriide, I'm gonna be a brrriiiiide," I was singing to myself when I woke up the next day. Darren went all out and got me the most beautiful ring. I know that most women would rather play a role in selecting the engagement ring that they would like to wear on their finger for the rest of their lives, but I didn't have to be one of those women. Darren was perfect with his selection. There wasn't one thing that I wanted to change about the ring. Also, if I picked my own ring, it would have taken away the element of surprise for me. I told Darren that I didn't want to have one of those long ass engagements that most black people have. Money wasn't an issue and my parents would be more than willing to pay for my lavish wedding, especially my mom. She always talked about my special day. My mom wanted me to have the kind of wedding she always dreamed of having. She wanted me to be happy on my special day, nothing was off limits. We never even talked about a budget because she knew that my dad's pocket was deep enough to cover whatever I wanted. After all, I'm the only daughter they have. Believe it or not, my mom and I used to talk about the day that I would be married.

My dad was especially happy to see that I didn't become a statistic. His biggest worry when I was growing up was that I would show up pregnant too soon. Well, he didn't have to worry about that anymore. I never got pregnant, not even by Darren. Getting pregnant at a young age nowadays to me was nothing short of foolishness and stupidity. I could understand how people could've gotten pregnant back in the day because birth control wasn't as prevalent as it is today,

213

but for a young girl to get pregnant without accomplishing anything in her life in this day and age is plain old stupid. A woman doesn't even have to pay for birth control if she's smart enough to research how she can get it for free. Different forms of birth control are being handed out at the free clinic like old government cheese. The responsibilities that come with children can be stupendous, and most of these young women usually find that out the hard way. I witnessed how a child completely changed the lives of a few people that I only feel comfortable referring to as associates when I was in high school; and that's all I needed to see and the fear of my parents kicking my ass and being disappointed in me to get me on the straight path. My mother also made it a point to take me back to Marcy Projects in Brooklyn to show me where I would end up if I ever got pregnant as a teen. Talk about scared straight!

My family had always been there for me, so it was only natural that I told them the good news first. "Darren proposed to me last night, mama," I said through the phone after she picked up. "No hi, how're you doing, or nothing, huh? Kids these days don't know nothing about greetings. What did you say, baby?" she asked because she obviously didn't hear me. "I'm sorry, mama. Hi. Darren proposed to me last night," I repeated. "Oh now that's why you couldn't say hi at first. I can understand that because when your daddy first proposed to me, I ran around the house butt naked to tell my mama how I was finally going to leave that crowded ass home with all them people living there. We had your aunts, uncles, cousins from down south and everybody else seemed to live in that house. I'm happy for you, baby," she said, after ranting about her own past. "Mama, I'm the happiest and luckiest woman in the world," I told her. "Well, you should feel lucky because there's a lot of women out there who don't know how to catch a good man. That boy Darren is a good man and you better make sure you keep him happy. I want me some grandchildren, you hear? Me and your daddy will retire soon and I don't wanna have to listen to his mouth for the rest of my life or I might just have to die a few years after retirement. I want me some grandchildren to keep my sanity. Your daddy's a good man, but he can be a pain in the ass, too. But that's with all men," she said. My mama was to doing a lot of talking that morning.

"Mama, I want to have my dream wedding. Do you think daddy will be okay with that?" I asked curiously. "You know your daddy is very conservative and frugal when it comes to spending. To hell with that, the man is downright cheap. But you're my baby and you deserve the best. Don't worry about a thing, I'll take care of your daddy," she assured me. "Thanks, mama. Is daddy there with you? 'Cause I want to tell him myself," I said to her. "Yes, he's downstairs watching CNN. Hold on a second while I get him." My mama put me on hold while she went downstairs to get my father. "Hi, baby girl," he said when he picked up the phone. "Hi, daddy, I'm calling to let you know that somebody's about to take your baby girl away from you," I said playfully. "I already know that nobody can take my baby girl away from me, what are you talking about?" he enquired. "Daddy, I'm engaged," I told him. "I'm happy for you, baby. Does that mean I'm gonna be taken to the cleaners?" he asked jokingly in a serious way. "I don't know, daddy, but I want to have a beautiful wedding," I mentioned. "Well, a beautiful wedding you will have. Don't worry about cost as long as you don't spend more than thirty thousand dollars," he said. "Now, daddy, how did you come up with that number?" I asked. "I watch CNN and they always have these news stories about how much certain events and things cost nowadays and thirty thousand dollars was about the average," he said. "I didn't say I want an average wedding, daddy. I said I wanted to have a beautiful wedding and a beautiful wedding might cost more than that," I said in my little girl voice. "We'll talk about it, baby, and I'm happy for

215

you. Are you engaged to that boy Darren that you've been dating since high school?" he asked. "Yes, daddy, it's Darren," I confirmed. "I always liked that boy. I'm glad he's gonna be part of the family," he said. "Me too, daddy. I'm glad he's gonna be part of the family, too. Tell mom I'll call her later. I gotta go call Will. Goodbye, daddy," I said. "Bye, baby girl," he replied before hanging up the phone.

I wanted to share my joy with my brother as well. Will always had a thing for Darren. He seemed to like Darren from the very beginning. He never liked any other dude that I brought around him, including Terrence. In a way, I guess he was a good judge of character. I wish he had been straight up with me in the beginning about his intuitions regarding Terrence. "Hello," the female voice said after picking up Will's phone. "Hi, may I speak to Will please," I said with hesitation in my voice. I knew I had the right number because his number was programmed on my phone. "Will, you have a phone call," I heard the female holler politely. "Who is it?" he asked. "I don't know, baby, but it's a woman." "It's probably my sister, tell her I'll be right there," he said. She got back on the phone and said, "He'll be right with you." I started thinking that the woman had to be Cassandra and my brother must've been getting pretty serious with her to allow her to pick up his phone. In the past, Will always guarded his phone like there was nuclear secret code hidden in it. "Is this Cassandra," I asked casually. "Yes, it is," she responded. "This is Tina, Will's sister." Since Will was taking his time getting to the phone, I decided to have a little chat with Cassandra and catch up. "Hi, Tina, how are you? Long time no see," she said. "I'm fine. How have you been? Is my brother treating you right down there?" I asked teasingly. "I've been fine and yes your brother has been treating me the best that a lady can be treated. I can't even keep up with his kind heart and generosity. That's a special brother you've got there," she said. The way she was gloating about my brother, I knew

Will had to be treating her right. He has always been a genuinely nice person for the most part, but because of his profession people always assume he's mean.

"Things must be getting pretty serious between you two?" I said to her. "Yes, I guess you can say that. I usually don't allow guys to meet my parents unless I'm serious with them, and my parents seem to love Will. He's like the son they never had. My parents only had girls, three to be exact. Your brother has won them over, but more importantly he won me over," she said. I could hear Will calling out my name as he approached Cassandra to get the phone. "Tell him we're having girl talk and you'll hand him the phone in a minute," I told her. "Will your sister and I are having a great conversation. You took too long to get to the phone," she told him. "You better not be letting out my secrets, T!" he yelled in the background. "Tell that boy he got no secrets left. The whole world knows about his life as a Falcon," I said jokingly. Cassandra was laughing and told Will that I said his secret was already revealed to the world as a football player. I liked Cassandra. She was most definitely a polite woman with southern manners and qualities. I could see her as my brother's wife. She and I ended up talking for about an hour on the phone. We really got along. By the time my brother came to the phone, I had already revealed to Cassandra that I was getting married. Will was really happy for me and pledged to help pay for my wedding if my daddy was being cheap.

Cassandra and I developed a bond and a friendship that day after our little conversation over the phone. From then on, she and I spoke on the phone almost every day. We became real close. She was the first true female friend that I ever had. When she asked about Terrence, I explained the whole situation to her, and she could not believe it.

Meanwhile, Darren and I had decided on a date to have our wedding six months later, which gave me time to do all the planning and hiring of the right people to give me the best wedding I had ever imagined. Darren also started spending time with his cousin, Joe, regularly, which bothered me at first because it was a known fact that he was a dog and a player. However, over time, I was able to see the change in Joe as a person, and I was glad that Darren finally got close to somebody other than me.

CHAPTER 49

Let the Planning Begin

It seemed as if Darren and I underestimated the amount of time that it would take to plan a wedding. A couple of months passed and all we had was the venue for the wedding, which was the Westin Hotel in Manhattan. The ballroom was magnificent and I wanted it regardless of the cost. I could hear my daddy gritting his teeth as the event coordinator told us the price to rent the place. That thirty thousand dollar budget he had in mind was right out the window. "I don't understand why people spend so much on a wedding these days, half the time the marriage don't even last longer than a year," he whispered to my mom. I heard his comment, but I didn't want to say anything. I wanted to maintain my jovial demeanor for the day. Everything was to be subcontracted, from the flower decorations, to catering, to the bridesmaids and groomsmen dinner. Even Cassandra got involved in the planning of my wedding; she was the one who looked over all the contracts that we signed with the different subcontractors. Cassandra and I became so close that I decided to ask her to be my maid of honor. It wasn't like I had a ton of female friends waiting to be asked, anyway. Nevertheless, Cassandra was a great choice.

My mother and I were always meeting with somebody to go over the specifics of everything. Meanwhile, nobody was keeping track of the cost. Every now and then, my father would make his little comment to my mother and me. "Remember, we only have a budget of thirty thousand dollars, ladies," he would say. My mother and I would both look at each other and chuckle because that budget was surpassed on the second day we started the planning process.

219

My daddy knew he was outnumbered and whatever the majority said was exactly what was going to happen. Besides, my brother pledged another fifty grand towards the wedding as my wedding gift. I felt lucky having people like him in a position where money was no object. The whole coordination of the wedding started to take a toll on me, I was stressed out and I needed a break from it all. I allowed my mother to take charge of everything. Even my father told her to focus on planning the wedding without having to work. He hired someone from a temp agency to help around the office.

My mother and I were conflicted about the color scheme for my wedding. I wanted an off-white theme while she felt adding colors would make it more vibrant. We ended up with my color of choice, of course. Everybody in the wedding party would wear off-white while the groom and I wore white. The bridesmaids' dresses were cut to fit every curve and very sexy with the back exposed. Since all the bridesmaids were slim and sexy, we didn't have a problem with people having to hide their bulges. The maid of honor's dress was designed more like a gown that Queen Victoria would've worn to a ball back in the day. That dress was also sexy and it looked good on Cassandra because she was tall. It wasn't hard to figure out anything for the men. All the groomsmen along with the best man would wear black tuxedos with off-white bowties and matching cummerbunds, while Darren wore all white, matching me. The floral arrangement was off-white as well as the table settings. It was almost like a winter in wonderland style wedding, but in off-white.

Coming up with the list of names of people we wanted to invite to the wedding was a chore in itself. I especially wanted my cousin Ray Ray to come because it had been so long since we had a family function where he was present. I knew that there were plenty of family members that I didn't know, but half of them would've been angry with my mother if she didn't invite them. However, I didn't want to spend my whole wedding night introducing myself to new family members, so I told my mother to only send out invites to the people that we'd seen at least twice in our lives and those who knew that she had a daughter. If a family member didn't know that I exist, there was no reason for them to be at my wedding. If I had never met or seen them throughout my life, there was no reason for me to spend two hundred and fifty dollars a plate for them. I made that clear to my mother and the same went for Darren's family as well. His family is just as big as mine.

Everything started moving right along over the months leading to my wedding day. Darren was sexing me regularly and his job only gave him assignments in the New York tri-state area so he could have time to help plan the wedding. Darren also decided to ask Joe to be his best man at the wedding. With that, I knew the bachelor party was going to be wild, but my brother was gonna be my eyes there. To ease my stress during the planning process, Darren would run me warm baths and make love to me as often as he could. He knew that a good nut would put me in a good mood and he made sure he kept them coming. We had the most sex during the six months leading to our wedding than any other time, while most people report rifts between the couples. I ended up having just three bridesmaids and a flower girl. All the bridesmaids were my cousins. Darren also had three of his cousins walk in the wedding as groomsmen. It was a family affair.

Darren and I also spoke about where we wanted to live. Initially, I wanted him to move into my house and just sell his, but Darren wanted us to have a fresh start and I agreed that we should buy a new house while both of us rented our places out. The money that we received as gifts from friends and family would be used as a down payment for the new house. However, we didn't have time to go house hunting because time was flying by quickly. We decided that we would wait until after the wedding to look for our new home. Darren and I may not have agreed on everything, but we were always able to come up with some type of compromise. Married life was going to start on a smooth course for us, and we made sure of it.

CHAPTER 50

The Last Few Days

A week before the wedding, Cassandra and Will flew up from Atlanta and they stayed at my house in the guest room. My parents loved her instantly after they met. Cassandra was undeniably beautiful and genuinely nice and my parents loved that about her. She didn't even get the third degree from my mother, as did all of Will's girlfriends in the past. While Cassandra and Will stayed at my house, I spent my nights over at Darren's to give them privacy. I knew my horny ass brother couldn't live without sex for too long. I wanted them to be comfortable. Besides, it gave me the opportunity to freely get freaky with my man. After Darren and I got back together, he spent most of his time at my place, so it was refreshing to be at his place for once.

Something about his place made me horny and dirty. I felt like a little girl who sneaked off to her boyfriend's house without telling her parents. That week, Darren wore my ass out in basically every single part of the condo apartment. It wasn't unusual for us to have sex two or three times a night. Darren's dick never seemed to want to go down and my pussy was always ready to get served.

That same week, Joe was planning a bachelor party for Darren at The Platinum Gentlemen's Club on Rockaway Parkway in Far Rockaway. Meanwhile, Cassandra and the bridesmaids had something planned for me at the apartment of one of the bridesmaids, who lived in Brooklyn. I knew that the fun at Darren's party would be limited because they were going to be in the confinement of a club, so I was a little more at ease about the whole party. All the guys, including my brother and Darren's cousins, left for the club about nine o'clock that Friday evening. They were going to have their fun and I was planning to enjoy the festivities with the girls.

When we got to my cousin's house, the girls had drinks, hors d'oeuvres, and all kinds of food ready for the party. At exactly eight o'clock that evening, two guys dressed in police uniforms knocked on the door. We were being pretty loud, but I knew what was up. "Ladies, you're gonna have to keep it down because the neighbors keep calling us about the noise," said one officer. "Why these white folks in Clinton Hill always gotta call the cops for no reason!" yelled one girl in the room. "Miss, we really don't wanna have to come back here because if we do, somebody's going to jail," he said. "We'll keep it quiet, officer," my cousin said. The officers left then we resumed with the noise. Twenty minutes later, two new officers showed up at the house. After my cousin opened the door, he informed her, "Ma'am, this is the second time we've been called to your home, I'm afraid we're gonna have to take you into custody," said the officer. Nobody said anything, but I jumped up and said, "This is some bullshit. We weren't making that much noise…" Before I could finish my statement, I was handcuffed and sat on the chair by the officer. "Anyone else want to join her? 'Cause if you do, you might want to take a seat and enjoy the show," he said as both of them pulled off their uniforms revealing their tiny underwear and bulging biceps and triceps. Those heifers really got me.

We had a ball that night and I think one of the women ended up leaving with one of the dancers afterwards. Neither of the dancers had a dick big enough to even compare to Darren's. I was thinking to myself that Darren would've been rich already if he had decided to become a stripper instead of an accountant. He had the goods and then some. The festivities ended around midnight. Cassandra was the one who paid for the whole thing. She was able to arrange everything with the help of my cousins. They planned it while they attended the formal dinner for the wedding party that was held the night before at this nice restaurant in Manhattan. My parents also got the chance to meet Darren's parents at the dinner that night. I thanked everyone for giving me such a great party, but I especially thanked Cassandra for being a good friend.

After a show like that I was naturally horny. I remember coming home that night to find Darren standing in front of the door butt naked with a rose clinched between his teeth. He must've been feeling horny after he left his bachelor party as well. He probably got up and stood in front of the door the minute he heard me insert my key into the lock. After taking the rose from his mouth, I didn't even have time to kick off my shoes he as pushed me back against the door after closing it, pulled up my skirt, and started playing with my pussy through my underwear as he kissed me. I didn't even say anything. I just stood there and let him do what he wanted with me. Moments later, he dropped to his knees and he slowly pulled my underwear off and had my legs spread wide open as I leaned against the door. Darren kissed my pussy softly then he licked my clit once before he started sucking on my pussy lips. I stood there with my hands up against the wall like I was surrendering.

Then suddenly I could feel his warm tongue curving through my pussy like a slow moving snake waiting to attack. My juices started flowing with anticipation. The movement of Darren's tongue increased as he started tongue fucking me while rubbing my nipples with his hand. He licked my clit, fingered me, rubbed then licked and rubbed while caressing my breasts. I was getting high on his love and I needed to support myself before I fell to the floor, so I grabbed his sexy bald head while he ate me. I could see the determination in Darren's actions to satisfy me as he licked my pussy with precision. Then I felt it, a nice nut converging on me as

Darren slowly brushed his tongue against my clit. "Oh shit!" I exclaimed, as my love juices came down my legs. Darren licked it all away.

After my nut, Darren came up from the floor and had me turn around to face the door. His dick was harder than ever, but I knew he just wanted to please me, so I didn't even bother gesturing toward my favorite beef link. While rubbing my ass, Darren spread open my pussy and eased his way in. "I've been waiting for this pussy all day," he whispered, as he leaned his body close to mine. He was winding and grinding his dick inside me and my pussy enjoyed every movement. Darren lifted my shirt and started caressing my breasts with his hands as he fucked me from the back. I could feel the head his dick going up against my g-spot. He started stroking harder and my spot couldn't take it anymore. Another nut was coming. "Give it to me, baby," I begged. Darren pulled his body away from me and stepped back to hold my ass as he pummeled my pussy. "Yes! That's it, baby," I encouraged. He clenched my hips and started stroking me with everything he had. I could feel my legs caving under me as my nut came running down my thighs. After a couple more strokes, Darren's body started to shake and he grasped me tighter as he released that nut he had been waiting all day to release. "I love you, Tina Stevens," he said. "I love you too, Darren Thomas," I confirmed. Darren never said a word about his bachelor party and neither did I.

CHAPTER 51

The Ultimate Day

The day that I grew up thinking about most of my life had finally arrived. I didn't want to think about anything but my special day. Cassandra, my mother, the bridesmaids, and myself had the whole day planned from seven o'clock in the morning all the way up to the wedding. I didn't want anybody out of my sight. Black folks always manage to screw things up and I didn't want anything to go wrong with my wedding. Nobody was going to be missing a shoe, underwear, stockings, earrings, nothing. I wanted them with me until after the wedding was over. My mother was the chief schedule planner that day. To keep any of us from getting tired, I decided to rent a limo to drive us around to run all the errands for the day. Each girl was picked up from her house in succession.   Before leaving anybody's residence, my mother, Cassandra and I made sure everything for the wedding was carried with them. My mother and I made up a checklist for each person and what they needed to bring with them for the wedding a couple of days prior.

The first order of the day was our appointment at this spa located in Manhattan. The ladies received the works, courtesy of my mother. That was her special gift to me. She wanted to make sure everyone was relaxed and stress free, which was the whole point of the spa treatment. We were at the spa for two hours getting everything done from facials to body scrubs, to our nails, to body massages and everything else we could think of. The ladies were very happy. After we left the spa, I treated the ladies to a Saturday brunch because I knew that as black people, the ladies just wouldn't fare well on empty stomachs. In between errands, I called

Darren to make sure he got his hair cut, picked up the tuxedos and shoes and everything else that needed to be done along with the rest of the guys. I didn't want anybody looking shabby in my wedding. I didn't have to worry about the ladies' dresses and my dress because I called the designer early and her assistant told me they were ready for pick up. After brunch, we went straight to this woman's shop in Manhattan who designed all of the dresses including my wedding gown to pick up the dresses. Vera Wang is great, but I wanted an original design that I personally created.

After picking up the dresses and trying them on to make sure that everything was perfect, I asked the driver to take us to the hair salon. I told my hairdresser about my special day, and she volunteered to make my hair look especially gorgeous for my wedding day. She also asked a couple of her co-workers to come in to help her out as there were six women, including my mother that needed to get their hair done. It was a huge favor, but she was well compensated for her time. Everyone had their hair done and wrapped for the unveiling later at six o'clock, the scheduled time for the church service. By the time we made it back to the hotel to get ready, it was almost a quarter to four. The three make-up artists I hired were downstairs waiting for us in the lobby of the hotel. They followed us upstairs to the three rooms that I reserved. I had my own make-up artist, while the ladies and my mother shared the other two. Everyone was ready by five o'clock. I felt like Cinderella when I went downstairs to get in my vintage horse carriage style limousine with my mother. The other ladies rode in a Hummer limo. The church wasn't too far from the hotel. I made sure it was close because I didn't want to mess up anything. We got to the church about fifteen minutes early. I also noticed Darren's limo got there early as well. I knew he wasn't going to be late, because I was checking on his whereabouts every chance I got.

228

I may have been planning to get everything done on time, but my black people never failed me. By six o'clock the church was still empty like there was a snow blizzard keeping people from getting there. There was no way I was going to walk into that church before the guests. Then around quarter past six, the crowd started rolling in. By six thirty, I was impatient and ready to walk in the church and get the ceremony over and done with. My mother went inside and spoke with the pastor and everything was ready. Darren's family sat on one side of the church and my family sat on the other. Two of my young cousins worked as ushers directing the family members to their appropriate side. "Are you here for the groom or the bride?" they would ask each guest and everyone was directed to the correct side of the church based on their answer. My little cousins didn't know every member of the family. Shoot, even I didn't and I'm older than they are.

The bridesmaids and groomsmen looked great. Even my cousin, the little flower girl, looked so cute in her little off-white dress. I was accompanied by my dad who wore a black tux. I'm not bragging, but my dress was the bomb. I came up with the design by putting together what I liked from about three different designers, including Vera Wang. Because I have nice breasts, I wanted to wear a dress that accentuated them. My dress was low cut in the back because of my smooth skin. It was tight around my bosoms to reflect my cleavage, a little loose around the waist so I could have room to eat later, and flowed down my hips with a train so long that it required four people to help me get out of the limo. Everyone was flashing pictures on my way to the altar. I smiled and so did my dad. I could see his eyes welled up, but he wouldn't let the tears go. When I arrived at the altar, Darren was looking as handsome as ever. "You look gorgeous," he mouthed silently to me. "So do you," I replied.

The ceremony took about forty-five minutes, and when the pastor announced that he pronounced us man and wife, I was the happiest woman on the planet. It actually happened. I got married. "You may kiss the bride," the pastor ordered and Darren pulled my veil up above my face and planted a big wet kiss on my lips. I didn't even care about messing up my lipstick because I kissed him right back. We went to Central Park with the wedding party to take pictures while the guests drove to the hotel for the reception. Hot hors d'oeuvres as well as cold ones were served as the guests waited for the wedding party's arrival. Darren and I took pictures for over an hour before heading to the reception. When we got to the hall at the Westin Hotel, everyone was talking and having a great time. The MC of the night announced the members of the wedding party one by one or couple by couple as they entered the reception room. People were clapping and everyone took their seat at the table reserved for the wedding party. Then finally, after our parents were announced, it was the moment that everyone had been waiting for. "Ladies and gentleman, I present to you Mr. and Mrs. Thomas," the MC announced. Everyone was up on their feet clapping and congratulating us as we walked through the cleared path to our seats. I winked at my cousin, Ray Ray, sitting there looking so handsome in a suit.

THE END

Please enjoy this excerpt from my upcoming book, Sexual Jeopardy.

If Looks Could Kill

I met Shauna in July 1994 while I was on vacation in Miami, Florida, during independence weekend. My friend Myles and I decided to fly down to Miami to relax in South Beach, Florida for a few days. We went down with no expectations. We simply wanted to go down there to ease our minds from the crazy life in New York City. We never anticipated meeting two of the most gorgeous women that the world has to offer.

We left the hotel early that morning after eating the free continental breakfast that was offered. We knew everything in South Beach was expensive, so we had planned to make the best of our free meals at the hotel everyday. We didn't go to South Beach to waste money, we went there to relax and have a good time. Myles and I shared a room with two double beds for economics sake. We both had just graduated from college and we didn't really have too much money to throw around. I had a great job waiting for me at the nightclub where I had been working part-time for the past couple of years, but I couldn't start working full-time until after the independence weekend.

Myles had just graduated from New York University with a degree in computer engineering. He was also waiting to start his new position with an engineering firm in New York City when we got back from our mini vacation. Neither of us really had much money to spend down in South Beach. We wanted to get away for as little money as possible and Miami was the cheapest vacation package we found. We arrived in Miami on Thursday night and we were scheduled to leave on

Monday so we could report to our new jobs on Tuesday. My mom and dad had given me some spending money as a graduation gift for my vacation. Myles's parents had also given him his spending money.

We both had about three hundred dollars each to spend for the five days we were in Miami. We had a very simple plan for our vacation, we wanted to spend all day at the beach, eat a light lunch everyday at one of the cheapest eateries on Ocean Avenue and at night eat dinner at some of the most affordable restaurants we could find. There was no room for splurging. At night, we would try to frequent the clubs that offered free admission so that we wouldn't run out of money before our vacation ended. We had a budget of about sixty dollars a day. We both had our credit cards in our wallets as back-up in case we ran out of money. But it was understood that we had a spending limit for every day we stayed in Miami.

Since it was our first morning in South Beach, we wore our bathing shorts and tank tops to the beach. We were halfway out the door, when we both realized how crusty and ashy our legs and arms looked. We each had brought a special bottle of baby oil to rub on our bodies to showcase all of our hard work in the gym and we almost forgot to use it. Myles was my work-out partner in the gym back home. We were both very muscular and toned and we knew that the baby oil rubbed all over our bodies would make us look like professional exotic dancers on the beach. Who the hell wants to look like male strippers? However, looking like a male stripper beats looking ashy any day. After realizing that we looked like we had already spent time on the beach by the amount of ash that was showing our skin, we took five minutes to rub oil all over our bodies. We each grabbed our sunglasses and a towel and threw the towels over our shoulders.

We stepped out of the hotel looking like Mr. Clean with our shiny baldheads. I could only see the back of Myles's head as he was a few inches taller than me standing at 6ft 2inches. He was joking about the fact that the glare on the top of my dome could cause someone to go blind. Myles had his moments with the jokes, but I had my own as well. He looked like a building standing on two posts. We both worked on our legs relentlessly in the gym, but Myles could never get his chicken legs to grow with the rest of his body. After he made his comment about my dome, I turned to him and said, "I saw a gang of chickens walking down the street looking for you. When I asked them what they wanted from you, they told me they wanted to get their legs back from you because chicken legs don't look right on humans." Myles started laughing because he knew that I had let this joke marinating over time before I unleashed it on him. He gave me a big dap and said "that was a good one."

We had been lying out in the sun on the beach for close to two hours and it was getting boring. We wanted to walk over to the Kenneth Cole store that we noticed the night before when the cab dropped us off at our hotel. I have always been a fan of Kenneth Cole fashion and I wanted to browse a little even though I didn't plan on buying anything. Myles didn't mind taking the walk with me. However, he was more a Ralph Lauren, Polo guy.

Myles and I were crossing the street to go to the Kenneth Cole store located a block up the street on Collins Avenue when it all happened. As we crossed halfway in the middle of the street, two goddesses driving a silver convertible Mustang GT appeared out of nowhere. For a moment, we were both lost in the women's beauty. We forgot we were standing in the middle of Ocean Avenue with a bunch of impatient motorists honking their horns at the convertible Mustang telling them to move it, not realizing that Myles and I were blocking their way. We slowly moved out of the way

233

to see the women drive by us almost in slow motion so we could get a better look at them.

We thought we had caused a small commotion by holding up traffic, but we soon realized that all eyes were on the two women sitting behind the wheel of the convertible Mustang. All that I could say excitedly to Myles was "Did you see that!" He turned to me and the look on his face said it all. We knew that we had seen the two most beautiful women that we had ever laid eyes on. It took us about a minute to allow the two women to fade away in traffic before we turned around to head to our original destination.

We found it strange that we didn't even say anything to the ladies as they drove by us. It was almost like we were caught in a trance and we couldn't say anything. They didn't bother to speak to us either. As Myles and I walked up the side street to the store, we were talking all kinds of crazy shit about the ladies. We were saying things like "they know they're fine and they're probably money hungry and hoping to score with the next big professional athlete on South Beach." We went on and on about them until we noticed they were pulling around the corner headed towards us again. They had apparently driven around the block and we must've caught their attention during our little stunt while crossing the street earlier.

This time, I was ready to say something as the ladies drove by us. As we started to step onto the street to start crossing before them again, we noticed that they both tilted their sunglasses to give us a look of interest. I immediately took advantage of their interest and asked them to pull over for a few minutes. The light skinned girl was in the passenger seat while the dark skinned girl was driving. Myles and I never had any disagreements on the type of women we liked and the type of women who were attracted to us. Because I'm dark skinned, I found it easier to talk to the light skinned women. They were almost more approachable to me and they often found me more attractive than dark skinned women. It's that "opposite attract" theory. Don't get me wrong, I think my mother is the most beautiful woman on this earth. She looks just like Cheryl Lee Ralph. I just have never met any dark skinned women who were not looking to date someone lighter than they are. That was just my experience.

Ever since I was a kid, I found it hard to talk to the women who shared my complexion. Most of them sometimes looked to the light skinned pretty boys for help with their self-esteem issues sometimes. It almost seemed like their self-hatred is so deeply rooted that if they could somehow dilute their bloodline with a light skinned man everything would be all right. The same could be said about a lot of dark skinned brothers as well. Personally, the first thing I notice about a woman is her smile, body, ass and intelligence. Complexion has never been a factor. However, the colonial mentality is still alive and well with a lot of brothers and sisters today.

I once dated a dark skinned woman who told me that I wasn't her usual type. When I enquired about what her usual type was, she told me that she usually went out with tall light skinned guys with green eyes, like I was supposed to be flattered by her ignorant ass comment. I left her ignorant ass sitting at the restaurant after she made that ignorant statement. Sometimes you have to fight ignorance with ignorance. My ignorant ass felt good leaving her ass sitting in the restaurant not knowing whether or not I was coming back. And I never went back.

I have been called prejudice by my own mother and father because I seldom brought home a dark skinned woman. What they never understood is that these women never want to give me the time of day. I have tried so many times to talk to dark skinned sisters and each time they tend to gravitate towards Myles. Like I said, Myles and I always knew the score and the dark skinned sister behind the wheel had a big Kool Aid smile on her face when she saw that Myles was headed to the driver's side of the car after they pulled over near the curb. She was gorgeous and fine at the same time. She had beautiful dark skin with shoulder length hair, cut in a bob style. From the way she was sitting in that leather seat, her thighs left the impression that her booty had the perfect dimension that men crave from a sister.

The light skinned woman on the passenger side was not only fine and gorgeous, she was extravagant. She was very natural with flawless skin and the sexiest red lips that I had ever seen. She wore her hair short like that style Anita Baker made famous during the late eighties through the nineties. My eyes didn't even get a chance to travel all the way down her thighs because I had to stop at her double D cups for a few minutes before I could regain my composure. They were both wearing their two-piece bikini bathing suits with a see-through skirt wrapped around their waists. Before we could start making small talk with them, we started taking inventory of their beauty and bodies. Myles and I couldn't believe our eyes. These ladies were as fine as God could make women.

I introduced myself as Ronnie to the light skinned one and she reached out and firmly shook my hand as she told me her name was Shauna. I responded "a beautiful name for a beautiful lady." I pointed over to Myles and I told her "that's my boy, Myles." She pointed to her friend sitting next to her and she told me "that's my girl, Chenille." Shauna and Chenille looked good enough to eat and we were hungry. Since we hadn't eaten lunch, I decided to invite the ladies to have lunch with us. That whole budget plan we had for five days was about to be thrown out the window. Myles knew that in order to spend any time with these ladies we were going to have wine and dine them. Women like that didn't just chill with a man for company.

Surprisingly, the ladies told us that they had eaten a huge breakfast and wanted to hold off on eating until dinner because they were watching their weight. So were we and the weight was distributed in all the right places. They suggested that we go lay out on the beach. They asked us to hop in the car so they could go around looking for a parking space. We jumped in the car and they drove back towards Ocean Avenue. As we pulled up around the corner on Ocean Avenue, we noticed this lady pulling out of a spot. I pointed it out to Chenille and told her to take it. However, before Chenille could pull into the spot this big muscular dude walked over and stood there claiming that he was holding it for his friend. I was thinking to myself "This steroid looking white dude is about to get his ass whipped over a parking space." I turned to Myles and I could see by the look on his face that he was down to put a beat down on the man if it came to that.

Myles and I usually don't like to start any trouble with people, but if it found us, we usually dealt with it. We wanted to wait to see how the ladies were going to react to the man's hostile approach to the parking space. We allowed them to talk to the man first. Shauna was closer to him, so she spoke "we've been going around in circles for about a half hour and we pulled up next to the car before you even got there. Is it possible for us to have the space?" With his chest pumped out to the street, that asshole laughed in her face and told her he wasn't going anywhere and that the space belonged to him. The steroids must've been going through his brain because he was overly cocky for a man who didn't know anything about me and Myles.

We told the girls to wait a minute as we jumped out of the car. Myles is taller and a little bigger than me, so he jumped out the car first. When that asshole took one look at Myles's bicep, he realized that he could be lying on his back quicker than Mike Tyson knocked out Michael Spinks. He decided to move out of the way and took some of the air out his chest so the girls could park. As the girls were parking, his friend pulled up and I decided to jump out the car for assurance. His friend took a look at me and Myles and told his friend there was a space down the street to hurry back in the car. With that little problem solved, the girls knew that they weren't about to hang out with two chumps. That little episode secured our position with the ladies for the rest of our vacation.

After the car was parked, we fed the meter for a couple of hours. Shauna stepped out of the car and for the first time I got to see her total beauty. She stood about five feet ten inches tall, which was taller than me and her body was a killer. She couldn't be bigger than a size six and her well-manicured toes were screaming to get sucked. Her body dimensions were perfect in every way. Her bathing suit was a bright fluorescent green color and the see-through fluorescent wrap around was tightly wrapped around her waist like a fitted skirt showing her assets to the world. She was even toned all around and her stomach was as flat as an ironing board. Shauna also had long killer legs that were smoothly shaven exposing her calf muscles.

Black men are increasingly being victimized by the police in New York and other major cities around the country. The violence has escalated to deadly force, most of the time without justification. In this controversial book, noted author Richard Jeanty, tackles the problem of police brutality and the unfair treatment of Black men at the hands of police in New York City and the rest of the country. The conflict between the Police and Black men will continue on a downward spiral until the mayors of every city hold accountable the members of their police force who use unnecessary deadly force against unarmed victims.

IN STORES!!!

NEGLECTED SOULS
Richard Jeanty

Motherhood and the trials of loving too hard and not enough frame
this story...The realism of these characters will bring tears to your spirit as
you discover the hero in the villain you never saw coming...
Neglected Souls is a gritty, honest and heart stirring story of hope and
personal triumph set in the ghettos of Boston.
In Stores!!!

Jimmy and Nina continue to feel a void in their lives because they haven't a clue about their genealogical make-up. Jimmy falls victims to a life threatening illness and only the right organ donor can save his life. Will the donor be the bridge to reconnect Jimmy and Nina to their biological family? Will Nina be the strength for her brother in his time of need? Will they ever find out what really happened to their mother?

In Stores!!!

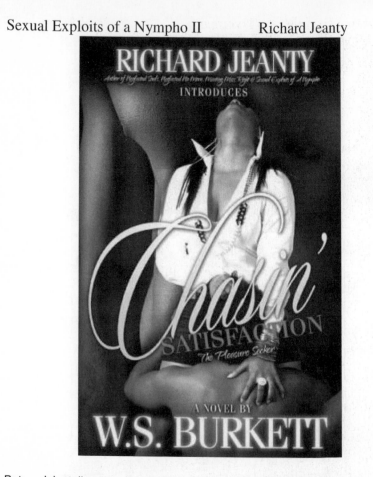

Betrayal, lust, lies, murder, deception, sex and tainted love frame this
story... Julian Stevens lacks the ambition and freak ability that Miko looks
for in a man, but she married him despite his flaws to spite an ex-
boyfriend. When Miko least expects it, the old boyfriend shows up and
ready to sweep her off her feet again. Suddenly the grass grows greener
on the other side, but Miko is not an easily satisfied woman. She wants to
have her cake and eat it too. While Miko's doing her own thing, Julian is
determined to become everything Miko ever wanted in a man and more,
but will he go to extreme lengths to prove he's worthy of Miko's love?
Julian Stevens soon finds out that he's capable of being more than he
could ever imagine as he embarks on a journey that will change his life
forever.

In Stores!!!

Ronald Murphy was a player all his life until he and his best friend, Myles, met the women of their dreams during a brief vacation in South Beach, Florida. Sexual Jeopardy is story of trust, betrayal, forgiveness, friendship and hope.

Coming February 2008

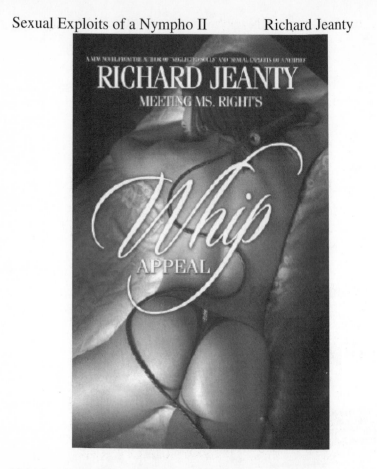

Malcolm is a wealthy virgin who decides to conceal his wealth
From the world until he meets the right woman. His wealthy best friend,
Dexter, hides his wealth from no one. Malcolm struggles to find love in an
environment where vanity and materialism are rampant, while Dexter is
getting more than enough of his share of women. Malcolm needs develop
self-esteem and confidence to meet the right woman and Dexter's
confidence is borderline arrogance.

Will bad boys like Dexter continue to take women for a ride?

Or will nice guys like Malcolm continue to finish last?

In Stores!!!

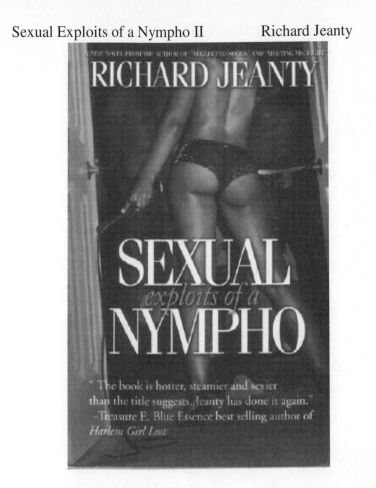

Tina develops an insatiable sexual appetite very early in life. She only loves her boyfriend, Darren, but he's too far away in college to satisfy her sexual needs.

Tina decides to get buck wild away in college
Will her sexual trysts jeopardize the lives of the men in her life?

In Stores!!!

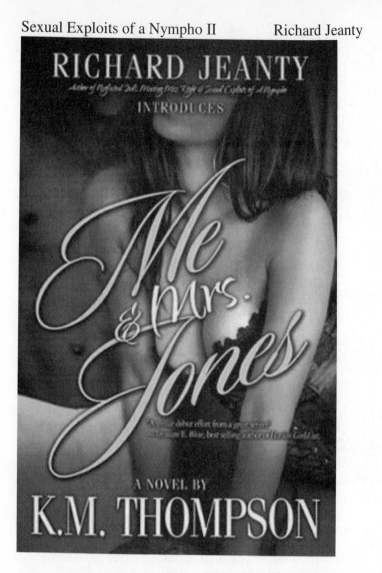

Faith Jones, a woman in her mid-thirties, has given up on ever finding love again until she met her son's best friend, Darius. Faith Jones is walking a thin line of betrayal against her son for the love of Darius. Will Faith allow her emotions to outweigh her common sense?

In Stores!!!

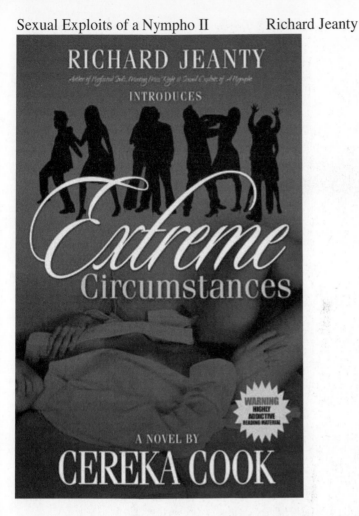

What happens when a devoted woman is betrayed? Come take a ride with Chanel as she takes her boyfriend, Donnell, to circumstances beyond belief after he betrays her trust with his endless infidelities. How long can Chanel's friend, Janai, use her looks to get what she wants from men before it catches up to her? Find out as Janai's gold-digging ways catch up with and she has to face the consequences of her extreme actions.

In Stores!!!

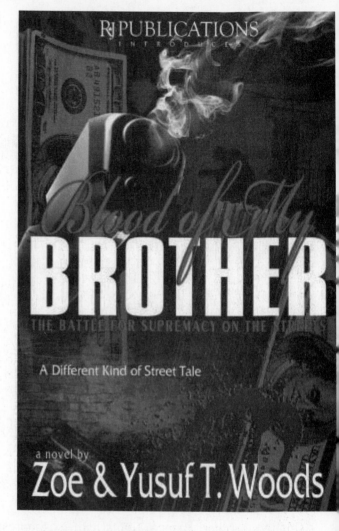

Roc was the man on the streets of Philadelphia, until his younger brother decided it was time to become his own man by wreaking havoc on Roc's crew without any regards for the blood relation they share. Drug, murder, mayhem and the pursuit of happiness can lead to deadly consequences. This story can only be told by a person who has lived it.

In Stores

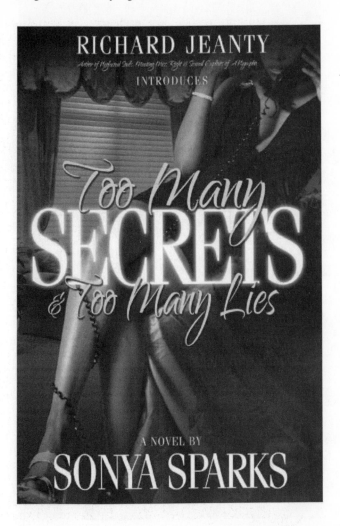

Ashland's mother, Bianca, fights hard to suppress the truth from her daughter because she doesn't want her to marry Jordan who's the grandson of an ex-lover she loathes. In this web of deception, author Sonya Sparks unravels a story that is sure to keep you on a roller coaster ride through the end.

Coming October 2007

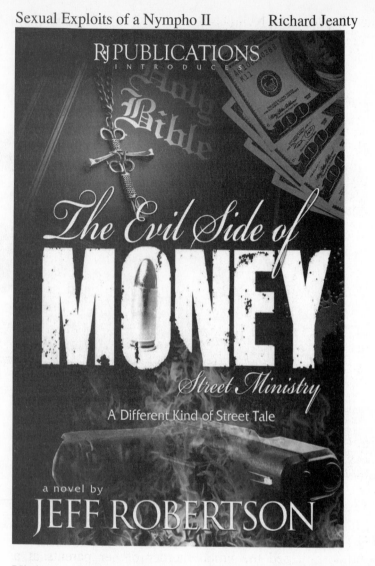

Violence, Intimidation and carnage are the order as Nathan and his brother set out to build the most powerful drug empires in Chicago. However, when God comes knocking, Nathan's conscience starts to surface. Will his haunted criminal past get the best of him?

Coming November 2007

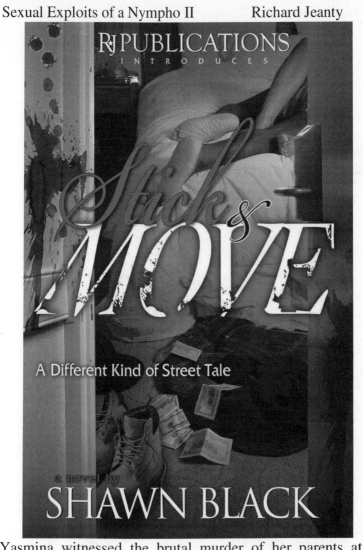

RJ PUBLICATIONS
I N T R O D U C E S

Stick &
MOVE

A Different Kind of Street Tale

a novel by

SHAWN BLACK

Yasmina witnessed the brutal murder of her parents at a young age at the hand of a drug dealer. This event stained her mind and upbringing as a result. Will Yamina's life come full circle with her past? Find out as Yasmina's crew, The Platinum Chicks, set out to make a name for themselves on the street.

Coming November 2007

Also coming soon…

Ignorant Souls
(The final chapter to the Neglected Souls trilogy)
By
Richar Jeanty

Bloob of My Brother II
By
Yusuf and Zoe Woods

Miami Noire
(The sequel to Chasin' Satisfaction)
By
W.S. Burkett

Cater To Her
W.S. Burkett

Kwame
The Street Trilogy
By
Richard Jeanty

Evil Side of Money II
By
Jeff Robertson

PUBLICATIONS
BRINGING EXCITEMENT, FUN AND JOY TO READING

Use this coupon to order by mail

1. Neglected Souls (0976927713--$14.95)
2. Neglected No More (09769277--$14.95)
3. Sexual Exploits of Nympho (0976927721--$14.95)
4. Meeting Ms. Right(Whip Appeal) (0976927705-$14.95)
5. Me and Mrs. Jones (097692773X--$14.95)
6. Chasin' Satisfaction (0976927756--$14.95)
7. Extreme Circumstances (0976927764--$14.95)
8. The Most Dangerous Gang In America (0976927799-$15.00)
9. Sexual Exploits of a Nympho II (0976927772--$15.00)
10. Sexual Jeopardy (0976927780--$14.95) Coming 02/08
11. Too Many Secrets, Too Many Lies $15.00 Fall 07
12. Stick And Move ($15.00) Coming October 07
13. Evil Side Of Money ($15.00) Coming 11/07
14. Cater To Her ($15.00) Coming November 2007

Name_____
Address_____
City_____State_____Zip Code_____

Please send the novels that I have circled above.

Shipping and Handling $1.99
Total Number of Books_____
Total Amount Due_____

This offer is subject to change without notice.
Send check or money order (no cash or CODs) to:

RJ Publications
290 Dune Street
Far Rockaway, NY 11691

For more information please call 718-471-2926, or visit
www.rjpublications.com

Please allow 2-3 weeks for delivery.

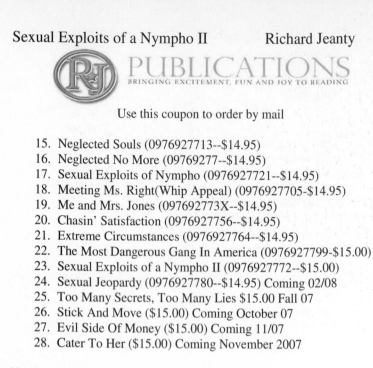

Use this coupon to order by mail

15. Neglected Souls (0976927713--$14.95)
16. Neglected No More (09769277--$14.95)
17. Sexual Exploits of Nympho (0976927721--$14.95)
18. Meeting Ms. Right(Whip Appeal) (0976927705-$14.95)
19. Me and Mrs. Jones (097692773X--$14.95)
20. Chasin' Satisfaction (0976927756--$14.95)
21. Extreme Circumstances (0976927764--$14.95)
22. The Most Dangerous Gang In America (0976927799-$15.00)
23. Sexual Exploits of a Nympho II (0976927772--$15.00)
24. Sexual Jeopardy (0976927780--$14.95) Coming 02/08
25. Too Many Secrets, Too Many Lies $15.00 Fall 07
26. Stick And Move ($15.00) Coming October 07
27. Evil Side Of Money ($15.00) Coming 11/07
28. Cater To Her ($15.00) Coming November 2007

Name_____

Address_____

City_____State_____Zip Code_____

Please send the novels that I have circled above.

Shipping and Handling $1.99
Total Number of Books_____
Total Amount Due_____

This offer is subject to change without notice.
Send check or money order (no cash or CODs) to:

RJ Publications
290 Dune Street
Far Rockaway, NY 11691

For more information please call 718-471-2926, or visit
www.rjpublications.com

Please allow 2-3 weeks for delivery.

PUBLICATIONS
BRINGING EXCITEMENT, FUN AND JOY TO READING

Use this coupon to order by mail

29. Neglected Souls (0976927713--$14.95)
30. Neglected No More (09769277--$14.95)
31. Sexual Exploits of Nympho (0976927721--$14.95)
32. Meeting Ms. Right(Whip Appeal) (0976927705-$14.95)
33. Me and Mrs. Jones (097692773X--$14.95)
34. Chasin' Satisfaction (0976927756--$14.95)
35. Extreme Circumstances (0976927764--$14.95)
36. The Most Dangerous Gang In America (0976927799-$15.00)
37. Sexual Exploits of a Nympho II (0976927772--$15.00)
38. Sexual Jeopardy (0976927780--$14.95) Coming 02/08
39. Too Many Secrets, Too Many Lies $15.00 Fall 07
40. Stick And Move ($15.00) Coming October 07
41. Evil Side Of Money ($15.00) Coming 11/07
42. Cater To Her ($15.00) Coming November 2007

Name_____
Address_____
City_____State_____Zip Code_____

Please send the novels that I have circled above.

Shipping and Handling $1.99
Total Number of Books_____
Total Amount Due_____

This offer is subject to change without notice.
Send check or money order (no cash or CODs) to:

RJ Publications
290 Dune Street
Far Rockaway, NY 11691

For more information please call 718-471-2926, or visit
www.rjpublications.com

Please allow 2-3 weeks for delivery.

PUBLICATIONS
BRINGING EXCITEMENT, FUN AND JOY TO READING

Use this coupon to order by mail

43. Neglected Souls (0976927713--$14.95)
44. Neglected No More (09769277--$14.95)
45. Sexual Exploits of Nympho (0976927721--$14.95)
46. Meeting Ms. Right(Whip Appeal) (0976927705-$14.95)
47. Me and Mrs. Jones (097692773X--$14.95)
48. Chasin' Satisfaction (0976927756--$14.95)
49. Extreme Circumstances (0976927764--$14.95)
50. The Most Dangerous Gang In America (0976927799-$15.00)
51. Sexual Exploits of a Nympho II (0976927772--$15.00)
52. Sexual Jeopardy (0976927780--$14.95) Coming 02/08
53. Too Many Secrets, Too Many Lies $15.00 Fall 07
54. Stick And Move ($15.00) Coming October 07
55. Evil Side Of Money ($15.00) Coming 11/07
56. Cater To Her ($15.00) Coming November 2007

Name_____

Address_____

City_____State_____Zip Code_____

Please send the novels that I have circled above.

Shipping and Handling $1.99
Total Number of Books_____
Total Amount Due_____

This offer is subject to change without notice.
Send check or money order (no cash or CODs) to:

RJ Publications
290 Dune Street
Far Rockaway, NY 11691

For more information please call 718-471-2926, or visit
www.rjpublications.com

Please allow 2-3 weeks for delivery.